Cónal Creedon was born in Cork, Ireland. Although he believes in eternal life, he admits he'll probably die like the rest of us.

# PASSION PLAY

## CÓNAL CREEDON

POOLBEG

Published 1999
by Poolbeg Press Ltd
123 Baldoyle Industrial Estate
Dublin 13, Ireland

A catalogue record for this book is available from the British Library.

ISBN 1 85371 698 7

Cover design and illustration by Blacksheep
Set by Poolbeg Group Services Ltd in Goudy 11/14
Printed by The Guernsey Press Ltd,
Vale, Guernsey, Channel Islands.

*For the main man, my da, Connie Pa.*

---

Special thanks to Joe Dermody, Maeve Saunders, Ross Crowley, Giovanni Milito, Geoff Gould, Fiona O'Toole, The Munster Literature Centre, The Everyman Palace Theatre and The Arts Council of Ireland.

**Pluto** (ploo´to), *n* (Greek Myth) God of the Underworld. God of Hades. (Astron) Furthest planet from the sun, invisible to the naked eye.

# 1

Eddie de Nut consoled my dad,

– Sometimes de need ta die is stronger dan de will ta live, he said.

* * *

When I was three years of age my mother went down to Pope's Quay. She sat on the bench across from the Dominican Priory, took off her rings and shoes, walked down the steps into the river Lee and drowned herself. She could have crossed the road to the church, but I suppose she must have tried that once too often. Nobody ever told me, I just always knew, but sometimes I wished they had lied, for Christ's sake they lied about everything else. Why the hell couldn't they have lied about my mother? Tell me she died saving a beautiful white swan and that the swan lives on to this very day and winters each year in the Lough out by Ballyphehane, where she rears one small downy baby cygnet. Tell me the swan comes back to Cork each autumn as a sign of respect to a courageous and beautiful woman who sacrificed her life that the most graceful of God's creatures should live. Tell me a lie . . .

I've no memory of my mother. I wouldn't know how she

1

moved through a room, or the sound of her voice or the shape of her face. To me she was just a photo on the mantel up over the fire. My days were spent staring at it, trying to get a grasp of who she really was, what space she filled, but I was fooling myself, she wasn't there.

If my mother was anywhere in our house, it had to be the stairs. I always felt it. Like she'd be waiting around the next turn, waiting to reach out between the banister rails and grab me by the hair. Or at night-time, lurking behind me in my reflection in the window. As sure as God she'd be standing there, made up like a Geisha girl, leering. I used to close my eyes and charge, taking the stairs two at a time.

She was forty-one years of age when she went to the river, and I missed her like hell. My sister Kathleen kept house for my dad and me, but I was reared by the Street, MacSweeney Street, and the lads who lived on it.

* * *

1:33

I turn up my radio, it's Elvis Costello. I suck in deep on my rollie, fingers glowing red in the dark. Alone, I'm surrounded by my past, everybody's here: Tony Tabs, Pa Crowley, Mrs Hickey, Grandda Buckley, Eddie de Nut. I see Imelda Kearney, Yvette, Veronica, Mags, Paulo. It's like they're appearing in front of my eyes, through the smoke with every reddening of the butt.

Tragic Ted told me a long time ago,

– Before ye dies yer life flashes in front of yer eyes!

– How do ya know dat, Ted?

– I knows a fella that nearly died, an' he told me! he said.

– Nearly dyin', an' nearly not dyin' are two different tings, Ted.

2

Tragic Ted, a right tulip all the same . . .

I can see the good days, the lads, Georgie, Pinko, Tragic Ted and Fatfuka. They're smiling, heads shaved, sunken eyes, pucking, throwing shapes and gatching around in crombies, parallels and boots. We're on a ferry to Liverpool, going to Manchester to see United thrash City in the League.

Fatfuka is lying on the deck, playing an air guitar and singing, *I Don't Want To Go To Chelsea*. Georgie, leaning over the railings, roaring abuse at some Liverpool dockers on the quayside. Music is strange, you know the way it can just trigger off memories like that . . .

– All Scousers are bastards! Georgie roars.

. . . now that I think of it, *I Don't Want To Go To Chelsea* wasn't even out at that time. What was he singing? I can hear the drum and the bass,

– Jeezus, wat was he singin'?

*Ba! Doom!*

*Going To See The Rollers,   Ba!   Doom!*

*Got A Ticket To See The Bay City Rollers,   Doom!*

*Going To See The Rollers,   Ba!   Doom!*

*Got A Ticket To See The Bay City Rollers . . .*

Fatfuka sings, mouthing drum-rolls at the end of each line. I smile, stub out my fag and listen.

Something sad about Elvis and the loneliness of late-night radio that's hard to put a finger on. It's a one-on-one sort of thing; like The Buzzcocks a different kind of tension, maybe got to do with some throw-back to stone-age man or something. Because as sure as night brings darkness, darkness brings fear.

I pull myself up from under my manky duvet, reach out for my tobacco, look for a topper. Not a sausage. I roll a new one. Familiar shapes, lit up by the bluish streetlamp out on Waterloo Terrace. 1:34 dazzling red from my clock radio. I suck in deep on my rollie, comparing the crimsons. Another sleepless night, just me and my radio.

Ever wonder what it's all about? It seems like the more I know the less I want to know. Just been listening to a science programme. It's frightening. Here we are, two thousand years since Jesus was a lad, on a planet that's spinning around at millions of miles a minute, spiralling off into outer space, travelling in what they call an elliptical path around the sun, and do you know what the scary thing is? I'll tell ya what is the scary thing? I'll tell you what is the stars. The sun is a star. And that's the scary thing. What if it's a shooting star? Did ya ever see one a' dem tings go? *VVVvvuuurrrooommm!* Flyin' across de sky. Well I tell ya, I don't fancy maintaining an elliptical path around one of them fellas. Madness! That's what it is! Pure and simple madness. Here we are, on the lifeboat to life itself, flying around a potential shooting star, and there's no way off. All around us crazy things going on: vanishing rainforests, nuclear testing, ethnic cleansing, holes in the ozone. Like, stop the gondola! I want to get off, but there's nowhere to jump. This is it. Here I am on the lifeboat to life; the Chief Engineer is down below doing some fine-tuning with a kango-hammer, the Captain is up on deck balming out under the sun balls-naked, sucking cocktails with about as much vision as a kami-feckin'-kaze pilot.

I suppose there's always hope, at least Jesus' dad must care. I mean, he created us in his own likeness, didn't he? Or did he? I was listening the other night to some expert on the radio, he asked the question,

– *What*, he said, – *What if God didn't create man in his own likeness, but on the contrary, what if it was man who created God in our likeness?*

Jeezus, some shaggin' expert. I mean there he was, an

expert and he's asking the questions. Experts should be giving answers, leave the questions to the thickos.

But he had a point, what if it's all some lunatic's plot, some power-tripping head-case of a balmpot, of a lunatic. What then? What if there is no God? What then, huh? What do you do when you live in a shoe? And if that don't beat everything, my landlady barged in here the other day and said I had to go.

Barged in she did, without even as much as a – Hello! or a – How are ya? I'm sitting here in bed, eating a cheese sandwich, listening to Gerry Ryan on the radio and she just barges in. I mean that's not right, is it? She said I had to leave. I just looked at her.

– Complaints! she said.

– Complaints? Complaints from who? I sat up in the bed.

– Never you mind from whom. All I'm saying is, I gave you a written notice to quit four weeks ago, and I want you out of here by Friday!

– Friday? Wat's y'r problem?

– There have been complaints!

– Complaints from who? Who! Brenda, Herman or de Monk? Complaints from dem? Ah! Get off de stage!

– Just take one look at the place!

– Wa's wrong wit' it?

– It stinks!

– Alrigh'! Alrigh'! So I missed de rubbish once or twice, but Jeezus . . .

– Look, I'm not about to enter into a discussion with you. I want you out of here!

And like most people who don't want to enter into a discussion, she had a lot to say.

– This isn't the first time I've had to talk to you about the condition of your flat, I've bent over backwards to facilitate you. I even bought you a new mop and broom. This is the end of the line. I want you out of here, and I want you out by Friday.

I couldn't help thinking that if she ever bent over backwards to facilitate me, she wouldn't have too much to be complaining about.

She stamped her feet, a big purple face on her. She turned to leave.

– A lot you'd know abou' brooms! I shouted.

– Pardon?

– Wat would you know abou' brooms? De only use you'd have for a broom is ta get ya around de town. Ya witch! Wat are ya? A witch, dat's wat ya are.

She just stared at me.

– Gowaan, shag off outa here! Ya can stuff yer stinkin' flat, but ya won't take my dignity!

– Dignity? she threw her eyes to heaven.

I flung a dirty underpants at her. It had been hanging on the end of the bed for over a month or maybe longer. She ducked, screamed and pointed at me.

– Ah shag off! I said. – An' take a dose a hormones or something!

I threw two fingers at her. I was sick to death of her and her antics, so I put my head down under the covers and finished my cheese sandwich. The door slammed shut.

That was three days ago. Ever since it's just been me, my clock radio and Easi-singles cheese. I mean in all fairness, you can't be thrown out onto the street like that, can you? I was talking to Jimmy the Monk from upstairs a few weeks ago, when I first got my notice to quit. He said that she couldn't just chuck me out like that. She has me totally upset. I can hardly sleep with the worry and I'm afraid to go out in case she comes and changes the locks or something.

– I'm not leavin'! Shag her! Dis is my home now.

# 2

Home can be happy or hell, so long as you keep going back there, that's what makes it home. We all saw what went on out in the street, like Georgie's mam walking up and down deranged after she lost her mind and Georgie – or Fatfuka's dad and what he'd get up to when he'd be locked out of his skull. But nobody knows the madness that goes on behind the doors of the homes. And at the end of the day everybody must go home. Our house was no different and that's probably why we had a coffin in the kitchen. You see, it all made perfect sense.

They say that you'd know a shoemaker's wife by the holes in the soles of her shoes and there must be a grain of truth in that. Because even though my dad was a master-craftsman cabinetmaker, we didn't have a stick of furniture around the house. I mean, we had the beds, the odd chair and all that but no shelves, no presses, no sideboards, nothing special, not if you don't count the coffin.

There it was in the middle of the kitchen on two carpenter's trestles, a sheet thrown over protecting my dad's handiwork and a few wads of white paper to save the sheet, and like the altar at Mass we'd gather around.

Kippers of a Friday, roast of a Sunday, one of the days

between Monday and Wednesday it would be bacon and cabbage and with payday on Friday, it was usually fried bread of a Thursday. Same old ding-dong.

– How's sc-sc-sc-school?

Strange, I never really took any notice of my dad's stutter, but some people said that's why he never got on.

– Fine, Dad.

– Any sl-sl-sl-slaps?

– Naw.

– Good! Good!

– More poppies, anybody?

Kathleen would plonk the handleless pot of steaming spuds onto the coffin.

– Ya can t-t-t-trow a few on d-dere, he'd point to an empty corner of his plate.

– Paul? she'd ask.

– Naw . . .

– Are ya sure?

– Certain.

– I-I hope you an' d-d-de lads aren't upse-se-setting G-Grandda Buckley? he'd put another potato into his mouth.

– Naw, Dad.

– Good! T-tis a fright to be old.

– More meat anybody? she'd be back.

– Ya can eh, t-t-trow a bit in dere!

– Paul? she'd ask.

– Naw!

– Are ya sure?

– Certain!

. . . and that's the way it would go, gathered around the coffin. Kathleen carting spuds in and out of the kitchen and me and my dad beating them back our throats. Same old

8

ding-dong dinner-time, same old ping-pong chit-chat, like Mass, night after night, every day of the week. Except that is for Saturdays. Saturday was my dad's day.

The pig is the one animal you can eat every bit of, this I know to be true. And where I come from, it was the head of the pig that kept the wolf from the door. Never the fur-lined devilish faces of the cow or the sheep. Always the pig, for some reason its human-like, hairless, fleshy jowls tasted easier on the conscience. But there's something evil when two eyes stare out at you from a pot. Maybe that's why he cooked them half-head at a time; split skull and jaw with hammer and axe, slit with carving knife down between the eyes, along the centre line of the snout right through the palate of the mouth all the way home to the jawbone.

– De p-p-pig is de one animal dat ya can ate every b-b-bit of, he'd say. – An' d-d'ya know why? I-I'll tell ya why! 'Cause we're C-Christians! Dat's why! 'T-t-tis de only ting dat de Catlicks an' de P-P-Prosidents has in c-common. We all ates de p-p-pig. Now, de Hindoos an' de-de-de-de Muslins an' de B-B-Buddas an' all dat shower has no God. De-dey don't ate no p-pig. Dat's why! Dat's why we ates d-d-de pig. An' here in C-Cork, we show our devotion to de one an' only true J-Jesus C-Christ Our Lord, by not wastin' one m-mouthful a' de G-God-given flesh a' d-de boar, de sow or de b-banabh.

This was his excuse for the weekly feast of entrails, off-cuts and offal.

– N-not only is it religious, he'd say, – b-but it's also part of our c-culture, de people a' C-Cork were atein' pigs' heads long before St F-Finbarre found us.

I'd sit there watching. His sleeves rolled up beyond his elbows and him tearing into and devouring a pig's head. Held firmly by the ear in the one hand and the snout in the other, scraps falling from his mouth to the white-paper-covered table. He'd gnaw into the prime cut of the cheek muscle just above the tooth-ribbed jawbone, grease and gristle seeping down over his black hands all the way to his elbows and the fat from the pig's eye socket, forehead and lock being smeared all over my dad's face as he struggled with the jaws of the beast. And, when he'd finish,

– L-l-like honey, he'd say, – A-an' who have d-de nicest pigs' heads in C-Cork?

– Peggy Foley's, Castle Street, I'd say.

– A-a-an' why F-f-foley's?

– 'Cause she knows a good pig's head when she sees one.

– C-c-chalk it down, P-p-p-luto boi! Chalk it down.

But Kathleen was getting older and he was getting more feeble, somewhere along the line she put her foot down, and said enough was enough. Eventually the boiling of the pig's head and crubeens stopped when my dad's pride gave way to his age and Kathleen took a tighter hold on the household. He was totally lost for a while. Just hanging around, like someone waiting to die.

I knew that my dad's traditionally trained taste buds had to be satisfied by an alternative compromise. I was saying nothing. But somebody must have said something, because one Saturday he arrived in with the makings of a dinner. Tripe and drisheen. A milky stew of sheep's stomach lining and chunks of curdled blood. Saturday was my dad's day again.

He wasn't really a drinking man, but after picking up the fixings down the English Market, he'd drop into Crowley's on Bridge Street for the one on his way home. Ten minutes into the Holy Hour he'd strike in the hallway, through the

10

kitchen and into the scullery, glowing. With the confidence of a Wimpy chef, and precision of a surgeon, he'd lay out the ingredients.

A slab of white tripe about the size of a small pillowcase, a roll of drisheen a foot and a half long, a pint of milk, the box of cornflour, two big onions or four smallish ones, white pepper, salt, the bread knife and board and a sack of poppies, Golden Wonders if in season.

Off with the jacket, up with the shirt-sleeves, he'd wet the hands under the tap. A quick rinse of the poppies in the sink, nothing too fussy he'd be peeling them anyway, and into the big pot for a boil.

While the spuds were on, he'd trim and cut the tripe into mouth-sized pieces, give it a good scald. By this stage it was all down to timing. The onions would be peeled and chopped, next the drisheen would be cut into chunks the size of your thumb. He'd strain the tripe and pour a kettle of boiling water over it just in case; boil again and strain again. Back onto the stove went the pot. Into the pot went most of the milk, the tripe, the drisheen, the onions, the pepper and a spoonful of cornflour mixed with the left-over drop of milk. Then a mad dash into the kitchen, grab the butter-bowl off the coffin, in went a knob of butter.

Kathleen would vanish into the front room, she couldn't handle the roaring and swearing from the scullery, as saucepans clattered, boiling milk bubbled over, hissing down on the cooker, and the whole house clouded over with steam. She couldn't handle it, but she got used to it.

A big pot of tripe and drisheen wrapped in a towel would be brought to the coffin. Me and him would gather around and eat. Kathleen would leave us at it. She'd go and clean up the battlefield.

– Ya w-w-wouldn't get de likes a' dis in d-d-d-e Metropole.

11

Would ya? he'd compliment himself.

— Naw, Dad. Not a hope!

— W-w-would ya like s-s-some more, Pluto son?

I'd make room on the side of my plate.

— You can throw a bit on dere, Dad.

— S-say when, and he'd begin ladling it out of the pot with a mug.

— Plenty! Plenty!

— W-w-well there's loads m-more where that ca-ca-came from, he'd say.

— Would ya pass over some poppies dere den, Dad?

Saturday was always special.

# 3

It's strange but Elvis Costello always reminds me of the old days on MacSweeney Street. Me and the lads just knocking around, travelling to England for matches and doing the gowl.

Our first trip. My first time out of Ireland. Drank our way from Cork to Dublin. Locked I was. Only a few miles from the North Wall or Ring's End or wherever the boat left from, and me up on deck with Palm-Olive, she was offering it to me on a plate. I was slumped back on a bench, steamed to the gills, too twisted to take it.

– D'yez have a bleedin' cabin? Or not? she was buckled from drink.

The boat dipped and lifted just enough for her to fall against me, cushioning herself with her big fleshy breasts, and like soap in the shower, she slid off in the direction of the railings. I held tight to the lifeboat.

– D'yez hear me?

She was back on the next wave. I could hear her, I could smell her, but I couldn't answer. She was saying something about twenty quid for a blow-job if I had a cabin, or ten quid for a hand-shandy in the Pullmans.

– Hang on! I slurred, – Me buddies has me jacket!

– Ah Jayzus!

She shook me, I just laughed, what more could I do.

I swayed there with every roll of the keel, just staring out into the blackness of the Irish Sea, the humming of the ferry in my ears, trying to straighten up.

– How much do yez have on yez! Do yez want it or don't yez? she was pressing on me.

My head was swimming. I couldn't breathe. I just felt like getting the gawks. It was lodged there at the top of my neck, like vinegar pouring from my gums, but I couldn't swallow, my throat was solid. Her left hand brushed against the grain of my velvety suede head, nails digging trenches into my skull, as her big watery, waxy lips clung onto mine. I'd never been kissed by a woman before, plenty aul' dolls mind you, but never a woman and definitely not a woman with make-up like Palm-Olive's. Polyfilla, that's what it was, plastered on with a trowel, dusted off with a roller, but like an old house you could see the shrinkage and settlement cracks.

Her mouth opened wide, tongue lashing wildly around my teeth, deep down into my throat and all the time sucking. Her hand squeezed into the tight pocket of my twenty-four-inch parallels. Fumbling and groping, she pulled out a scrunched-up fiver.

– Dis'll do, she hissed.

– Uh! is all I could manage, and she pushed me to the wet bench that ran the length of the deck. Her body eased down heavily, she tugged at my zip.

– Come on, baby! she whispered. – Come on! Yeessss! and her lips locked onto mine.

My head spun to the sound of the crashing sea, throbbing of the engine, motion of the ferry and fumes. The full weight of Palm-Olive's bulky overdressed body pressing down, her sink-plunger lips layered with sticky lipstick, perfume blending with the cigarette-smoke, drink and diesel. I opened

14

my eyes. Her mouth was slithering against my numbed lips. I could see her caked crust of make-up shatter along her cheeks with each movement.

And then it happened. It was like it came from nowhere. I tried to move my head, her left arm pinned me to the bench. I was helpless. My stomach turned.

Power-driven vomit, travelling at a ninety-six miles an hour, pumped from my gut past Palm-Olive's tongue and partial denture. The mixture of vodka, beer and bits of food thundered around the inside of her cheeks, all the way to her tonsils. Somewhere back at the top of her throat it turned and ploughed back at me like a tidal wave only to be met by the continuing flow from my gullet. The meeting of the waters clashed somewhere in the middle, spraying the most foul-smelling, green-coloured bile out along the faulty seams at the corners of our lips. Our mouths held the solid bits, but only for a fraction of a second until the lip-seal was blown apart by the force of the second wave. I don't really remember much after that.

* * *

– Are ya right there, Pluto? Fatfuka nudged me with his boot.

I was wet and freezing, face down on the deck, covered in gawk, naked to the navel, my jeans down around my knees. Palm-Olive was gone.

– Dere's yer jacket.

I couldn't talk, I had a pain in my body.

– Jesus look at the state a' ya! Georgie pointed. – Yer destroyed!

Chunks of carrots and a scattering of peas all down my front, the greenish slime stretching from my mouth, over my chin all the way to the deck.

– Well, did ya get it last night?

– Huh?

– Did ya ride her?

15

– Olive is it? my head was splitting.

– Oh it's Olive now, is it?

– A brasser dat's wat she was! Georgie laughed.

– Yeah, and she looked like she hadn't seen soap in a while, Fatfuka said.

– Palm-Olive soap! Georgie pushed me and laughed.

I never saw her again after that night on the ferry, the night I split my bottle of Blue Smirnoff with a fifty-year-old dipso brasser. I don't even know if Olive was her name. But for ever after, anytime me and the lads would talk about that trip to see United, she was always Palm-Olive to us.

– Well, did ya get it? Or didn't ya?

– Did I wat!

– Gowaan! Wat was it like?

And I gave it to them, every gory detail, from the bench to the lifeboat and rolling across the deck, the waves crashing over us, from there to eternity. My night of glorious lust and passion with Olive, a real woman, the lads lapping it up.

In all fairness, I didn't even know if the vomit was mine or not. All I knew was that my fiver was gone. But I told them the story anyway, and got my money's worth.

Sixteen years of age, myself and the lads from MacSweeneya, my street, heading to England. The last of the Boot Boys. We lived for each other, me, Fatfuka, Tragic Ted, Georgie, Pinko and the lads, we'd have died for each other. But the writing was on the wall, the gang was falling apart. I suppose I should have seen it coming, I mean like Georgie was getting more and more into selling the papers, Fatfuka was only on his Easter break from the Christian Brothers and he was going all the way to take the Cloth, Ted was talking about moving to England, he wanted to try out for Notts Forrest, he'd followed Forrest since Miah Dennehy, our Miah Dennehy of Cork Hibs signed for them. But it didn't matter, we were young and heading to Manchester to see United thrash City.

# 4

My dad said that the smell of the brewery held the city tight that night; the night they found my mother's shoes and rings. It was Mrs Hickey who found them. Coming out of St Mary's after confession; she didn't recognise them as my mother's at first, but thought it an odd place for someone to leave a new pair of shoes, you know, on a bench down Pope's Quay. But new shoes were big news on MacSweeney Street, and gradually the tragedy of how my mother's shoes ended up on the bench dawned on her when she found the rings stuffed into the toes.

They say Mrs Hickey came running up Cypress Street and into MacSweeneya with the shoes held up over her head, she was screaming . . .

– Jeezus! Will somebody help! She's in de river! She's in de river!

Two days before they found my mother's body, dangling from the cross-strutting beams under Horgan's Warf. Low tide. Some people said it looked like she was trying to climb out. But I don't know, maybe that was so that it would go easier on me, Kathleen, and my dad. Because whatever they say about death, suicide's hardest on those left behind.

\* \* \*

1:37.

– God save us! It's Jim Reeves, a request for some fella called Stan de Man. People! I ask ya? *Anna Marie* by Jim Reeves? Jeezus, I ask you.

Three days, and I haven't set foot outside the flat. Three whole days sitting in this bed, listening to the radio. I haven't seen a soul. Nobody calls. Nobody cares. Even I don't care. There's nothing out there for me anyway, just the babble of bull.

No bread, all the cheese is gone too. I think of The Witch, she's probably tucked up in her bed; electric blanket, central heating, weather-glaze, the lot. Shag her anyway.

\* \* \*

1:36:58

On nights like this, she always finds it hard to sleep. She sits up on the bed, throws her legs to the floor, her husband moves.

– Huh? Alison, huh? What time is it? he mumbles.

– Shh! Go back to sleep, she whispers.

He turns, mutters something and snuggles back into his pillow. She wraps herself in her night-coat, tip-toes out onto the landing and downstairs to the kitchen, pours herself a glass of milk, places it in the microwave and switches it on.

Alison owns a string of houses rented out in flats, all are doing very well, all except Waterloo Terrace. A dinosaur she inherited from her father. She has more trouble with that house than all the others put together. Her eyes roll across the sterile surfaces of her state-of-the-art kitchen, the hand-painted and glazed tiles, the custom-built Irish hardwood cabinets. For the most part life is good, but tomorrow will be one of those days. She knows it. There's a guy, Paul O'Toole, she's faced with evicting him. She hates the show-down, but it goes with the territory. She doesn't like herself when she's the landlady, but that's the way it's got to be, you can't show the soft side to these people, they only ride the situation. She knows they call her The Witch; she lives up to her name.

– *Ding!*

The milk is ready.

\* \* \*

Waterloo Terrace. I have lived in flats all over this town, but I should have known better than to get one off an ad in the paper. It was a kip. I mean how good can a flat be if they had to advertise it. There's always queues of people waiting to get into the decent ones.

You see, I was under pressure. Just moved out of Veronica's six months earlier. A fella I used to work with in the Post Office put me up for a while, but that was a short-term thing. His wife spelt that out to me in the first two weeks, always asking things like,

– *Any luck with the flat-finding, Pluto?* or – *I suppose you'll be leavin' us soon, Pluto?*

. . . you know, things like that. After six months I just couldn't take any more of it. So, that's how I ended up in this dump, it was a rushed job.

I hired a Hackney for the move. Never knew I had so much stuff, two big cardboard boxes and a few Quinsworth carrier bags. Even the driver said we'd hardly fit it all into the cab, but we did.

I unloaded my gear from the car onto the terrace, paid the

man his two-fifty and took one look at the place in the clear light of day. I knew this could be my Waterloo. It wasn't like any of the other gaffs I had lived in. Don't get me wrong, I had lived in some pretty shitty dives over the years, but this was different.

See, flat-land has a culture all of its own. It's like in every city there exists a free republic of flat-dwellers, totally removed from the possessions trip. It's ever-changing, moving in, moving out, a sort of a buzz about it. But not here. I'd heard about these places before. We called them the Cancer Wards. Stagnant. The people living here were going nowhere. They were older, a good twenty years on me, and this was their home. They were too tired to move and too poor to buy; an elephant's graveyard. It didn't bother me though, I was only passing through.

Mine is the ground floor. Flat 1. Jesus! The first day I arrived I couldn't get in the hallway with all the junk. Some guy on the top floor, Jimmy the Monk they called him, was collecting it for his imaginary cottage in the country. Up to the ceiling it was. Eventually, when I did manage to batter my way to the door and finally get into the flat, it wasn't up to much. Just one room, with a bed, a cooker, sink and a partition in the corner with the bathroom, although it didn't have a bath, just a toilet bowl and a shower that never really worked, but it was mine. It's nice to have your own toilet.

Down the hall I shared a bathtub with the rest of the house. It looked like it hadn't been used in years; plaster falling from walls and ceiling, curtains shredded and black, wormed floorboards exposed in parts and graffiti dating back to the Status Quo.

One big scrawl in faded red marker read,

– *Screw Me! Brenda Is A Brasser!*

and a drawing of a naked one with her legs wide open. I

20

guessed that was the woman up in No. 3, the landlady mentioned somebody by the name of Brenda living up there.

I didn't sleep much that first night, not that I was afraid or anything, but, it just seemed like there were people moving about into the early hours, up and down the stairs. Around half-one the Monk comes home, locked out of his skull, he's bouncing off the walls spluttering, groaning, farting and cursing. Hard to sleep with that sort of carry-on going on, but after a while you just get used to it.

The front hall was so choca-block with the Monk's rubbish that for my first few weeks I came and went from my flat by way of the window. It all sounds fine and dandy, but really, it was a fierce inconvenience. Handy enough for the shopping and all that, but there's something inhuman about using a window instead of a door, and I didn't like the idea of leaving it unlocked either, climbing in and out the window would only give some people around here ideas. Anyway, somebody reported me to the guards, and that put a stop to it.

It was like the first day of Spring, and there I was trying to get my bicycle out the window to go for a spin out the country. It wasn't really my bike at all, only minding it for a fella that I met down in the unemployment centre. He was going away somewhere, so I said I'd keep an eye on it. Anyway, there I was battling with the bike, four feet off the ground. From nowhere this squad comes screeching up the Terrace. I fell off the window-sill with the fright and nearly broke my neck. Two bluebottles jump out of the squad.

– Hoi! What're you doing there!

– What am I doing here? I says. – What are any of us doing here?

– Are you tryin' to be smart or something?

But before I could answer him, the one with the red face barges in,

21

– Is that your bike?

– No, I says. – I'm only minding it for a fella I knows . . .

– And I suppose you're mindin' his flat as well, and that's why yer climbin' out the window?

– No! I says. – The flat's me own.

– Well, if the flat's yer own, why aren't ya using the door like a normal person?

The cops were treating me like I was some class of an gowl or something, so I explained the situation to them, they only laughed.

They were very helpful in all fairness to them. One of the guards even gave me a hand with the bicycle, but that was the end of it. So I mentioned to Brenda up in No. 3 about the Monk's rubbish in the hall and all that. She said she'd speak to him. Not long after that Brenda the Brasser had it out with Jimmy the Monk, and since then he has kept some sort of a passageway clear along the hall, well at least he's tried.

. . . and after a while you settle in, and everything becomes normal. That was eight years ago.

\* \* \*

1:38

He's tall and lanky, fresh out of Templemore Garda Training College. The size of his ears exaggerated by his haircut. He's sitting at the desk in MacCurtain Street Station waiting for his partner to arrive. One of the other Guards has warned him what to expect. The guy he's teamed with is a bit of a blow-hole, none of the other Guards will work with him. That's why he ends up with the green-horns.

He hears him before he sees him, he's big and burly, more like a farmer than a Guard.

– So you're de new rookie? his farm hand reaches out. –

Jez, ye new lads are gettin' tinner an' taller every year. Dey say dat you know yer gettin' older when de Guards start gettin' younger. I tinks they should change dat to: you know yer gettin older when Guards' ears start gettin' bigger! You've a fine set a' antlers dere yourself, he laughs.

The fella with the ears smiles.

– So dis is your first posting in a city? the burly fella asks.

– My first posting, full stop.

– A green-horn! Well, you're in good hands with me, I've been poundin' de beat of dese streets for over thirty year now, I'll show ya de ropes.

It crossed the fella with the ears, mind, that any cop who'd been pounding the beat for thirty years can't be much of a cop.

– Come on, says the burly fella, – We'll go for a spin around de town. Here, you drive.

He throws him the keys for the squad car, and leads the way out of the station, – An' bring yer ears with ya!

He says something about how he's always given the job of breaking in the new recruits.

– They wouldn't trust nobody else with de new lads, he brags.

# 5

Like my grandda and my grandda's dad, my dad was a cabinetmaker. The lads up in Mulla's Yard said he was a genius, he could make a full piece of furniture, no nails or screws used.

I swear to God, you can never really know what goes on in another man's head, but it's hard to believe that something as slapless as a wooden dowel could turn my dad away from the cabinetmaking. It was like up until then his whole life swung around Mulla's and then one day, snap! No more. The day of the dowel dawned.

Maybe it had to do with the fact that Mulla died and his son, the Graduate, took over the running of the yard or that the Graduate ran the yard from the office and he didn't know one end of a hammer from the other. Maybe it was because there was no *meas* on the wood joint any more nor the men who knew how to make them. Whatever the reason, enough was enough and my dad's head was turned.

– S-s-s-sure dis isn't f-f-furniture, he'd throw the mallet down.

– Look! Either you make it or the Chinese make it! Take yer pick! the Graduate would say and walk away.

– D-d-dockets an' dowels, he'd mumble. – 'tis all d-d-dockets an' dowels dese d-days.

24

It was like he saw his craft die in front of his eyes and with it he caught a glimpse of his own mortality. Somewhere along the line it dawned on him that he couldn't face into eternity in some thrown-together plywood box, fastened with a few aul' dowels. He was a cabinetmaker and only a casket fitting for a master-craftsman would do. That's why at the age of fifty-eight he decided to make his own coffin in the kitchen at home.

He drew together boards from trees grown on different continents. Boards hand-picked from the shipments as they'd arrive into Mulla's Yard. Boards brought together, planked and hobbled away home. It took over a year but he was in no rush. He wanted the finest collection of grains to be found either side of the hardwood jungles of Burma and the Amazon Basin for his masterpiece.

– L-l-look a' dis, son, he'd say. – D-d-dat's a dove-tail, an-an-an' dat la, d-d-dat's a T-T-T-joint. An' s-s-see dis one here la, dat's me own s-s-s-secret F-joint, and I'll s-s-show ya how t-t-te make one a' dem one a' d-d-dese days.

My sister Kathleen lined his coffin with quilted yellow, green and black silk, the colours of Glen Rovers. And in the true tradition of quilters she stitched in a square that didn't match the pattern, a planned mistake so as not to challenge God's pride by creating perfection: split down the middle, half-red and half-white, for Cork.

\* \* \*

I was crossing Patrick's Bridge, about two weeks ago, and who did I walk into only Fatfuka's small brother. I wouldn't have

25

recognised him, he was a man. We got into the stupid talk, you know like,

– Ah, Pluto!

– Huh?

– It's me. Peter! Peter Crowley, MacSweeney Street?

– Peter?

– Peter Crowley! Fatfuka's small brother!

– Ah Jeezus! Peter boi, I wouldn't ha' recognised ya. How're tings?

– Not bad, not bad.

– Do ya ever see any of de crowd from MacSweeneya? You know, Pinko, Ma and Pa Hickey, de Buckleys?

– Naw, not in years, he says.

– How's Fatfuka?

– Fatfuka? Didn't ya hear?

Peter's face changed.

– Hear? Hear wat?

– Fatfuka's got cancer, his words were cold.

– Huh?

– He's not good, he's not good at all.

Fatfuka's small brother just continued talking and giving the details, but I was stunned. I don't know if I said goodbye, I just walked off with Fatfuka in my mind.

So, I went to visit him in the hospital the next day. That's where I bumped into Pinko. He was looking like a million dollars, the business was going well for him, he said he was writing a book. Then he told me Tragic Ted was dead.

– AIDS! he said, and he sort of laughed and he looked at me trying to avoid eye-contact. He was on edge in my presence, unsettled by my unemployment, embarrassed by his own success. I stood there outside the nurse's office on the cancer ward, eyeballs spinning in my head, as stoned as a gourd, but I still sensed Pinko's unease. I thought this was

26

odd. I had known Pinko all his life. I was there the day he came home from the hospital after he was born, and here he was acting the prick with me.

I remember that day like it was only yesterday. Strange, I'm two years older than Pinko and yet I've such a clear memory of it. Sometimes I think memories are a mixture of stories, truths, untruths and other people's memories.

The Kinks always remind me of the old days down Cypress Street, playing soccer with Pinko's big brother Georgie. Georgie Worst, after Georgie Best.

The pace was fast. Coursing like greyhounds after a hare, up and down. No grass, just pavement and concrete walls to skim along. The ball never stopped on Cypress Street, unless of course a car came.

– Hold the ball!

. . . and just like that, everything stopped. Unfair advantage never taken, everybody standing statue-like until the traffic passed and the all-clear was given.

– Ball's off!

I think it was Man United versus Liverpool, the score, 17-2 . . .

. . . Cypress Street was an ocean of motion, short pants, dirty exposed knees, quarter-irons knocking sparks off the road. Georgie Worst made a break up the wing by the high footpath, a glory hunter, he wouldn't let the ball off. Tragic Ted, well-placed at the far side of the gate, an open goal.

– Cross de ball! Cross de ball! Ted was screaming. – On de head!

Georgie sold me a dummy, with a quick flick off the footpath, no one to beat only the goalie.

– Remember 1916! he shouted.

– On de head! On de head! Ted was frantic.

Backward-running, shirt-tugging, red-faced, panting.

– Oooough! The frenzy brought the Stratford End to their toes, The Kop rose up as one,

> – *Georgie Worst, Super Spa*
> *He walks like a woman,*
> *An' he wears a bra!*

– On de head! Tragic was manic.

Georgie's eyes darted. The goal was wide open. But then he stopped, he just stood on the ball and stopped it dead. We all stopped too, expecting traffic, but the street was clear. Georgie stepped over the ball and as if in a trance, walked straight across the goal mouth, his pace quickening to a trot.

There turning the corner were his mam and dad, Eddie de Nut. Their arms full with bags and boxes and flowers, half-eaten bunches of grapes and half-empty bottles of Lucozade. By the time Georgie reached his mam, his eyes were popping out of his head.

– Do ya have him, Mam?

She just nodded and there bringing up the rear was Georgie's Nan carrying his new baby brother. Georgie just stood there. Me and the lads swarmed.

– Gis a look! Gis a look! we were screaming.

Georgie, like Moses at the Red Sea, calmly made his way through the mob.

– Is dat him, Nan? Is dat me baby brudder?

– We'll get him home first, an' den you can take a look'v 'im, Nan smiled.

– Ah gowaan! G'is a look!

For once The Stratford End and The Kop were united.

– Dere, Georgie, she leaned over. – Dere's yer baby brudder, now wha' do ya tink a' him?

She peeled back the swaddling. He had a small crinkly

face. Georgie never saw a baby before. Georgie's eyes were like saucers.

– So what do ya tink a' him? Nan repeated.

Georgie just stared.

– He's very pink, isn't he? he mumbled.

– He is pink! Nan smiled. – He's very pink! she laughed. We all laughed.

That was how Pinko got his name.

The ball was put away. Grapes and cracked cups of Lucozade were handed out the window. The celebrations began. For weeks Nan would retell the story, about the day she carried her grandson home from the hospital, and how Georgie's eyes were like saucers, and how he said, – *He's very pink!* And everybody would laugh, and Georgie was a hero.

* * *

I was there the day Pinko came home from the hospital. We drank cracked cups of Lucozade to his health, and there he was, in the hall outside the cancer ward, freezing me out. Imagine that, just because he's wearing a £200 suit and I'm in an army parka. Jesus, Pinko's a right gowl all the same.

Pinko's attitude didn't bother me though. I was visiting Fatfuka. Fatfuka, now there's another fella that got his nickname young. His da, Pa Crowley, was in the pub celebrating the arrival of yet another child, his ninth.

Pa Crowley had a foul tongue in his head, anyway there he was buying drink all round . . .

– Congratulations, Pa boi, so eh, is it a boy or a child?

– It's a fat fucker! Pa laughed and shook hands with the free-drinker.

. . . and just like that the name stuck, odd isn't it, just like that everybody started calling the baby Fatfucker. His dad, his eight brothers and sisters, aunts, uncles, everybody, everybody except his mother. But she soon gave in and after a while it didn't mean fat fucker at all, it was just a name. I mean he was christened something else, but everybody called him Fatfuka, just plain and simple Fatfuka. And you know, the funny thing was: he grew up to be a tall, thinnish young fella, but it didn't matter, Fatfuka was his name. I suppose it's sorta like having a name like Smith or Carpenter when you don't hold a trade. It's just a name, and it doesn't really matter.

# 6

Fatfuka's dad wasn't an alcoholic, but he used to drink an awful lot. People said he was in the IRA, or at least he was connected. Everybody knew that Fatfuka's uncle was jailed during the border campaign back in the 50's, and of course the fact that his grandda had shot dead three Black and Tans from the roof of the bank during the troubles, was part of history.

He spent three whole days up on the roof just waiting for the right moment to strike terror into the heart of the Empire. They had a book in the house with him in it and everything.

Fatfuka's dad never saw action though, that was probably why he drank so much. But sometimes when he'd be well-oiled, he'd get all patriotic like and walk out into the middle of the street to reenact his father's day of glory. It always began with a sort of a speech,

– Tree days an' tree nights, he lay in dat gully on de roof of de Munster an' Leinster Bank. Tree days an' tree nights without shelter from de torrential rain or de howling November winds. Tree days an' nights with only a ponnie a' milk, a loaf a' bread and a baulk a' cheese to keep life in his

31

body. Old Pa Crowley didn't care about life, not his nor no-one else's. No! Not at all. My fadder would have gladly sacrificed his worldly self dat Ireland might be free! Free from de tyrants' yoke. Eight hundred years of oppression, dey stole our language, our culture, our youth, our land, but worst of all dey stole our dignity. An' after eight hundred years, tree whole days don't seem dat long to have to wait.

Fatfuka's dad would then reach for the nearest thing that looked like a rifle – you know a stick, a hurley or a brush, or something. He'd hold it under his shoulder and up against his cheek, running his bloodshot eye down along the barrel. Slowly the speech would begin again, very quietly, but gradually working himself up into a frenzy. He'd stand there like a monument, gun pointed to the road, as if he were perched on a roof-top looking down. He always began in a whisper,

– Tree whole days! Tree whole days! Tree whole days! Tree whole days!

Tree whole days! Tree whole days! Tree whole days! Tree whole days! and then he'd stop.

– I have 'em in me sights, tree of 'em. An officer flanked by two privates.

I have 'em in me sights, three a' de bastards.

Steady, wait a second. Steady! Steady! No, not yet, not yet . . .

I thinks of me wife an' me two sons, I whispers an Act of Contrition.

I pray to God dat if I die dis day, he'll take me quickly.

I take aim.

*Bang!*

A shot in de head, de fucker's dead, glory-oh!

De Officer fumbles tryin' to get his revolver from his holster. De second Private turns with his rifle pointin' skyward.

*Click-click!* I reload.

*Bang!*

I get de bastard clean through de heart, and blow de fucker arse over head. De Officer is still struggling with his holster. I stand up in full view, raise me gun up over me head an' roar,

*Remember 1916, ya bastard!*

De Officer looks up an' sees de vengeance in me eyes. I shouts at him,

Die, ya Imperialist cunt! Die! I raises me rifle to me face.

*Click-click! Bang!*

I plant one right between his fuckin' eyeballs. He falls backwards onto de footpath, two hands stretched, like Christ on de cross.

Fatfuka's dad would then rise a clenched fist above his head,

– *Remember 1916!* he'd roar, he'd stop.

– . . . remember 1916, he'd whisper.

Fatfuka's dad was a pity, a bit like James Dean really.

It became our war cry, it didn't matter if it was cops and robbers, or cowboys and Indians, even the simplest game of chasing, it would always be,

– Remember 1916!

\* \* \*

It hit me like a sledgehammer, when I heard Fatfuka had cancer, I just couldn't believe it. Fatfuka of all people, one of the few lads from MacSweeneya to get his act together. I mean, the whole street was really proud when he joined the Christian Brothers. He was like a hero going off to join the Foreign Legion or something. Fifteen years of age at the time, we didn't see much of him after that, but you would always hear the bits and pieces.

Anyway some years later he quit the Brothers and went

teaching, married a girl from the northside. They had everything; the house, the job, the car, two kids, the lot. But then they found some growths on one of his organs or somewhere. It just seemed so unfair. A real sound bloke, you know like. If you met him in the pub, he'd chat away with ya, sound out, but then he got cancer.

* * *

I checked the nurse's office, nobody there, that was when I noticed Pinko coming down the corridor looking well in a suit and a bunch of flowers under his arm.

– Hoi Pinko! he didn't recognise me. – It's me Pluto, Paul O'Toole, Pluto, from MacSweeney Street.

– Ah! Pluto, How're ya getting on? Haven't seen ya in a lifetime.

– Jeezus, Pinko, you look like a million dollars, how're things?

– Pluggin' away, he said.

– Somebody said you opened a shop?

– Eh? A newsagents? I've three now.

– Did ye give up de sellin' on the street?

– Naw, my father still has the streets.

– Eddie? Eddie de Nut? How's he?

– He'll never change, he said.

– Ya didn't get married?

– Naw, but I heard you married a French one, Pluto.

– Not for long though! and I laughed.

Next thing I know he's telling me about this book he's writing. I don't know how we got on to that but I think he asked me what I was doing, and I was telling him that I was drawing the dole, but before I could say "the dole", he cut me off mid-sentence.

34

– I'm drawing . . .

– Really? I'm doing a bit of writing myself, he said.

– What sort of writing? I asked, skipping over the whole dole thing.

– Well, it's sort of a novel.

It was about a fella who went off to join the Christian Brothers and after a few years he knew it wasn't for him so he quit. It was like he joined to please his mother, or something. Anyway when he came out he met an old boyhood friend, they fell in love, like steamers, and everything was hunky-dory. They had everything that two men who loved each other could wish for. But just as things were heading into the happy-ever-after stage, didn't the ex-Christian Brother have a conscience attack. He decided to do the right thing and give up his buff-hole surfer, find that girl-next-door type and marry her, even though he still loved his old boyhood friend with all his heart. Meanwhile the boyhood friend couldn't live without his ex-Christian Brother lover. Anyway the upshot of the whole shebang was that the boyhood friend went and threw himself into the river.

– Pig's head?

– Yeah! Dead. His body was washed up by Blackrock Castle. And he did all this just to conform to a set of morals that were imposed on him by his family, friends and a social code laid down by the Catholic Church, Pinko explained.

– Phew! Heavy stuff! I said.

But I couldn't help wondering who the hell would read such a corny story.

– So eh, wen do ya tink it'll be finished? I asked.

– It'll probably never see the light of day!

– D'ya know? Dey say most first novels are autobiographical or is it biographical – anyway, you know wat I mean.

– Really? said Pinko, and he stood back. It was as if all of a sudden he didn't want to be with me. There was a long silence.

– Ya here ta see Fatfuka? I broke the ice and asked the obvious. – Very sad wha'? Pinko just nodded his head. – Do ya know wat room he's in? I asked, he just shrugged his shoulders.

– Well maybe we could go into one a' de wards an' ask someone?

– Not a good idea, Pluto. This is a cancer ward, wait for the nurse.

He stood back, distancing himself from me.

– Jeezus, we could be here all day!

My eyes scanned the hallway.

– Are you in a hurry somewhere, Pluto?

– No, no, no, I mumbled.

That's when we began to talk and Pinko told me all about Tragic Ted dying of AIDS. A smack-head.

I was glad to see the nurse coming, Pinko was so bloody edgy.

– Ah nurse! he smiled.

– Gentlemen, can I help you? she stood into the office doorway.

– We're looking for a friend of ours.

– Yeah, Fatfuka, he's up here somewhere! I added.

– Pardon?

– De, eh, cancer ward! Eh, Fatfuka! and I pointed down the corridor.

– Fat fuc . . . ? she looked confused.

– Sorry, you'll have to excuse Pluto! You see, everybody calls our friend Fatfuka, Pinko butted in, – But eh, his real name is, eh? His real name is? Pinko looked to me for inspiration.

– His real name is, she echoed. – What is his real name?

36

– Eh? Would you believe it, Pinko sorta laughed. – I know him all my life and for the life of me, I can't remember his name!

– It's Fatfuka! I said. – Everybody calls him Fatfuka.

– Hmm, right!

The nurse scanned the registration book.

– His da's name was Pa Crowley if dat's any help.

– Ah, Crowley! relief on her face. – Yes! Yes! Yes! Crowley, Crowley James. Here, James, James Crowley. Here, he's in this room here!

The nurse opened the door into Room 305.

Jesus, he was like death, not a hair on his head, eyes sunken deep into sockets, skin stretched drum-tight over decaying bones, exaggerating the skull-like structure of his face, totally wasted, unrecognisable. Pinko's face dropped.

– Eh, Mr Crowley? These two gentlemen here . . .

She guided us towards the bed.

– Ah, Pluto? Pinko? Fatfuka raised his arm.

He was weak and looked dazed. He even sounded different, sort of like a Christian Brother. Pinko reached out, held Fatfuka's hand, kissed him on the cheek and stepped back like someone viewing a corpse. This was strange, I mean I'd known the lads all my life and we never did the huggy-kissy stuff, then again Pinko was always a bit weird. I decided to act as natural as possible.

– How's she cuttin', Fatfuka? I made to shake hands trying not to look at his derelict body. – Yer lookin' great, boi! How're ya feelin'?

Fatfuka's mouth stretched to a smile, the nurse snorted a bit of a giggle, her shoulders shook trying to hold it together. Fatfuka's smile turned to a laugh. Pinko belched out a guffaw.

– Ya never lost it, Pluto boi!

Pinko shook his head and just laughed out loud.

– Is dere something I'm missing here, lads?

Fatfuka and the nurse were in convulsions of

uncontrollable hysterics. I stood there confused, Fatfuka groaning between laughter and tears, Pinko and the nurse doubled over. Maybe it was because I was a bit stoned, but I just didn't get the joke. I mean, in all fairness, I never saw Fatfuka looking so bad, as long as I'd known him. But I laughed all the same and they laughed louder.

When all that died down, we just sat there on the side of the bed, three friends talking. We talked about the old days, Tragic Ted, Georgie, Grandda Buckley and life on MacSweeney Street. Fatfuka gave a blow-by-blow breakdown of street football on Cypress Street. Games, not exactly as I remembered them, but then again memories are sort of personal things. It was just like old times, but it wasn't. We were strangers to each other and that was the painful part. It was like we were pretending to be friends, it was over-played and old-hat. We had moved on from those days, and all that was left on the shelf were the glossy book-ends of hot summers and happiness.

– Great days all the same, eh? Pinko smiled.

Fatfuka nodded and groaned a bit.

– Did ya hear about Tragic Ted? I changed the subject.

Pinko's face stiffened.

– What about him? asked Fatfuka.

– Tell him Pinko! Tell him wat ya told me.

Pinko looked daggers at me.

– Ah, 'tis nothing, he said.

– What about Ted? Fatfuka pulled himself up in the bed.

– He's died of AIDS, isn't dat right, Pinko!

Pinko didn't answer.

– What? Ted's dead? Fatfuka looked shocked.

– Langer!

– Wat? Wat did I do?

– AIDS? Fatfuka whispered. – Poor aul' Ted . . .

He sighed, shook his head and slumped back down onto the bed. There was a deadly silence.

38

When we came out Pinko read me the riot act for being so insensitive, I told him to go fuck himself. Anyway I haven't seen Pinko since, and thanks be to Christ for that, is all I can say.

* * *

The last time I met Tragic Ted I didn't even know he was sick. It was a few years back, in London. I heard Mags was over there. I was hoping I could persuade herself and small Paulo to come home. I never found them. It was my first time in London, I didn't realise how big the place was.

Piccadilly was jointed. Every class of colour and creed bustling shoulder to shoulder like ants. And there he was in the distance, looking like a crusty.

– Ted! Hoi Tragic Ted! Is dat you, Ted?

I wasn't sure, I hadn't seen him in a while.

– It's me, Ted, Pluto!

– Huh?

– It's me, Paul O'Toole, Pluto, MacSweeney Street, eh Ted?

Maybe it wasn't him?

– Ah Pluto man! and he smiled exposing decaying stumps of yellow-green and brown teeth. – Pluto?

I looked at Ted. He was a mess.

– Jeezus it's good ta see ya, Ted boi, good ta see ya.

– Yeah right, he stumbled over the words. – Good ta see ya too, Pluto man.

And we fell into a crazy conversation of nothingness. I wouldn't mind, but I knew better than to ask an old friend where they're living or what they're up to. It always leads to an embarrassing silence or a string of lies, but I tripped into my own trap. He was living somewhere, working nowhere and not up to much. He was in bits, an addict, dealing smack in Piccadilly

Underground. He unsettled me. You can never trust a junkie. So I said goodbye and walked away. It nearly killed me. Tragic Ted stood there with a hopeless smile on his dirty face, like a well-worn rock causing a ripple in the constant stream of commuters.

– Eh! Ted? I turned.

– Pluto? his eyes widened.

– Ya haven't seen Mags around, have ya?

– Who? he stretched his ear towards me.

– Eh Mags, me ex-aul' doll, and her child Paulo?

– Is dat de French one? he strained his memory.

– No, no, no! Not Yvette! Mags! Mags and Paulo! Me ex-aul' doll and our kid! Y'know, from Cork!

– Eh! What do she look like, Pluto man?

– Ah! forget it, I said.

Sure Ted wouldn't have a clue who Mags was.

– Bu' ? Bu'?

Ted wanted to talk. I had nothing to say to him.

– No problems, Ted boi. No problems, gotta go, see ya around, Ted boi.

– Yeah right! Pluto man.

– Keep de faith, Ted.

And I walked away.

I turned to wave, he stood there rooted, with that stupid smile on his face. I waved, he just raised his eyebrows, brightening his big blue watery eyes. It nearly killed me, so it did. I was his oldest friend, and that one-minute chat was probably the only conversation he'd had in a long time. I should have taken him with me, but I had nowhere to go. I just walked away. There was nothing I could do for him. He was destroyed. To the masses he was just another dirty old junkie with natty hair and black hands, but all I could see was the Tragic Ted I knew. A wide-eyed, macaroon-eating, nine-year-old dirty-face, who moved into our street, must be nearly twenty-five years ago, and it cut me to the bone just to walk away.

# 7

It wasn't something they talked about all the time, but every now and then it would crop up.

– And just to think, they'd say. – She took off her rings and shoes and placed them neatly on the bench next to her before she bare-footed it down de steps into de black river, just imagine . . .

I never understood the big deal of it all. Those shoes were her good shoes. She picked them out herself from Barry and Hyland's window. She paid for them on the never-never over the three months coming up to Christmas. My dad told me that each time she cleared a bit on the slate, she'd try on the shoes and admire them in the mirror, as if justifying the extravagance.

That's why. That's why my mother didn't bring her new shoes with her to the river. It'd be such a waste.

* * *

Rory Gallagher's *Moonchild* comes to an end. I light my rollie and switch the radio off. 1:59 on the clock. Another sleepless night, of nightmarish memories and painful dreams. I'm alone but I'm not lonely. I look around my flat, my castle, my hole. Is this what it's all about? Is this the grand total of thirty-three years of living? One big struggle, one painful experience after another. It wasn't always like this, we had some good times, down MacSweeneya in the old days, me, Pinko, Georgie, Fatfuka, Tragic Ted and the lads.

And here I am on Waterloo Terrace. Not ten minutes from MacSweeney Street but worlds apart, sharing my front door with a bunch of no-mind misfits. Brenda the Brasser, Herman and the Monk, maybe I'm being a bit heavy on them, but I swear to God, everything about this kip is bad news and that's the truth.

Take No. 7, the top of the house. It's been locked up for the past couple of months. The last tenant was a national-school teacher, fresh out of Mary Immaculate Teacher Training College in Limerick, like a little lay nun ready to take on the world and teach the youth. She was a quiet sort of country girl who kept herself to herself. I never really talked to her. When I'd pass her in the hallway she always held her head low.

Anyway, she was only here a couple of weeks and one night, heading for half one in the morning there's a most unmerciful commotion up in her flat and a thundering down the stairs. She comes charging down shoeless, in her night-dress, screaming. She runs out into Waterloo Terrace and vanishes. Never comes back to collect her things or anything. That was the last we saw or heard of her. No. 7 has been vacant ever since.

Herman was on the stairs that night. He said she was like a crazy person, eyes bulging, hair wild, night-dress shredded, face scrawled and bleeding. He said it was the first time she had ever talked to him . . .

– Get outa' my way! she screamed.

– Is zere somethink wrong? Herman asked.

– Get outa' my way! The Divil's in my room! The Divil's in my fuckin' room!

– Der Divil?

Herman held her shoulders trying to calm her. She stared at him for a split second then her right hand shot out and scrawled his face. He released his grip. Like a flash of lightning she was gone, down the stairs screaming, vanishes into the night. The following day, the handyman came around to nail and padlock her door. Myself and Herman cornered him on the stairs, you know gettin' the low-down.

Seemingly it was the same as always, when she got home from work that evening. Although the flat was cooler than usual and there were traces of smoke lingering in her room. She didn't pay much attention to it, these old chimney-breasts always leaked. She did notice that it smelt of turf or wet straw, but the people in this part of town have been known to burn their own floorboards to keep themselves warm. So she turns up the Super-ser to three, the place is still freezing. She decides to get into bed for the warmth.

As she's pulling her night-dress down over her head, she catches a glimpse in her mirror, sees what looks like a man lying on her bed. She turns around, but no-one's there. She switches off the heater and sits into the bed. Strange, because even though it's skinning with the cold, there's a warm patch running right down the middle, as if somebody had been lying there. This freaks her out a bit. She decides to get up and make a cup of tea for herself. She throws back the bed-clothes, sits up on the bed and makes her way over to the wardrobe where her dressing-gown is hanging. As she opens the door of the wardrobe, once again in the mirror she sees the same man on her bed. She turns her head, he's gone, but the bed is smouldering with hot embers and soot scattered all around. She reaches for her dressing-gown. That's when she

43

notices smoke rising from the bottom of the wardrobe. She looks down: two black cloven legs, the hooves of a beast. She makes to scream. His hands shoot out from behind her hanging clothes, two reddish-brown hands with long black curling nails and arms covered in the fur of an animal's pelt rather than human hair. This is when she first comes face to face with the Devil. An evil, keen, ruddy face, surrounded by a shock of tight black curls, a beard neatly trimmed to a point and two small snailshell-like horns twisted tightly, one at each corner of his temples. He's snarling, foaming at the mouth as he tears at her. She battles with Satan,

– But vot did der Divil vant from her? Herman asked.

– Jesus, I dunno! said the handyman. – Maybe her soul or something. Anyway they fought and made total shit of the flat, so they did. And then she broke free and made a run for it!

– Ah! Zat must haff been ven I met her on der stairs.

– So eh, wat's de story with No. 7 now? I asked.

– Well, the boss told me to lock the place up, said the handyman.

– Lock de place up?

– The Devil! he pointed up the stairs.

– Surely she don't believe dat de Devil's up dere?

– Look, I don't know what the landlady believes, I only does what I'm told. But I tell ya dis much, if the Devil is up there, I'd say it's better to have the door locked and nailed shut, just in case like.

I just looked at Herman, we both turned our eyes to heaven.

And that was the last we heard of the Devil, the schoolteacher and the handyman.

And what about Herman up in No. 4? What the hell is he doing here? A German? Nobody emigrates to Ireland. Brenda the Brasser was telling me that as far as she knew, he was in Insurance or something and he met Maebh, a girl from Donegal. She was working in an Irish bar in downtown Dusseldorf. Herman fell under her spell. It's a common enough thing, when a man meets an attractive, sweet and charming young woman who smiles each time he demands more beer, laughs at his corny jokes, encourages his smutty comments, just takes his money and smiles. A bit like prostitution, everything has a price, but not everything is for sale. I suppose that's why publicans employ bar-maids – well it's not to improve the taste of the beer. Anyway, Maebh introduced Herman to the magic of Irish music, I think it was The Clancys, or The Dubliners, or The Wolftones, U2, or maybe it was Johnny Logan, or somebody, it doesn't matter. Well, it didn't matter to me or Brenda. It certainly mattered to Herman, he was hooked.

Summer comes, summer goes and Maebh returned to Dublin, her boyfriend and Trinity. Herman, like a love-sick tomcat, chucked the job in Dusseldorf and followed her. He began his search for Maebh in beautiful Bundoran in Donegal. Slowly he drifted southwards along the west coast of Ireland. It was a ten-year odyssey and by the time he found himself in Cork by the Lee he had a son in Kinvarna, a daughter in Spanish Point and was playing the bodhrán, dabbling in Art *agus ag caint cúpla focal Gaeilge* – speaking a few words of Irish. He never found Maebh though.

That was eight years ago, ever since he's been living here on Waterloo Terrace. He's given up the bodhrán, thanks be to Christ, although he still dabbles in the Art and the *cúpla focal*. When he's flush he usually takes No. 6, calls it The Studio. The Studio if you don't mind? A flat, is a flat, is a flat.

– The bloody Studio? Some people! I ask ya?

* * *

Sometimes it's easier to see yerself in the people that surround you. I mean like, if all your friends are balmpots, well the chances are that you're a balmpot. Then again you wouldn't be hanging around with them if they were balmpots, would you? Not unless you didn't realise they were balmpots in the first place. Anyway, I think that the crowd who live in this house are a bunch of balmpots. I'm not too sure what I'm doing stuck in the middle of them.

So here I am in this no-minds'-land, and I can't help but ask myself,

– Is dis it? Is dis wat it's all about?

Jesus, not a teabag or an Easi-single in the flat. Is this it? All my life lies, nothing but lies: Santy Claus, Fairy Godmothers, frog-kissing Princesses, Adam and Eve. Years of confession, confusion and Mass, years of getting knocked about by some arse-hole of a so-called teacher for not knowing my *Modh Coinníollach* from my *Tuiseal Ginideach*, and all for what? Crap jobs, signing on the labour and it's not getting any better, might get a Community Employment Scheme. Is that it? To live out my life on Rent Allowance, Health Board hand-outs. Unemployment benefit! Bastards! That's what they are.

I've had my run-ins with that shower, they put me through hoops. It's like there's an invisible line, the only thing that separates us from them is power. The more people on our side of the line, the clearer the line is, the more power they have. They tell you nothing. Their job is to give you as little as they can get away with, and when they realise you're on to them, they don't like it. They don't like it when you question the system. Bastards! That's what they are. And here I am facing back into all that again.

46

Nothing, no food, no job, no flat, no friends, no wife, no aul' doll, no sleep, no nothing. Nothing but a half bottle of JD and two hits of acid, and do you know what? I don't even drink whiskey, not to mind do acid. Herman brought me the whiskey about a year ago, duty free from Germany, and the acid came from Tony Tabs.

* * *

Everybody knows Tony Tabs, but Tony Tabs knows me and that's the difference. It's like we always knew each other, not that we were ever really friends or anything, we just knew each other. You know like, pass him on the street,

– Howzit goin, Tone?

– Plugging away. Yerself, Pluto?

You know that sort of thing. Sometimes he'd even stop and we'd chat, you know, about nothing.

– Howzit goin, Tone?

– N'too bad. Yerself, Pluto?

– Strugglin'.

– Are ya still over in the other place?

– Naw I'm gone from dere, but I'm livin' up above now.

– I thought ya were gone from there.

– Naw, dat was de last place, you know over across like. How bout yerself, Tone?

– Ah, I moved about two year back.

– Gowaan, where are ya now?

– I'm back in the old gaff . . .

Anyway it was in one of those chats, that he gave me the two tabs. He insisted. I told him I hadn't done acid in about five years, but he insisted anyway seeing as it was Christmas time.

– Great tack! he guaranteed, and told me there was plenty

47

more where that came from if I wanted some. He said he'd be surprised if I didn't get back to him after I tried it.

– Great tack! he repeated.

I sort of felt my brain wasn't as elastic as it used to be, to be going messing with any psychedelic stuff.

– You know like, it might never spring back! I explained. He laughed.

– Gowaan ou' that! and he pushed the tabs into my hand.

– Happy Christmas! he said and walked away.

. . . and there they are wrapped in tinfoil, on my dresser ever since.

# 8

Drugs? I can take them or leave them. But, sometimes I wonder what if? What if I had stayed away from them altogether? Then again what if I never took that bus, or had that chat, or bent down that day to tie my laces, what if? What if? You can't live a life of what ifs? I mean, what if this was China, sure we'd all be eating rice. But sometimes you'd wonder, you know, what if?

I asked the doctor about it that time the burn holes on my forehead got infected,

– Do ya tink if I never done drugs dis wouldn't have happened, Doctor?

– Get over yourself and get on with it!

\* \* \*

Growths! It was a nightmare, pimples I could live with, but this?

I balanced my rollie on the edge of the sink and leaned over, my nose touching the mirror.

– Jeezus! I couldn't believe it. – Twigs?

About ten of them, tight, gnarled, twisted, contorted twigs. Hard twigs sprouting from my forehead, just above my right eyebrow.

– Jeezus Christ!

Hard little crusty horn-like twigs, each one almost identical, about a quarter of an inch long and growing to the right, tight against my forehead in the direction of the window, probably had something to do with the way I slept. They were crisp and crunchy to the touch, with clusters of green waxy leaves bursting out along the branches. What do you do when you've got twigs growing out of your head?

I noticed the rows of small pimples above my eye before I went to sleep, small hard green-tipped pimples, but twigs? Jesus! What do you do with twigs?

This was something I had to deal with on my own, I mean like, what could a doctor do for me? Send me to a horticulturist? Well, shag that for a game of soldiers! I'm sick of being a Health Board guinea-pig; drug the rest of the population into submission with pills and painkillers and antibiotics for all I care, but not this lab rat, no more. I'm going alternative!

I knew combing my hair down over the growths wouldn't really work, for one thing, people would notice, you know like,

– Hey Pluto, ya changed yer hair style, John, Paul, George, Ringo and Pluto! The fifth Beatle, wha?

Anyway, even if the hairstyle did hide the twigs, how long would that last? God only knows how quickly these things grow. What if they start flowering?

– Holy Fuckaroni!

What if they sprout berries? Fruit-trees growing out of my forehead, just above my right eye, Jesus! I know nothing about plants; never had gardens on MacSweeney Street. But one thing I did learn from the odd gardening programme on de radio was, you don't get rid of bushes by chopping them down, it only makes them stronger and they come back thicker.

So, I jammed my thumb-nail sharp at the base, in under one of the growths, just at the point where the skin turned to wood, and prised it in as deep as I could, deep into the fleshy stem. A quick flick.

– *Chitch!* it snapped off.

One by one, the twigs fell to the sink but that wasn't the end of it. There lined up across my forehead, three rows of bumps, hard, green, pointed bumps. Rip them out by the roots was the only way.

So, I dug deep, deeper than the roots, deep enough to draw blood. It had to be done. Blood streamed down over my right eyebrow, across the bridge of my nose, and dripped into the sink. I examined the ten bloody craters, no sign of any roots or saplings, thanks be to God! But what if they grew back? I flicked the ash from the top of my rollie, and took a drag, reddening the tip. Slowly, precisely, I burned out all traces of vegetation or root fibres in each of the stem sites. Ten burnt-out craters across my forehead, it hurt but it just had to be done. And then for good measure, I reached under the sink where there was an old bottle of weedkiller. The landlady had given it to me that time the grassy stuff started growing under the skirting-board behind the shower. I rinsed my face and the back of my neck with it. And that was the last I ever saw of the twigs. Well, if you don't count that time the following spring, when I noticed a bump on the top of my head. I tried to check it out in the mirror but because of the angle and my thick growth of hair, I never actually got to examine it. Luckily I knew the treatment. So, I picked it off until it bled, purified the wound with a cigarette-tip and a few drops of weedkiller, just to be sure, that put a stop to that.

\* \* \*

Alison empties what's left of her milk down the sink and puts the glass into the dishwasher. She feels sorry for Paul O'Toole, she knows of his history of mental illness, the Health Board informed her all about that before she took him on as a tenant. But she just can't cope with him any more. It's always one thing after another. She doesn't like to think of him without a roof over his head, but what do you do? All she wants is a trouble-free existence.

Her accountants tell her that she's actually losing money on the Waterloo Terrace property. She'd be a lot better off if she gutted the place and converted it into top-class apartments. But there is a sort of an unwritten code; you see, some of these tenants have been there since her father's time and she can't raise the rent. Then again, the place is a bit of a tip. It's swings and roundabouts really.

\* \* \*

I stub out my rollie and push myself down into the bedclothes, damp musty sheets, three whole days.

– Shag dat witch, and anyone who looks like her! that's all I can say.

I lie here in silence trying to sleep, images spiralling around my demented brain, I laugh. My chest is full of pain and sadness. I just want to cry. I know crying will solve nothing, it never has. Nothing changes unless somebody hears your cries, there is nobody to hear mine. I dig my head deep down under the smelly bedclothes and cry anyway.

\* \* \*

– Huh! 2:03, footsteps on the ceiling, probably Brenda the Brasser or someone . . .

# 9

– My little man.

It's a terrible thing to have no real memories of someone who means so much to you. That's the way it is with my mother. Not one memory, and my dad had very little to say about her. But one thing he used often say was,

– My little man . . . t-t-that's wat she used c-call ya, Paul, an' de-de-d'ya know dat for de first t-t-two years of yer l-l-life she'd never let ya out a' her arms. Upstairs, downstairs, on de s-s-street or over to de sh-sh-shop, always in her arms, and it was always de s-s-same. My little man.

\* \* \*

2:03.

They're cruising the streets in the squad car, the fella with the ears enjoying the power he's experiencing behind the wheel, the burly fella rambling on about his years on the Force, crime and law and order.

– Law an' order is a bit like chalk an' cheese really, you know like, very similar but poles apart, the burly fella says. – Drugs! Dat's wat it is, 'tis all drugs dese days. Ye can hang a right here. See down dere, dat's de red-light district. Get yer

53

rocks down de docks! Dat's what dey say. I tell ya, I've seen a few changes in dis town over de years. Sure dere was no crime in de old days, you know like, if a fella stepped outa' line ya gave him a flake over de back a' de neck with de two-pound flashlamp, and dat'd be de end of it. Tellin' ya! De shame of de law callin' to de house would nip most of it in de bud. But dese days? Naaw! Dey've no respect for de law at all. 'Tis too easy dey has it. Up agin' the wall an' shoot de lot of 'em, dat's wat I says! See 'tis all drugs dese days!

Hoi, slow down, ya can turn up left dere . . .

\* \* \*

2:03.

*Knock-knock! Knock-knock!*

He can hear the tinny sound of her radio in the background. It sounds like Neil Diamond.

*Knock-knock! Knock-knock!*

– Hang on a sec! Brenda's voice cackles from behind the battered door.

– Is me, Herman! he shuffles outside on the small landing.

– One sec! her voice muffled by the sliding of bolts, rattling of chains and latches. The door eases open, revealing a face only a pimp could love. Faded eyes, smeared lipstick on wrinkled lips, wild bleached-blonde hair down, exposing silver roots and all this smelling of drink.

– Ah! Brenda! Neil Diamond, yes?

He points over her left shoulder into the flat.

– *Vot a beautiful noize, Ba, Ba, Ba, Ba . . .* He sings along with the tune.

– Jeezus! Herman boi, what do ya want? 'Tis two o'clock in the mornin'!

– Eh, sorry, sorry, I worry for Pluto!

54

– Pluto?

– Ja! Down in No. 1.

– What about him?

– I haff not seen hide or hair off him in two or three days now.

– So what!

Brenda doesn't really have the energy to be dealing with Herman.

– Vell, maybe zere is something wrong! Pluto has not been out of his flat, is this not strange?

– How do you know he hasn't?

– Vell, I talk to Jimmy.

– Jimmy?

– Ja, Jimmy ze Monk up in No. 5.

– Oh, dat Jimmy?

– Ja, ze Monk, he has not seen Pluto either!

– What do ya want me to do about it, Herman boi?

– I am concerned for Pluto's well-being!

– Take it from me, Herman luuv! Pluto's fine, I mean I can hear his radio being switched on and off, all hours of the night like.

– But, maybe he is, vell you know!

Brenda knows what he's getting at. It was Herman who found Pluto the last time he tried to kill himself.

– Look, I'm not one to gossip, Herman boi, but he had a bit of a barney with herself on Monday, I'd say he's just a bit low.

– Herself?

– The Witch!

– Oh! Ze Witch!

– Yeah she wants him out by Friday, I think he's takin' it fairly bad, but I'd say he'll be fine, Brenda tightens the belt on her robe.

55

– Yes, he tells me last week of his friends, one who dies of AIDS, another who has cancer. Maybe I call down to him to talk, cheer him up, yes?

– At dis time a' de mornin'?

Brenda knows that the last thing Pluto needs is to be cheered up by Herman.

– Maybe he just needs to be on his own, she says. – I mean like he has a lot on his mind.

– Hmmm! Herman raises his right hand to chin, – I don't think he ever really got over der break-up mit his girlfriend Mags, yes? Und his wife, huh?

Herman would like nothing more than to stand there chatting about Pluto's problems and love-life for the night, but Brenda has other plans.

– Eh? I dunno boi, she steps back. – Look I'd love to invite ya in, but I'm up to me eye-balls at the moment.

– Oh, by all means Brenda, Herman waves his hand, – So you think ve should do nothink about Pluto, yes?

– Eh? Not for the time-being anyway, luuv, not for the time-being.

– I keep you informed of any developments, yes?

– That'd be great, Herman luuv.

And she closes the door gently but firmly in his face, deadening the radio and Neil Diamond. He waits on the landing for a second or two then heads back up to his own flat or studio.

* * *

– *Thud!*

2:05. Sounds like Brenda's door closing.

– Maybe I'll have a fag.

So I reach for my rollies. – An' d'ya know wat? I'll

56

have a drop a' whiskey, it's me birthday. Thirty-three today!

I sit up on the bed, click on the radio.

   *. . .What a beautiful noise,*
*comin' up from the street . . .* It's Neil Diamond.

What a load a rubbish, if I owned a radio station I'd make it a rule,

NO CRAP MUSIC

I mean of all the great tracks in all the world, some tasteless, tone-deaf, poulanus of a DJ, with a flick of a switch can just inflict Neil Diamond on the whole country at two o'clock in the morning without warning, sure that's crazy! Somebody should phone them, or something.

I make for the window, take down the half bottle of JD, blow the dust off and rise it to the light of the street lamp. As usual, outside there's murder. It sounds like it's coming from the Lower Road, down by the station. But night-time is strange that way, sound travels further in darkness. I pour a drop into my Man United mug and take a mouthful. I hold it there afraid to swallow, and slowly it draws moisture from my cheeks and gums, and overflows trickling down my throat.

– Aaaah! Not bad! Not bad at all.

I take another sip, and head back to bed and Neil Diamond.

# 10

I visited Fatfuka again in the hospital, the day after the flare-up with Pinko. I suppose I sorta felt I had some unfinished business. It was like Pinko cramped my style. I just wanted to meet Fatfuka on my own.

It had only been a day, but you could see he was wasting away. It was like he was rotting there in front of my eyes. We hadn't talked in twenty years. I'd say things like – *Hi!* or – *How's yer mother?* And things like that, but we hadn't really talked. It was strange, just the two of us, waiting for God.

Fatfuka had no shortage of visitors, they had him pestered,

– Don't get me wrong, he explained. – I love to see my wife and kids. But Jesus, her mother and the crowd from work? Don't be talkin' to me! I usually pretend I'm asleep, he laughed.

– Wat about me?

– Not at all! Not at all! Pluto boi, a breath a' fresh air, that's what you are.

After that there was no stopping me, I was calling every day. We'd just sit there, chatting about nothing and everything like old friends. It was like there was a desperation in our new-found friendship, two of us realising life had no real future for us. Just the pain of the present, and the pleasures of the past.

– Did you ever get to Sherkin Island? he asked.

    – Sherkin? Sherkin Island?

    – Remember you used always be saying it was the best place in the world.

    – Jeezus, I forgot all about Sherkin.

* * *

Sherkin Island? It's amazing the impression a place can leave on you. Two and a half years of age I was; too young to remember anything of it. But it was the best holiday we ever had or so my dad would say. It was the only holiday we ever had.

A fella by the name of Franky, Franky Driscoll, from Sherkin who worked up in Mulla's Yard with my dad convinced him it would be a great place to bring meself, Kathleen and my mother for the weekend. My dad wasn't sure, but Franky talked him into it, filling his head with stories of sandy beaches, fresh air, warm seas from the Gulf of Mexico and pubs that never close. Done. So on the Friday of the August Weekend, with sacks and bags and cases and boxes held together with twine, we took the bus to Baltimore for the ferry to Sherkin Island.

When Franky saw us arriving at the pier,

    – Napoleon travelled lighter, he said.

My dad spent the rest of his life looking back on that weekend.

    – The b-b-best time of our l-l-lives, he'd say.

That's how it would always begin. He'd reach into his jacket and pull out the wallet. There folded in the side pocket a battered, dog-eared, faded photo of himself standing on a beach. His trousers rolled up to the knees, stripped to his vest, and his braces dangling, Kathleen at his feet with a bucket and spade and me perched there in his arm, the three of us squinting from the sun and smiling.

– D-d-do ya remember? he'd say, and show the photo, never actually allowing it to leave his hand, he'd put it straight back into the wallet again.

I always wished it was my mother holding me in her arms on the beach that day. It was the following Christmas time she went to the river, a photo would have been great. But it wasn't to be.

I have no living memory of that weekend, but my dad told us about it, hundreds of times.

– . . . de first night meself an' y-y-yer mother were up in de p-pub. It was comin' up to c-c-closing time, we had a-bou-bou-bout a pint an' a gl-glass left, he'd say. – So I g-g-goes up to de bar an' called a do-do-double round, no problem. Anyway dere we were t-tippin' away, it was heading towards t-ten t-t-to twelve an' de bar was pouring go-go-go-goodoh, so I says to yer mother,

– M-m-arie, will I, will I try for another one?

– Ya may as well t-t-try for two while yer at it, s-s-says she.

So, back up to de b-b-bar and I c-called for two more p-pints a' Murphy's, a drop a' J-Jameson an' two g-g-glasses a' Murphy's for herself. Yer man is p-p-pouring de p-pints sayin' nothin'.

So I s-s-says to him . . .

– Wen do de b-b-bar close?

An' j-just as de words left me m-m-mouth I knew I'd blown it. D-de whole bar stops t-t-talkin' an' looks at me. I wished de ground would ha' opened-up an' s-swallowed me on d-d-de spot. D-de barman s-stands back from de c-counter, c-closes one eye an' looks at d-d-de clock, it's almost midnight, t-t-total silence in de bar. He t-t-turns to me.

– When d-d-do we shut de bar? he says.

It was a s-s-stupid question, b-b-but it was out.

– Well?

He turns to dis b-b-big red-faced fisherman fella s-s-standing next to me an' he re-repeats de question.

– When do we s-s-shut de bar, Mickey?

Mickey stubs out his f-f-fag, puts his p-p-pint on de c-c-counter, turns, looks at me an' s-s-says,

– Good Friday!

His f-f-ace curled up an' he laughed. We d-drank away into de e-early hours a' de m-m-morning, drinkin' until we had enough or t-t-too much, whichever came first.

– G-g-good Friday! Ha! G-gas or what?

My dad would close his eyes taking full pleasure. Then he'd give an account of every moment of the weekend, from when we got on the bus at Parnell Place on the Friday, until we got back home on the Sunday night and the big fry-up of fresh mackerel caught that morning off the rocks.

Saturday was the day though. My dad told stories of eating eggs so fresh that even the hen didn't miss them. And then the beach, and how he went out in a dory fishing with Franky and they caught enough fish to feed the whole island for a week. Islanders love fish, so my dad was a hero. Stories of rabbits on headlands and swooping seagulls, crashing waves and warm seas from the Gulf of Mexico. It was heaven.

– Why c-c-couldn't life be like dat, a-a-all de time? he'd ask, and the stories would continue.

. . . then in the evening myself and Kathleen were entertained by Nan Driscoll, Frankie's Granny, with stories of underground passages, Algerian pirates and the Sack of Baltimore. My mother, my dad and Franky went off to the pub and lucked into an Island Wedding. It was the most wonderful night of their lives, they had the best of food and drink. Then they danced over crystal-glossed floorboards, my mother even sang a song. And while the wedding was at its peak, my dad took her by the hand and said goodnight to Franky. They walked arm-in-arm across the island past the Horseshoe, past Long Strand and when they came to Silver Strand they climbed up onto the headland and snuggled down into a soft green hillock looking out over the Atlantic watching the sun go down on America. My father would tell how at one stage, just as the sun vanished below the horizon the sky lit up with streaks of reds and golds and orange,

– It l-l-looked like New York was on f-f-fire . . . he'd say – Ah yes, d-de best night of our lives! W-w-wouldn't trade it for de w-w-world. An' who would tink dat your poor m-m-mother would be gone only a sh-short s-six months after . . . hah? Who would t-tink it, Pluto boi?

Who would think it indeed? It was probably that weekend on Sherkin that pushed my mother over the edge. It was like she had been given a glimpse of paradise only to have it snapped away from her forever. She was faced with living out a life of purgatory on MacSweeney Street.

\* \* \*

– So, did ya ever get to Sherkin? Fatfuka asked.

– Naw, I said – Do ya know, I was only on Sherkin once in me life and I was only two an' a half years of age at de time but I tell ya, I can picture every stone, pothole an' blade of grass on de place.

– Were you ever on any of the other small islands around Ireland?

– Yeah, England! I smirked.

Fatfuka laughed.

– What about that first time we went to Manchester?

– De time we went to see United thrash City!

– Yea, and you got off with the brasser on the boat, Pluto?

– Palm-Olive?

– Doubt ya, Pluto boi, ya!

* * *

. . . it's hard to explain the feeling of freedom when you're in a foreign land, especially that first morning we glided up the Mersey into Liverpool docks. A new world, a new day; police constables, milk-trucks, streets, shops, buildings, voices, words, sounds, everything, everything like it was in the comics.

– All Scousers are bastards! Georgie roars again.

Inside the ferry terminal. Tragic Ted's lip is burst open. Pinko's eye is bloodshot and half-closed, a gash runs along over his eye.

– Jeezus? Wha' happened ye? Georgie asks.

– Your brother! Ted points at Pinko. – He could ha' got us killed! Next time you start! Yer on yer own, Pinko boi!

– Fuck 'em! says Pinko. – City fans are slapless. Anyway I was only singin' a song!

– Singin' a shaggin' song? Ted shakes his head. – Dere was about twenty-tree of 'em dere, an' he gets up on th' table, knocks all deir drink and started singin' *In The Mosside Slums*. Only for me ye'd be dead, boi!

– Man City fans from Dublin! Pinko explains to Georgie. – Dey were slaggin' off Cork!

– Where did ye have 'em? asks Georgie.

63

– Down in de lounge on de second deck! says Ted. – Made shit a' de place, so we did!

– Just de two a' ye, against twenty-three of 'em?

– Well, there was a gang of Leeds fans from Drogheda and three Everton fans from Mallow jumped on for us, Ted says. – No one likes Man City.

– D'ya know? Pinko says. – I had one a' dem down by de hair, bootin' him in de face, an' it crossed me mind dat I didn't know if I was kickin' him because he was from Dublin or because he was a Man City fan.

– But Jeezus, wha' happened you, Pluto? Ted asks.

I'm standing dere stripped to the waist, my jacket tied around me.

– Dat's the way I found him dis mornin'! says Fatfuka.

– A night a' passion.

– Did ya get off with yer one?

– Did I wat!

– Palm-Olive! Isn't dat right, Pluto!

– Dats right, Georgie boi!

From nowhere, the place erupts with,

> Yer gonna get yer fuckin' heads kicked in!
> Yer gonna get yer fuckin' heads kicked in!
> Yer gonna . . .

There's about a hundred of them, City fans. Eyes glaring, fingers pointed like pistols. The back of my neck tingles as the noise echoes around the ferry building. They're being corralled by a line of bobbies, herding them to the buses. Pinko climbs the crowd-control barriers, scarf around his wrist,

> In the Mosside slums, in the Mosside slums,
> Ye look in the dustbin for something to eat,
> Ye find a dead dog and ye think it a treat,

> *Ye shit in yer pants every time that we meet*
> *In the Mosside slums . . .*

I didn't stop to think about it at the time, but there's something odd when a bunch of Manchester United fans from Cork are slagging off a bunch of Manchester City fans from Dublin by singing a song about a place called Mosside, and this is all happening at the crack of dawn, down the docks in Liverpool or on a ferry, out in the middle of the Irish sea. But that's football for you.

We're all up on the barriers, me and the lads from MacSweeneya. Cans and bottles are pouring down on top of us, but we're just singing a song in the rain. The cops hold their line and clear the terminal.

– Gowaan, ye Dublin fucks! Pinko roars – We'll get ye on de boat on de way back.

We jump a Black Taxi. The five of us fit into the back, no problem. Meself and Ted sit on fold-downs right behind the driver, it's dinky. Amazing, my first time ever in a taxi, and I'm in Liverpool.

– Lime Street Station! says Georgie.

The taxi takes off.

– You lads from Ireland? asks the driver.

– We're over to see United thrash City!

– Yer first time in England then, lads?

Nobody answers.

– Well, I've been to Lourdes wen I was younger, with me Mam, says Pinko.

– It didn't work! Ted shouts. – 'Cause you're still a spa, Pinko boi!

Fatfuka locks onto Pinko's head and wrestles him off the seat onto the floor of the taxi. Georgie cracks open a bottle of duty-free vodka.

– What are ye doing back there?

Georgie takes a slug of vodka and passes it on. He unties his scarf from his wrist, raises it above his head.

> *Ahhh! Me Lads,*
> *'u should ha' seen us comin',*
> *de fastest team in de league, de rest are always runnin',*
> *All de lads and lassies, smiles upon deir faces,*
> *Runnin' down de Waaaaar-rrick Roooaad,*
> *T'see Matt Busby's Aces!*

– What are ye at back there? he shouts again.

– Shut up an' drive th' fuckin' car!

> *Ahhh! . . . Me lads . . .*

. . . all the way to Lime Street Station.

* * *

– D'ya remember de time we ran into de Liverpool skinheads in de station at around seven o'clock in de mornin'? Dey were headin' south to London to see Liverpool and Arsenal in de Cup or something. We were goin' north to see United an' Oldham Athletic. Ted spotted three or four of 'em outside Lime Street an' led a charge. Do ya remember? Dey legged it into de station and us after 'em like a pack a' hounds screamin' for blood.

– Jeezus yeah! Fatfuka pulled himself up in the bed – Remember, the clatter of boots across the platform, Tragic Ted out in front and he's shouting, *Come back and fight, ye Liverpool shite!* Right into the middle of them, about two thousand Liverpool skinheads waiting for the trains to London. The crack a' dawn and here's five drunken paddies lookin' for a scatter, do you remember, Pluto? Next thing we were de ones running, lucky to get out alive. I think Ted took a few boots in the arse alright, but that was about it.

Myself and Fatfuka laughed at the memories.

– I remember de first time I met Tragic Ted, I said.

– Gowaan? Fatfuka's eyes widened.

– I suppose he was about nine or ten. He'd just moved into our street. Dere he was, a filthy face on him, eatin' a Macaroon bar!

– Gowaan?

– Yeah, he'd just been taken in by Mrs Hickey.

– Das right, Fatfuka said. – He was adopted, wasn't he?
I just nodded.

– My mam said Mrs Hickey was his auntie. His real mother died when he was a baby, and his dad just went on the batter or something.

– I remember me dad sayin' dat Ted would have starved to death only for de Nuns and Mrs Hickey.

– I tell ya, for a fella dat was taken in, he spent a lot a time on de street . . . eatin' Macaroons.

– Jesus, what a start to life! and for some reason we laughed.

– Still all the same, we're masters of our own destiny, he said.

– How d'ya mean?
I wasn't sure what he was on about.

– I mean, I'm not taking away from the rough start he had and all that, but really, Ted was miserable. Where d'ya think he got the name Tragic?

– D'ya know, I met Tragic Ted abou' fifteen years ago, he was home for Christmas. D'ya remember dat time he won a fortune in de Sweeps or de Pools or something?

– Oh yeah! Won forty grand or something.

I knew the amount was more like four thousand, but it didn't matter.

– Somethin' like dat, I nodded.

67

Patrick Street was mad, it was pissing out of the heavens, a gale-force wind. Christmas lights thrashing around above our heads. Carol-singers, shopkeepers, hawkers, everybody looking for money. I got the job of postman, doing double shifts. Only three weeks' seasonal work, but it was worth it, you need money for the Christmas. Anyway there I was, two hundred quid in my pocket, Christmas Eve and not a present bought. So I knocked off early and headed into town. I knew exactly what I was looking for.

A cap for my dad for bingo; stop him getting soaked waiting for the bus to The Glen Hall, he'd love that. For my sister Kathleen and her husband I was getting a big box of biscuits. See, they'd have loads of people calling around, the biscuits would be handy, and for the niece and nephew, I was getting two Cadbury Deluxe selection boxes. And of course, I had to get something special for my beautiful Yvette.

This was our first Christmas together as man and wife, our first Christmas in Ireland, her first Christmas away from home, and it wasn't going too well. She had all these fairytale memories of French Christmases, Yule-logs, sleigh-rides, Eggnog, Port and Brandy. I was working my balls off, getting the post out. She was spending most of her time moping around the flat. Anyway I decided I'd make it up to her by getting her something special, something nice, something romantic. A bottle of perfume and some sexy underwear. The French love that kind of stuff.

So, there I was Christmas Eve, two hundred quid in my arse pocket, outside Roches Stores, and who did I meet only Tragic Ted.

– Jeezus Ted! Long time no see.

– Ah Pluto man, how're tings?

– Good! Good! Workin' like a dog, dough. Christmas postman, double shift. Just snatchin' a bit a' time to do a bit a' last minute shoppin', how's yerself?

– Strugglin' away, ya know yerself, just back for de Christmas.

– How's England?

– It's a kip. Have ya time for a pint?

– Jeezus I'd love to, but to be honest, I really has to get me shoppin'.

– I'll come along with ya, we can go for de one after.

This wasn't exactly the plan, but what could I say. Anyway I was delighted to see Tragic, hadn't talked to him in years.

First stop the men's department Roches Stores for my dad's present. One blue peaked cap. Perfect. No delays. We queued at a cash till.

– So eh! What do ya think, Ted? I held up the cap.

– Not bad, not bad, he closed one eye. – But eh, what size is it?

– Size?

– You know like, seven, seven an' a quarter, seven an' a half, seven and three quarters, eight, eight and a quarter, you know like.

– Size?

– Like what size is yer dad's head, Pluto?

– What size is me dad's head? Jeezus Ted, I don't even know de size a' me own head? I didn't even know that heads had sizes.

– Well, you'd want to know his head size before ya go gettin' him a hat, he said.

I explained I had no time to be measuring my dad's head. All I wanted was a cap to keep him dry for bingo.

– For bingo? Why don't ya get him somethin' like a book, you know, like a book on bingo.

– Do dey have books on bingo, Ted?

– Dey has books on everything.

A book on bingo. It was settled, we could get it later. I left the cap on the counter and walked out of the shop.

There I was, standing in a check-out line, a mile long in Dunnes Stores, one big box of biscuits and two Cadbury Deluxe selection boxes in my arms.

– So eh! Who are dese for anyway, Pluto?

– Me sister Kathleen an' her kids, I said.

Ted gave me one of those looks.

– Somethin' wrong?

– No, no, not at all. I'm sure yer sister'll be delighted.

– But?

– No buts. But eh! I don't tink too many mothers would want all dat sugar an' sweets comin' into de house, ya know like.

He was dead right.

– So eh, what do ya suggest, Ted?

– I suppose you could always get 'em a few books. He wasn't joking.

I explained that we weren't really a book family.

– I mean like to dis very day de best book I ever saw was *De Commitments*, got de T-shirt, de video, de lot, but I still don't have de book, you know what I mean.

But Ted was making sense. So before we went to de book shop, I had to get Yvette's present.

I wasn't too happy having Tragic Ted traipsing after me around Cash's perfumery and women's underwear departments. Not the easiest thing for me to be doing on me own, not to mind having Tragic Ted and a langer-load of store detectives in tow.

70

He talked me out of the perfume, saying that you can't just buy a scent for a woman, it was something more personal than that, anyway he had me convinced that the biggest insult you could give to a woman, especially a French woman, was to buy her the wrong perfume.

– It's as personal as dog's piss to a bitch! he said.

So, we scrapped the perfume plan and headed off up to the Ladies' Underwear. In one way, I was glad Ted was with me. I mean like I'm the sorta fella who's too embarrassed to buy condoms, not to mind fingering me way through rows of lace, silk and satin suspender-belts, stockings, corsets, bustiers, basques, bras, boob-tubes, seamless, strapless, crotchless, thongs, G-strings, French-cut, low-cut, half-cup, cotton, camisoles, baby-dolls and teddies; and that was only the first three racks. At the end of the shop I could see the leather, rubber and the odd ostrich feather.

– Jeezus! And they say men're sex mad!

I looked to Ted. He's busy burrowing his way through the stock.

– Eh, can I help you gentlemen?

– No, no, we're just lookin'.

– Don't mind him, says Ted. – We're lookin' for something nice for me buttie's aul' doll. For Christmas, don't ya know?

– Does anything catch yer eye? she asks.

I push my eyeballs back into their sockets, – Anything at all, says I.

– So, eh, what size would you like?

– About the same as yerself – a 32B I tink – but maybe a bit keener in de waist.

She gave me one of those – Men! looks.

– What about this?

She lifted up a bit of a lacey thing.

– Perfect! says I. – Put it in a bag.

71

– Hoi!! Hold it! Hold it! says Ted. – Ya can't just take de first thing dat's waved under yer nose, Pluto man. Ye gotta check out de merchandise.

– Ah, come on, Ted boi, will'a. I just wanna get outa here.

– Chill out man, now that we're here we may as well do it right, like. Eh, excuse me miss, you might show us dat one dere, like a good girl. Do ya have it in red?

. . . and off they went down through the shop. I stood there like an expectant father in a maternity ward. Eventually, my choice was made for me. A nice silk French-cut knickers, with matching lacy brassiere and suspender-belt, pink in colour,

– Nothing smutty like black or red, says Ted.

. . . and two pairs of stockings, one black and one white. Perfect, Yvette would love this.

– So, will I gift wrap it for you?

– Naw, says Ted. – We'll eat 'em here.

He laughs, she wraps.

. . . and then Ted turns to me.

– Are ya sure 32B is her bra size?

– Well, dat's de size of de bra she has at home, like.

– Yeah! But not all bras are de same.

– How'd ya mean not all bras are de same? A 32B is a 32B, isn't it?

– Ah! For God sake! A bra isn't like a sock, Pluto boi. It's not like one size fits all.

– Look dis is a 32B, an' she's a 32B, an' no more about it!

I was begining to get sick of Ted and his advice at this stage.

– 32B or not 32B, that is the question . . . but have it your own way, said Ted and he stepped back, but he had planted the seeds of doubt in my brain.

– What exactly do ya mean, Ted?

72

– I'll put it dis way, he said. – A 32B, is a 32B, is a 32B, but dere's no guarantee it will fit her. Different cuts, fabrics, structures an' suspension, 'tis like buying a cover for a two-seater couch, ya has to try it on.

– So wha' are ya sayin', Ted?

– I'm sayin' put 'em back on de rack, and save yerself a bellyful a' heartache, 'cause believe you me, if it's too small, she'll tink dat you tink she's gettin' fat, an' if it's too big, she'll tink her Bob-a-louis are too small.

– Her Bob-a-whaties?

– Look! I'd say you'd save yerself a lot a grief if ya bought her a good book.

That solved everything, all I had to do was get a few books. So, I went to the Hi-B for a pint with Ted. We chatted about the old days on MacSweeney Street. He told me he had tried out for Notts Forrest a few years earlier. I asked him if he met the Sheriff of Nottingham, he laughed and said he was glad to see the back of the place. I told him I had just got married to Yvette, and how I met her in Amsterdam about six months earlier and how I really loved her. He told me about winning the four thousand pounds. I asked what it was like to be a millionaire, he just threw his eyes to heaven and laughed again. We finished our pints, and headed for the bookshop, stopping off on the way at Elbow Lane to roll a joint. Jesus! Tragic Ted; one miserable shagger to go shopping with.

So that was it, that was the Christmas I bought my dad *The World Book of Anthropology*, Waterstones were clean out of books on bingo. I got my sister and her family an atlas, they'd never been outside Cork in their life. And I got Yvette a book on French cookery. It was my first Christmas with the beautiful Yvette, and my last.

# 11

So there I was, talking to Fatfuka about Grandda Buckley, the oldest man on MacSweeneya, confined to a wheelchair, a local hero.

– Da's right, I said. – Imagine dat? Losing his legs at de age of seventeen in de trenches at de battle a' de Somme, fighting for England! England I ask ya'? Meanwhile de bloody Brits were over here, after oppressin' us for almost 800 years dey had the gall to execute Patrick Pearse and his band a' poets, schoolteachers an' geriatric shopkeepers for causin' a minor disturbance in a Post Office of a Bank Holiday Monday . . . Madness, pure an' simple madness, dat's what it was!

I took a breath.

– You didn't swallow that one, did you? Fatfuka settled himself in the bed.

– Wha', about de Brits an' de 1916 rising? Sure you should know all about dat, didn't yer own granddad shoot three Black and Tans dead from de roof a' de bank?

– Ah, now! I wouldn't be too sure about that.

– But didn't ya have a book at home with him in it an' everything.

– He was in the book alright, but it was a photograph of Terence MacSweeney's funeral. He was in the crowd outside

74

the church, you could just about make out the top of his head behind another fella's hat, if yer man had moved over just about two inches you'd get a good view of me grandad.

– But what about yer dad an' de tree whole days on de roof of de bank, an' all dat?

– I'd say that was all in my dad's head, said Fatfuka. – Anyway what I'm talking about was Grandda Buckley losing his legs in the First World War. Not Patrick Pearse and the lads in the GPO in 1916.

– Ya mean to say?

– Sure Jeezus, Grandda Buckley had children and grandchildren, Pluto!

– Ya don't need legs to have children.

– But sure, what about the years he worked down in Fords?

– Hmm? I suppose you've a point. But, I mean like he was gettin' a pension from de army. De whole street knew about dat, and dere was no denying, but he had no legs, an' what about all de stories?

– Stories? Fatfuka looked at me.

– Yeah, stories! You know like de time he bombed Dresden an' de scuttling of de Scappa Flo, not to mind de day he was carrying de dying drummer-boy through de death, gore, blood an' barbed wire a' no-man's-land, only to have a big Nazi shell knock him arse over head and take his legs clean away from under him.

As I sat there spewing out the stories the truth gradually dawned. Not only was it highly unlikely that any one soldier would find himself fighting in the Infantry, the Navy and the Airforce, on three different fronts at the same time, but the memories spanned the two World Wars. Not to mind the odds against Grandda Buckley fighting in the Second World War if he had lost his legs in the First World War at the delicate age of seventeen. I couldn't believe it! My only childhood hero, he lived on our street, just five doors down from our house, was being held up to the light, and I could see right through him.

Fatfuka obviously noticed my pain, as the myths of childhood crashed down around my ears.

– Do you remember? he said. – Do you remember Grandda Buckley used call us by our rank, like, – Hoi, you, Corporal Pluto! Salute in the presence of an officer!

The memory brought a smile to my face.

– Or, – Sergeant Pinko! A message for the front line. Run up to the shop an' pick up supplies. Two Woodbine, and hurry, dere's a good lad. Do you remember?

– Yeah, I said, – . . . and wat about when we'd be on our way to school, he'd be sittin' outside de house in de wheelchair like a Sergeant Major surveying de troops. We'd file by, one by one, sacks on our backs, saluting as we passed, an' he'd shout somethin' like, – *Keep yer heads down lads! Come back in one piece, and troops! REMEMBER 1916!*

– Grandda Buckley ha!

– I remember, Fatfuka smiled. – It must have been summertime, because there was no school and the weather was warm. Meself and Georgie, Pinko's brother, were just hanging around, messing with a piece of twine . . . the sun was low in the sky, cutting long shadows along MacSweeney Street. Georgie was making shapes, and snakes, and trains, and things with the twine.

– Well, I think it's a good idea.

He stood up from the footpath as if to walk away.

– Alright, Fatfuka gave in, – but I still think it's stupid, I mean like, cowboys an' Indians no problem, but cowboys an' cowboys? You want us to make a lasso outa' dis bit a' twine, and round up all de dogs on de street? Da's a stupid idea!

But Georgie was always the leader, so cowboys and cowboys it was. They mounted up, and slapping their arses they rode out, into the furthermost reaches of their minds, west of Cactus Creek across the Salt Flat Plains and just beyond the ridge; Indian country and Dry Gulch Canyon.

– *Whoa!*

Georgie pulled on the reins, Fatfuka's steed prancing sideways.

– What is it, Georgie? *Whoa!*

– There! Looks like a stagecoach, an' it's been shot up pretty bad.

Georgie drew his Colt from his holster.

– Probably Sioux! Fatfuka squinted his eyes.

– In Apache country? Doubt it.

The stage driver was dead, body draped back and lifeless.

– *Geeeup!*

And they moved in for a closer look, eyes scouring the horizon for savages, this could be a trap.

– Looks like he's breathin'. Cover me, Georgie.

Georgie cocked his firing pin. Fatfuka dismounted.

– Here, hold Tonto.

He moved towards the stagecoach. – You okay there, par'ner?

He poked the lifeless body with his pistol.

– Wha', wha', wha?

It was Grandda Buckley, asleep in the chair.

– 'S OK, Grandda. We thought the Apache got ya.

– 'T'would take more than a few pesky Apache to get me! – and he spat out onto the footpath. – Troops! he rallied.

Fatfuka and Georgie stood to attention.

– Take me up the Line, de Front Line!

This usually meant he wanted his chair moved across the

street, to the sunshine. Georgie dismounted from his imaginary pony, and moved to the rear of the wheelchair.

– *Hoi! Hold it, hold it!* – Grandda Buckley stretched out his hand. – Here, show us tha' piece a' string there.

Georgie handed over the twine.

– Here now, turn around there like a good young fella.

Grandda Buckley threaded it in under Georgie's armpits and behind the back of his neck like a bridle, and flicked the two loose ends.

– *Geeup!* he said.

Funny how old man and young boys share the same headspace.

Slowly the "stagecoach" pulled off picking up speed.

– *Geeup!* Grandda Buckley tugged the reins. – *Geeup!*

Fatfuka got under the harness.

– *Wee Haw!* Grandda Buckley yelped.

The bockety wheelchair trundled off down the street, Grandda Buckley whip-cracking and howling all the way.

Stagecoach was the new game on MacSweeney Street. Even the lads from neighbouring streets would arrive down with their bits of rope. It seemed like Grandda Buckley spent his days a woopin' and a hollerin', flying up and down the street in the wheelchair, towed by gangs of small dirty faces.

Saturday morning. Meself, Fatfuka, Pinko and Georgie were hanging around outside Buckley's.

– Knock at the door! Georgie ordered.

– Dey're probably still asleep.

Pinko was chicken.

– Pinko's right! 'Tisn't even nine o' clock yet.

– I'll do it meself!

Georgie drew his .45, rapped on the door and stood back, slipped it back into the holster. Nothing happened.

– Maybe we should go away and come back, Pinko suggested.

– You must be jokin', and let de crowd from Dominic Street come down an' have him.

Georgie was having none of it. He drew his Colt again, this time with purpose, and flaked the door.

– *Jeeezzusss!*

The upstairs window shot open, it was Mrs Buckley, Grandda's daughter-in-law, her hair in curlers, chalky-faced, more frightening than any Apache brave.

– Jezus! What d'ye want dis time a' de mornin'? She wasn't happy. We huddled in by the wall, out of sight. Georgie stepped out onto the footpath in full view, smoking gun in hand.

– Can Grandda come out to play?

Mrs Buckley's face cracked.

– Come back in a half an hour! and she smiled.

By twenty past nine, Buckley's door opened and Grandda was wheeled out. We were all harnessed up, chomping at the bit and ready to go. Grandda Buckley knew the routine, holding his end of the reins, with a gentle,

– *Giddy Up!*

We moved off along the footpath up the slight slope towards the bookies. Always the bookies, but it was closed that hour of the morning.

– *Whoa! Whoa!* Grandda called and slapped on the brake. We unharnessed and turned the stagecoach around. The full stretch of MacSweeney Street before us. We were prancing, tugging, shoving, ready for action.

– *Whoa! Whoa!* Grandda Buckley fought for control. – *Whoa!*

– Look! Fatfuka pointed. – It's the Dominicas!

And there turning the corner at the top of the street was Nicky Flynn, Danker and the lads from Dominic Street.

– Apache war party! Apache war party! Grandda Buckley tugged on the bit.

79

The Dominicas broke into a trot.

– Apache war party! Grandda roared.

The Dominicas were howling and almost on us.

– *Weeee! Haw!*

Whip cracked, brake dropped.

– *Yee! Haw!* REMEMBER 1916! he screamed.

And like a flash we were off, tearing down MacSweeneya, old buckled wheels hopping off the broken and battered pavement, shooting into the air and screaming.

– Faster! Faster! Grandda Buckley's eyes were bulging. – They'll have our scalps. *Yee! Haw!* the whip clattered over our heads.

The Apaches were closing in, we could see their war-paint and smell their breath, this was no Sunday School outing, dem Indians meant business, they wanted whiteman's scalps to decorate their teepees and lodges. Our scalps! And they were gaining on us.

But digging deep into our inner souls we prayed to the Almighty for the strength to outrun these heathens. One last surge, one final push, just to get us beyond the redman's range and out of open country.

As if God-given it happened. Like we were catapulted forward, wings at our feet, spurred on by fear. We sped off to the safety of the rattlesnake-infested canyons, leaving the Apaches to swallow our dust.

– *Whee haw!*

– *Whoa! Whoa! Whoa!* Grandda Buckley roared.

But we were stampeding, hoofs thundering across the burnt clay of Dry Gulch Canyon.

– *Whoa! Whoa!* Grandda Buckley screamed.

– *Hold it lads! Hold it!* Georgie tugged on the reins. – *Hold it lads!* he shouted.

But our mustangs were out of control and bolting.

– Grandda's out of his chair! Hold it!

There he was, Grandda Buckley, being dragged along the footpath behind us, his wheelchair up-turned on the street, slipped off the kerb in the chaos to get away from the Dominicas. Grandda Buckley looked shook, like an upturned beetle, wriggling on the ground still clutching his ends of the string.

By the time we got back to help him into his chair, the Dominicas had vanished and Mrs Buckley was out on the street. That was it. That was the last game of Stagecoach on MacSweeney.

\* \* \*

2:08.

I stub out my rollie, pour myself another whiskey and sip. Louis Armstrong on the radio, *What A Wonderful World* . . .

– Doubt ya, Louee boi, I whisper. And close my eyes to what dreams are made of.

\* \* \*

Up in No. 4, Herman cradles a cup of coffee, 2:09.

> . . . *Und I thinks to mein self,*
>       *Vot a vonderbar vurld* . . .

He likes to sing along with the radio, it improves his English. His stomach is tight, more apprehensive than fearful. He worries for Pluto, he senses it, not your usual run-of-the-mill Thursday night. Herman knows the sounds of the night, he is a night person. Herman sips his Lavazza.

# 12

2:09.

Down in No. 3 Brenda gets ready for bed, rubbing under her armpits and between her legs with a rough well-worn face-cloth. The shower never really worked, water only trickles out of it. It's either scalding or freezing and leaks underneath, dripping down into No. 2, into what was Jimmy the Monk's kitchen before he moved up to No. 5. It's not like the Monk would complain or anything but he mentioned it once and once is enough. Brenda hasn't used it since then. She mentioned the leak to the landlady a few years back, she's still getting around to it. As for the bath in the bathroom downstairs, well nobody had used that in years.

Brenda wraps herself in her pink robe, flicks off one of the bars on the electric fire, lights a Silk Cut extra-length and leans back listening to the radio. She likes Louis Armstrong. Life isn't so bad.

Brenda has lived on Waterloo Terrace for the best part of twenty-five years. This place is her home now. She knows that everybody calls her Brenda the Brasser. It doesn't bother her any more. She's known it for years, back as far as when there were students living here. She'd hear it around the halls, see it on the bathroom walls . . .

SUCK MY COCK! BRENDA IS A BRASSER!

. . . and a drawing of a big banana-shaped penis. It nearly killed her when she first saw it. She tried to clean it off with her towel, but it would be there again in some other form the following day. What really hurt was the time the landlady confronted her.

– Ah! Brenda, I've being meaning to ask you about the writing on the bathroom wall?

It was an open-ended question.

– What about it?

– Well, I might very well ask you the same question?

– You don't think I wrote it? Brenda looked at her.

– Look! I'm not inquiring as to who did it. I'm questioning the content of the message. The Witch folded her arms, she wasn't leaving without an explanation.

– How do ya mean?

– Well, are you, or aren't you?

– Am I, or amn't I what?

– Look, I'll put it this way, the landlady took a breath, – This is a respectable house and we won't tolerate any of that kind of carry-on!

– Carry-on? What carry-on?

– You know what I'm saying – Just consider this your first and final warning!

She turned and walked away. That was over twenty years ago.

* * *

I don't know if your life flashes by in front of your eyes before you die, but in a way that's what it was like every time I went to visit Fatfuka in the hospital, he just wanted to talk about the old days.

– Don't mind Stagecoach! Fatfuka pulled himself up in the bed. – What about the time we all went to see *Mackenna's Gold*?

– *Mackenna's Gold*?

– Remember the Western? In the Savoy!

– A cowboy filum? my mind was drawing blanks. – You'd think I'd remember dat, I mean, it wasn't like we were going to de flicks all de time or anything.

– Ah Jeezus, ya must remember!

– What was it about?

– What was it about? What was it about! How would I know what it was about? You must remember, Pluto boi! Remember it was Pinko's birthday and his Mam said she'd pay for us all to go to the pictures. Do you remember?

Pinko's birthday rang a bell, the memories were starting to shift.

Pinko's Mam gave Georgie the money for the lot of us to go to the pictures. The first thing Georgie did was to go and buy twenty Consulate. We went down to the carpark behind Roches Stores for a smoke. Four each, they were gone in a half an hour.

– If I get caught smokin' I'll be mombolised, Tragic Ted said.

– My dad says I can smoke when I can pay for 'em, said Georgie.

– Dere was a fella in school caught smokin' by his mam an' she brought him home an' sat him down an' made him smoke twenty Woodbines one after de other, to make him sick, like! said Fatfuka.

– Gowaan?

– . . . and when he finished the last Woodbine, his Mam asked him what he had to say for himself.

– An' what did he say?

– He took twenty Major outa' his arse pocket, put one in his mouth an' asked her for a light! Fatfuka laughed

– I'm tellin' ya there'll be no laugh if I'm caught, Tragic said.

– Well, yer safe out, Ted boi. Consulate are like vodka, dere's no smell off 'em.

– I don't know what's the problem wit cigarettes anyhow! said Georgie.

– They're supposed ta be bad for yer health. Stunts yer growth like!

– Stunts yer growth? Tragic Ted freaked, – Well, I wants ta play soccer for Notts Forrest when I grows up, like Miah Dennehy.

– If ya grows up!

– Ye could always play in the Midget League, Ted.

– Midget League? How small do ya have to be to play in de Midget League?

– I'd say you're a bit too tall as it is, said Georgie.

– What! No! Too tall for the Midget League. Too small for the real league!

– Don't worry, Ted boi! Fatfuka put his hand on Ted's shoulder. – Notts Forrest field a Midget team and maybe Miah Dennehy will put in a good word for ya.

– Do ya think he would?

– 'Course he would.

– Well, I'm not smokin' no more.

– But what if ya start growin' again? I mean like there's only so much Miah Dennehy can do for ya.

A look of worry came over Ted's face.

– Don't mind him, Ted boi! Fatfuka said – Sure look at John Wayne, he's no midget an' he smokes.

– Hmm! you could hear Ted thinking.

– Come on, we'll be late! Pinko was afraid we would miss the trailers.

– Plenty a' time.

– Yea, said Tragic – What about de cartoons, might be Bugs Bunny or someone, and we haven't even got our sweets yet.

– Right, said Georgie, – We'll go, but first we has to get another pack a' fags for inside.

The Savoy wasn't just a picture-house, it was a world of its own. Five steps and glass doors shielding us from reality and the rain. Inside, two kiosks flanking a sweeping marble staircase the width of the building, climbing all the way up to the gods, branching off at different levels as it rose. Like a fairy palace, all golds and reds and carpeted wall to wall. Velvet flip-up seats in rows, sloping from ceiling to screen, scattered with feeder tunnels that led out to the marble staircase.

. . . five packets of Perry, ten two-a-penny Black Jacks, eight-pence worth of Acid Drops, a big bottle a' Tanora and another twenty Consulate.

– Come on! shouted Pinko.

We must have been standing outside in the rain for a full quarter of an hour, a look come over Georgie's face, lips moving, like he was saying his prayers or counting or something.

The queue was huge, stretching all the way as far as the Gas Company. Somewhere at the back of the line, the chanting started . . .

– Honker! Honker! Honker! Honker! it got louder and louder, everybody jumping up and down and chanting – *Honker! Honker! Honker! Honker!*

And then he appeared, out onto the steps like a Russian General in his red cap and coat, gold trimmings and buttons, a small old man and, like his uniform, his skin was about three sizes too big for him. There it was, stuck right in the middle of his face, the biggest honker I had ever seen in my life.

– *Honker! Honker! Honker!*

He flipped the Cinema sign to *OPEN*, up went a roar, now was the time.

– *Heeeavvve!* a surge towards the door.

– Get back, ye little skuts! Honker roared flaking wildly with his flashlamp.

– *Heeeavve!*

– Get back, ye little skuts!

– Lads! Lads! I think we've a problem? Georgie was under pressure.

– Get back, ye little skuts!

– *Heeeavvve!*

– Lads, we haven't enough! Georgie said it a little louder this time.

– How'd ye mean, not enough?

– Get back, ye little skuts!

In the background the sound of – *heeave, heeave, heeave*, coming like waves.

– We've spent too much money. Probably the fags!

– De money? Pinko stopped.

– Lads! Lads! All out!

– We're gonna miss de cartoons! Pinko was almost crying.

– No one's goin' missin' nothin', Pinko!

– Wha's the hassle? Ted was shifty.

– Dere's a problem lads, we've spent too much money!

– We've spent too much? You've spent too much, Georgie boi! Ted snarled.

– Look, it don't matter who spent what. De money's gone.

87

– But de picture is startin' in a minute, and it's my birthday, Pinko sobbed.

Look lads, it's as simple as dis, Georgie explained. – I haven't enough to pay for the lot of us, only three can get in.

– But it's my birthday! Pinko was crying.

– Would you ever shut up, Pinko! – La, de best we can do is for tree of us to go in and de other two go down Printworks Lane, I'll see if I can open de fire doors to let ye in.

– Do ya think dat'll work?

– All we can do is give it a try!

It didn't sound like a great idea, but it was an idea and it was all we had to cling to.

– Okay, I'm lookin' for two volunteers.

Tragic Ted and Fatfuka stepped out. Georgie gave them their cut of the sweets and four Consulate each.

– Just in case, he said – Now ye'll have to wait a while, I won't open de door 'til de trailer is on and it's dark inside, just to make sure dat Honker is out of de way, like. And wen I do open it, follow me back to de seats an' for God's sake be quiet!

Ted and Fatfuka headed off around the side of the building towards the fire escape. Georgie, Pinko and myself barged our way back into the top of the queue – *heeave!*

Halfways through their second fag, sitting in the doorway on Printworks Lane, listening to the laughter from the full-house matinee.

– Must be th' cartoon! said Ted. – Do ya tink dey've forgotten about us?

– Never! I'd say Honker's up by de toilets and dey're just waitin' for him to go away.

– I hope so.

– Jeezus! Look who's comin'!

It was Nickey Flynn and Danker, from Dominic Street. Ted melted into the doorway, but too late, they had been lamped.

– Dis is all we need, whispered Fatfuka.

– Gis a drag! Nicky pointed to the fag.

– Dere ya are.

Ted held it out. Nickey reached for the butt and took a pull.

– Consulate are shit, he said.

– We could have sworn ye were two steamers! Danker slagged.

– Why? Are ye lookin' for two steamers? Ted bounced it back.

– What are you sayin'!

– I'm not sayin' nuttin'!

– Easy Danker! Easy! Nickey tugged on his jacket.

– Langer!

– So what are ye up ta? Nickey looks to Fatfuka.

– We're waiting for Georgie.

– Georgie?

– Yeah! He's gonna open this door an' let us in to the flicks, Ted said. Fatfuka's eyes darted, he couldn't believe Ted could be so thick.

– Into de flicks?

– Yeah, a cowboy one! De lads are inside already, said Ted.

– And dey're opening dis door for ye?

– Yep!

– Danker! Nickey barked, – Run around to Pot Black an' tell de lads we're goin' to de pictures. Hurry, Danker! Hurry!

Fatfuka realised there was no point protesting, he could do nothing but watch as Danker limped down the lane and disappeared around the corner in the direction of the pool hall.

Inside, the Savoy was mad, over a thousand wild kids in control. Raids on the ice-cream lady under cover of darkness, scuffles between rival gangs, popcorn and chewed chewing-gum thick in the air. Honker charging up and down the aisles shining his torch in people's faces, failing miserably to keep a lid on the whole thing.

– Right! said Georgie, – Meself and Pluto will go out and let the lads in, You stay here and mind de coats, Pinko!

He handed Pinko the bottle of Tanora, – and don't drink it all, OK!

We made our way down the centre aisle, across in front of the screen and through the door that led to the toilets. Ladies to the right, Gents to the left and there at the end of the hall, the fire exit out onto Printworks Lane.

– Keep an eye out for Honker, Pluto! . . . – Are ya out there, Ted! he shouted through the slit in the door.

– A course we're here! Wha' kept ye? Fatfuka's voice was made faint by the door. – Nicky Flynn from Dominic Street's here as well.

– Who? Georgie strained.

– Nicky Flynn, Dominic Street! . . . another muffle.

– Who? Georgie raised his voice.

– Shh! Take it easy, Georgie, I think I see Honker's flashlight, and it looks like it's comin' dis way! I said.

– Nicky Flynn, from Dominic Street!

The voice from the far side of the door was garbled. – Now open the shaggin' door!

– What are dey sayin', Pluto?

– Jesus! I don't know, but open de door! I tink Honker's comin', I shouted.

90

Just a split second before Georgie gets his hand to the spring lock, the door into the cinema opens, there stands Honker eyes beady from the dark, flashlamp in hand.

– What's going on here, ye skuts?

– Nothing sir! Georgie stood back.

A few thumps from the far side of the door.

– Open the shaggin' door, will ye!

It sounded like Nicky Flynn from Dominic Street, meself and Georgie just looked at each other, as if to say, what the hell is Nickey Flynn doing out there?

– What's going on here, ye skuts?

– I tink dere's somebody at de door, sir.

– Here, let me see.

Honker slipped the torch under his arm and pushed down on the lock. The door sprung open out onto the dazzling brightness of Printwork Lane, there stood Fatfuka and Ted.

As our eyes adjusted to the light, it looked like every kid from the northside was out there. For a split second, total silence, nobody moved, like rabbits caught in headlights of Honker's buttons, they just stood there. Honker stretched out his arms in the doorway. From nowhere came the cry,

– *Remember 1916! Charrrrrgggee!*

. . . and they did. Like the Sioux at the Little Big Horn. Honker was General Custer slashing and hacking with his flashlamp, trying to hold his ground, his arms lashing wildly, but he was outmanoeuvred, outnumbered. He spiralled as he was pushed nose first against the wall.

– I'll remember yer faces, ye scuts! Ye're all barred!

Honker jammed between the wall and the door shouting useless threats. Ted grabbed the hat off his head and we just scattered to the safety of the picture-house and darkness.

* * *

– And you're asking me what the film was about!

The hospital bed shook, Fatfucka laughing. – Sure we spent the rest of the afternoon throwing Honker's hat from row to row in the cinema, driving him demented.

– Remember on de way home we met Pinko's dad, sellin' de papers outside de bank.

– Eddie de Nut?

– Yeah! An' he asked Pinko what de filum was like, and Pinko couldn't tell him, do ya remember? An' Georgie just said – It was a Cowboy film, Dad! And Eddie de Nut just nodded his head. Do ya remember?

– Do I what? Fatfuka held his sides, laughing.

I noticed a nurse peeping into the room through the small little glass window in the door, probably just checking up on all the noise.

# 13

2:11.

I can hear Brenda moving about upstairs . . .

She tries not to think of the past, it only gets her down. She tries not to think of the landlady, an ignorant woman with money, that's all she is. Brenda clicks off the second bar of the heater, pours herself another vodka and slips into her lonely bed.

– Shag that witch!

Although the bathroom hadn't been used in years, each new generation of tenant would come across the faded graffiti, and the name Brenda the Brasser would live on. A living lie, that's what it was. Brenda had only one lover in all her life, and her crime if any was her loyalty to a lost cause.

She met Sammy Daly a long time ago. She was seventeen and working in The Wimpy; not what you'd call a first-sight love. Sammy was a fine fella, nice and mannerly, charming, but no Don Juan. He was over-nourished, overdressed, older, always in a suit, always a joke on his lips, he'd arrive in after the pubs laughing, red-faced.

– An' how's Beautiful Brenda to-night?

He always called her Beautiful Brenda. It made her feel

warm. She'd serve the burger n' chips, extra onions and plenty of tomato sauce, that's how he liked it.

– You make the best burgers this side a' Texas, Brenda, do ya know that? The best this side a' Texas.

Brenda would keep her head low, never acknowledging but always loving the praise. Brenda didn't get much of that growing up.

She remembered her first kiss. It was just like any other night, except Sammy hung around until closing time. He sang a verse of *Rose Marie*, a drinking-straw held between his teeth like a rose, and offered her a lift home. A bit forward, she thought, but he was carrying a few extra pints of courage that night.

They drove down by the Marina, where he parked, looking out on the moon dancing across the river Lee, saying nothing. He held her hand, and squeezed it gently. Brenda had never held a man's hand before. It was warm and safe and sweaty. They sat there for what seemed like forever just looking at the river and listening to the car radio. Without warning, Sammy turned to her and looking straight into her eyes, said,

– I love you, Brenda. You're the most beautiful woman in the world, he whispered.

Everything stood still. Never before had anybody looked into her eyes. The words just echoed around her head. That was the moment she fell in love with Sammy Daly.

Gently his lips pushed against hers. His face was bristly. She didn't know what to do, but she felt safe. He prised open her mouth with his tongue, she moved her lips invitingly. It was wonderful; Percy Sledge on the car radio, *When A Man Loves A Woman*, and like a million other lovers from Luxenburg to Cork and back again, it was their song. Brenda remembered that night as if it were yesterday. It was the night of her first kiss. It was the night she fell in love with Sammy Daly and the night Sammy Daly's wife was in hospital giving birth to their second child.

Love blossomed on trips to the Marina, but after a while Sammy stopped calling to The Wimpy. He'd just wait outside in the car, and they'd park around the corner, in the lane behind the *Examiner* office.

– Who needs romantic views when we have each other? Sammy would say.

Brenda wasn't really happy with the situation. Once or twice she asked Sammy about his wife, he'd only get angry. Brenda loved Sammy, she didn't want to lose him, but always felt cheap doing it in the car. She mentioned this to him and within six months he had rented the bed-sit up on Waterloo Terrace. It was their love-nest. Brenda moved in and he'd call around when he needed her. The fact that he paid the rent gave her a sense of security, that feeling of being loved. Sammy did love her, he needed her, he cared for her; but he cared for his wife and kids more. It almost killed Brenda that time he nearly died with a heart attack, not knowing, not being able to visit the hospital, so excluded, but that was the love she chose.

Over twenty years flies by, and how little things change. She still loves Sammy and he still pays the rent, and calls around, not as often, not as sober, but he still cares. He tells her his worries, drinks a few vodkas, smokes a few cigarettes, maybe gets a back-rub. That's about it! But Brenda's happy with her lot. She'd rather be lonely and loved, than not be loved at all. She pitied Sammy's wife, sometimes. But most of all, she hated Christmas.

She unplugs the heater, stubs out her cigarette, switches off the light and turns down the radio. *The Flower Duet* from *Lakme*, what a lovely way to end a day.

*   *   *

2:12.

I never was much for that classical stuff, but I suppose it's not bad this time of the morning, you know like, night-shift workers and people who can't sleep. It's mellow. I sit up in the bed and pour another whiskey.

# 14

2:12.

– Ya can park her in dere, says the burly fella.

– Here, is it?

The squad car rolls to a halt, rubber brushing the kerb.

– Yeah right, see dat place dere, always has a bit of after-hours on de weekends. Ah 'tis harmless enough, but eh, I like to swing around every now and den just to let 'em know we're not asleep, d'ya know. De trick to good policing is to maintain a presence.

– That small pub?

– Owned by a lad by de name a' Tony Kelly. Ah, a fine sort. You know the type, young family and all dat. But still though, ya wouldn't want 'em tinkin' dat ya weren't on de case like.

Tony Kelly, or Tony Tabs as he was better known, was born on St Martin Street. He's been dealing ten-spots from the age of thirteen, over twenty years ago. Since then he's made his fortune and moved on. He bought the pub a while back after he took a bundle on a cocaine deal. Not really in the drugs scene any more, he still gives a bit, takes a bit, sells a bit; but he's no major mover, not since the kids came along. He made up his mind back then that he wasn't going to jail. The bit of dealing he's doing just about covers the tax, rates and accountant's bills

97

run up by the pub. Tony Tabs is a high-living low-life, he finds alcohol-addicts harder to handle than drug-addicts.

Most Thursday and Friday nights, Tony, Mickey the barman and the lads stay back, have a few jars, smoke a bit of blow, that kind of thing. This Friday was no different except Tony had picked up a few wraps of coke; the boys were in the back lounge sucking it up their hooters.

– Cut out another few lines there, Mickey! Tony orders and carries on exactly where he left off. He's speeching on his favourite subject, world domination.

– Then I'd buy another pub in New York, that'd pay for the Night Club in London, while the apartment building in Spain would pay for the other pub, and the first pub in Germany would . . .

The lads know that it's all in Tony's head. Tony is flying.

*Knock-knock! Knock-knock!* on the door.

– Mickey, go out an' see who that is – Tony clicks his fingers and points.

Mickey heads to the window, pulls back the curtains. – Jeezus! he hisses, – It's the Law.

– Shit! says Tony.

Another knock at the door.

– Did they see ya?

– I think so!

– Fuck! Clear up all that there! Tony points to the table covered in coke dust. The lads break into a flurry of action. Tony breathes in deep and gets himself together, slowly he walks to the door and opens it.

– Ah, good evening, Guard . . .

He's trying to control his pace, because as stoned as he is, he's aware of the fact that he's speeding.

– Ah Tony, havin' a bit of a late-night session, are we? asks the burly fella.

– Mick the eh, barman is gettin' married in a few eh, weeks, and we were just havin' a few jars after work like.

– At half two in the mornin', Tony? Come on now!

– Well, eh, we finished a long time ago, we're just eh, cleanin' the place after the night now!

Tony's eyes are bursting out of his head, his nose is running. It's like a hollowness at the back of his head from the Charlie. He feels the taller Guard staring down on him. He's never seen a pair of ears so big in his life,

– Must be something trippy cut through that shit . . . he thinks to himself.

He's beginning to sweat.

– Well, if ye're finishin' up, I'll let ye to it so den, says the burly fella. – By the way . . .

– Eh, yea?

– This is the new man on the beat.

He introduces Tony to the rookie. Tony tries not to look at his ears. They're huge, starting to freak him out. The burly fella cracks a joke about seeing more of each other. Tony shakes hands and laughs nervously. They say goodnight and walk away. Tony Tabs closes the door and sighs.

– See what I mean? says the burly fella. – It's just a matter of keepin' 'em on deir toes.

Mickey asks Tony if everything's cool.

Tony nods his head and says,

– Just the new pig, ears like frisbees. Cut out another few lines there, Mickey.

\* \* \*

Names are funny things, you'd often wonder do names become things or things become names – you know like, it's the old story of if we call an orange an orange, why don't we call an apple a green. Then again I suppose, no matter how many times you mix yellow and blue, you'll never get apple.

I was talking about my own name last week, one of the days I went to visit Fatfuka in the hospital, he was telling me that Pluto was the God of Death . . .

– God of Death, sure that's not why I was called Pluto! P-L-U-T-O, Pluto! It's fairly straightforward really, I explained, – Me nickname is a mixture of de letters an' sounds in me real name, Paul O'Toole, Pluto. Pluto, Paul O'Toole, do ya get it?

– As far as I remember, you were named after Mickey Mouse's dog, Pluto!

– Pluto the dog? Naw!

– Figure it out for yourself.

– Ya mean to say dat all dese years I've been called after a cartoon dog?

– Think about it, Pluto!

– Pluto? Jeezus, why Pluto?

– Do ya know? Fatfuka changed the subject. – I never saw you at Grandda Buckley's Funeral?

– Funeral? I didn't even know he was sick!

– Ah Jeezus! That was almost eighteen years ago, Pluto boi!

I couldn't believe I'd missed it. He said he saw it in the paper. I don't really read the death notices, but still though, you'd think I'd have heard about it.

– Ninety-eight years of age he was.

– Gowaan?

– They were all there, all the old crowd from MacSweeneya.

– Jeezus, I wish I'd known about it.

– Mr and Mrs Buckley, the Murrays, the O'Connells, the Riordans, Ma Hickey and Tragic Ted, even Pinko, his Mam and Eddie de Nut turned up.

– I can't believe I missed it.

– Ah, 'twas mighty! But do ya know what was really sad?

– What?

– When they were carrying out the coffin, all the old crowd were there, ya know like, the crowd from MacSweeneya, and all that.

– Yeah?

– Yeah! And there by the side of the hearse were three or four small dirty-faced young fellas, and they were standing to attention saluting the coffin, like a guard of honour.

– Ah gowaan?

– Yea! Just like us, Pluto, just like us when we were small.

– Old habits die hard, wha'?

– 'Twas like a time warp.

– An' did ya get a chance to talk to any of de old neighbours? I asked.

– Did I what! Sure didn't most of us go down to the Metropole for a jar after the removal!

– De Metropole? Dat was a bit swanky!

– The only place that'd hold the crowd.

– Gowaan?

– Brilliant! Meeting all the old crowd, talking about the old days, Pinko's Mam even told the story about how Pinko got his nickname.

– Pinko must be sick of hearing dat one.

– We're all sick of it! Fatfuka laughed. – But, it was great though all the same, someone said that Grandda Buckley had lived a long and full life, so there was no real tragedy about his death, just happy memories. Do ya know who was there? – Fatfuka sat up in the bed.

– Who?

– Imelda Kearney! She asked me if I ever see you around, Pluto.

– Imelda Kearney?

101

– Eddie de Nut said the last he had heard of ya, you were off in darkest Africa converting the natives.

– Pinko's dad is a head-case! I laughed.

– Stone mad!

– Imelda Kearney? I took her to me Grads! She fainted every time I tried to get me hand inside her dress. Has she still got de buck teeth?

– Not at all! Fatfuka shook his head. – She's a fla!

– Gowaan, and de glasses?

– Must have contacts.

– And ya say she was askin' about me?

– Ah now, Pluto! I hate to shatter yer dreams, she was with her husband, an Estate Agent I think.

– I don't mind sharin' me women! Not so long as dey're good-lookin'.

– Imelda Kearney had no problem sharing her men in the old days, Fatfuka sneered.

– Do ya remember? We'd always get the birthday kiss from Imelda.

– I know, said Fatfuka. – She was the first girl I ever kissed.

– Me too! I was only fourteen, she was fifteen and a half.

– D'ya remember? None of us would go out with her, 'cause we thought she was a loose woman.

– At fifteen? – and we laughed at our innocence.

– Jeezus, by the time I was fifteen I was getting birthday kisses from her every few weeks! Fatfuka laughed. – Happy days, eh?

– And ya say she's a fla? – I looked stony-faced at Fatfuka, he nodded. – And ya say she was askin' for me?

– Ya missed your chance, Pluto boi! Ya missed your chance.

– Imelda Kearney? A fla! Jeezus! Dere is a God!

And we just fell about the place.

It was good to see Fatfuka laughing, I'd never seen a man so sick look so happy.

– Ya say ya were talkin' to Eddie de Nut? I asked.

– Yeah, he was looking great. They say he made a fortune out of the papers.

– Was dere any mention a' Georgie? I asked.

And as always, the pain of life was never too far behind a laugh.

– Eh, not really! Fatfuka paused. – I was really only talking to Eddie de Nut for a few seconds in the loo.

* * *

Eddie de Nut was a head-case. They first moved into MacSweeney Street after my mother found the three of them huddled in a doorway down by St Mary's.

– Like the H-Ho-Holy Family, my dad used say. That was before Pinko was born. Georgie was the baby, wrapped up in a blanket, asleep, with only a drawer for a cot. As pale as a swan, my mother used say. They lived with us for a while, then they got one of the flats down Cypress Street.

Eddie never had much schooling, but he was a good provider. All he ever wanted was to be his own boss. But there aren't too many openings to the business world when you're coming from the tenements. Eddie was a trier, or a bit of a loser, it was much of a muchness. But he never gave up. He had a dream. And one day his boat came in, a bit of a leaky tub. He jumped aboard and lashed himself to the main-mast.

Eddie took to selling newspapers. The more he sold the more he made. He'd buy twenty, sell twenty, go back and buy forty more. Eddie knew this was only chicken-feed. The whole thing of traipsing over and back through town to get papers was costing him. So when Georgie was old enough, he took him

103

along. Georgie could hold the pitch with a couple under his arm while Eddie went back to dispatch. Sales skyrocketed.

Pinko never worked the papers. His mam wouldn't have it. She felt one of the lads should get an education. Eddie didn't agree, but she was his Queen and he'd do anything for her. Georgie was Eddie's man.

Tuesday after school, Georgie was holding his corner while Eddie went back for more supplies. He wasn't gone very long, but when he returned he found Georgie crying and a bigger lad, standing there, selling the papers. Eddie lost the head.

– Hoi! Wat're you doin' on my corner? Eddie wasn't messing.

– Your corner? the lad wasn't backing down. – I don't see no sign sayin' 'tis your corner!

He might have been young, but he was tall, with a saucy look on him.

– Dis is my corner! Eddie roared.

No budge out of the lad. Eddie felt vulnerable and defenceless, his left arm carrying papers, his right hand coins, but this had to be sorted and sorted now.

– What are ya doing tomorra? Eddie asked.

– Huh? The lad was confused and, in the split second of hesitation that followed, Eddie leaned back his head as far as it would go,

– Eh, tomorra'? the lad repeated.

Eddie's head whipped down, forehead connecting full-on with the lad's nose, making shit of it.

– Get that stitched! Eddie mocked.

The lad dropped the papers to the pavement and shuffled off down Quay Street, groaning, and holding his shattered, blood-dripping nose.

Eddie waited for days for the inevitable reprisals but

nothing ever happened. He learned a lot that day about business. It was kill or be killed, survival of the fittest and most importantly, as he constantly reminded Georgie,

– No man can give you power, do ya hear me, Georgie? Ya has to reach out and take it for yerself!

And that's probably why Georgie was such a leader, he was just like his old man.

Anyway it wasn't long after that before Eddie realised he could use the same strategy on every street corner right across the northside. Street by street Eddie opened up new frontiers, nutting anybody who got in his way. That's how he got the name Eddie de Nut. Soon we were all working for him, meself, Fatfuka, Tragic Ted and a bunch of the lads from school, everybody. Everybody that is, except Pinko.

Eddie was a self-made man and he knew it.

> – Me floor space is eight miles of city streets,
> Concrete an' asphalt.
> Me premises is de tarmac an' me anorak.
> I pays no electricity,
> I pays rates to no man,
> 'Cause me lightin' an heatin' is God-given.
> I've no lease,
> I'm the owner of none,
> But, what I have I hold,
> 'Til I'm dead in the grave or too old.
> The King of street corners, traffic-lights and bridges,
> I'm Eddie the Nut an' dese are me Lads.

He'd rattle it off to anybody that had the time to listen. The papers were Eddie's life.

We did well out of it, just standing there dealing news,. Eddie driving around in the van keeping us stocked. We were Eddie de Nut's Lads and everybody knew it. The Empire was expanding, from Wellington Bridge to The Lower Road, back as far as The Parochial Hall, down into Blackpool all the way to the top of Mayfield. Georgie was only fifteen years of age, but he was like a man, he was like a manager. Always picking up the slack, just like his dad.

* * *

Fatfuka was racking his brain about Grandda Buckley's funeral.

– So eh! There was no mention of Georgie at all? I asked.

– Jeezus, that was almost twenty years ago, Pluto. See I was only talking to Eddie de Nut in the toilet, he was a bit steamed, and he called me Ted or something. He always got my name wrong.

– He always got all our names wrong! I said.

* * *

The Coliseum Corner. It took at least three of us to service the Coliseum. The busiest pitch in town, gateway to the city. A four-way intersection, eight pavements of punters, sixteen lanes of traffic travelling every which way, fifteen hundred newspapers an evening.

I think it was Bona Night, a few of the lads never turned up. Eddie de Nut was like a lunatic. Georgie volunteered to do the Coliseum on his own.

– Sure ya can't do it on yer own!

Eddie was bullin'.

– Look, I'll give it a shot, Dad!

– Well, shag 'em anyway, dey're all sacked!

Eddie sacked fellas every day.

– Come on, Dad, dere's no sense cryin' about it! Drop us down to de Coliseum.

– Fifteen hundred papers, an' dose little shits wouldn't turn up!

106

– Ah come on, Dad!

– Alright! Alright! I'll swing around when I'm finished de deliveries, ta give ya a hand!

But Eddie de Nut wasn't happy. – Fifteen hundred! he muttered.

Georgie surveyed the situation, he liked a challenge. There had to be a way. He saw that the traffic lights changed systematically, Lane 1, 2, 3, 4, and then the two filter-lanes had the green only. The fact that Brian Boru Street was one-way meant he didn't have to bother with it, if he serviced MacCurtain Street, the Lower Road and Summer Hill properly. Timing would be everything, selling to pedestrians would be tricky though. Then he figured it out.

Four bundles of papers, one at each corner. Then with a few under his arm, he started. Lane 1, 2, 3, 4, selling to the first eight cars in each stopped lane, eight was about all that got through the lights at each change. He could dash back to restock at each corner in rotation, servicing the filter-lanes and pedestrians along the way as he moved through the junction.

Eddie de Nut had finished the deliveries, it must have been about three quarters of an hour later. Traffic was thick. He was heading back down MacCurtain Street, towards the Coliseum. Up ahead he noticed a fuss, people gathered on the footpath, watching. And then he saw him in the distance; it was Georgie. There he was, a small scruffy young fella, papers under his arm weaving in and out of the traffic like a, well like a dancer; ducking, diving, spinning, but all the time selling. Eddie hadn't been exposed to much Art, Theatre or Drama in his life, and he'd never seen anything like this.

It was like a pain in his throat, for the first time in a long time Eddie became emotional, tears trickled from his eyes, tears of pride. Georgie was his boy. He just sat there behind the steering wheel in a dream-like world watching this beautiful performance, content in the knowledge that the future of his empire was in safe hands with Georgie.

The traffic moved, dream broken. Eddie blew the horn, Georgie didn't hear him. He beeped it again and whistled out the car window. Georgie turned, all he could see was his Dad's teeth, beaming white, a big broad smile, behind the windscreen.

– Doubt ya, Georgie boi! Eddie roared.

– Sorted, Dad! Sorted!

Georgie gave a thumbs up, and retraced his steps back across the intersection, breaking the rhythm he had so carefully worked out. Eddie de Nut could do nothing but watch, horrified, as the rear wheels of a truck just chewed up Georgie, crushing skull to tarmac, splattering pavement and papers with blood and guts.

He cradled Georgie's mangled body in his arms until the ambulance men prised the small corpse from him, and kneeling there in the middle of the road, he wept out loud.

Eddie de Nut was never the same after that.

\* \* \*

– Although, I do remember,

Fatfuka was still talking about Grandda Buckley's funeral,

– towards the end of the night, I heard Eddie de Nut consoling Mrs Buckley on the death of Grandda, and he was saying how all the kids loved Grandda including Georgie. Mrs Buckley asked him how long Georgie was dead.

– Three years this August, Eddie whispered, and he just broke down and started crying like a baby.

– We were all a bit steamed, but I suppose Eddie de Nut never really got over Georgie. I think, he sorta blamed himself, Fatfuka said.

– De Coliseum, wha'?

# 15

At the age of seventy-four my dad took the sheet off the coffin, stood it upright and tried it out for size. Found it a mite tight, must have put on weight. Kathleen blamed it on the years of pig's head.

– All fat an' bone, she said.

Anyway he took to training, you know walking and things, getting fit for the coffin. With all this new-found interest in death, it was like a change came over him.

Maybe it was out of boredom, or maybe it was because he hadn't cooked the pig's head or the tripe and drisheen in a few years, maybe he just wanted to keep his hands busy, whatever the reason; one day he rubbed his fingers along the grain, not a knot, not at all. He took the pencil from his ear and drew a few lines. That's how it began and it all began simply enough. A little bit of inlay here and there, a simple scroll along the side.

But then he carved the full forty-nine lines of St Patrick's Breastplate, you know the one,

*Christ be behind me, Christ be before me, Christ be above me . . .*

. . . right down the length of the lid. And with oak, walnut, ash and cherry veneer he inlaid the symbols of his craft: the mallet and chisel, the tenon-saw and plane, the pencil and pot of glue and the square and dividers, one at each corner. It was medazza, but he just didn't know when to stop.

Somebody mentioned that the square and dividers was a Freemason's sign and suggested that St Patrick might have been a Protestant. I mean, St Patrick did spend most of his time up with the Unionists, didn't he? So he carved the Virgin Mary on the end panel up where his head would be, draped around her feet he inlaid the tricolour in mahogany, ash and pine.

– N-n-not only am I an Irish Catlick, b-b-but I'm an I-I-Irish Republican C-Catlick, he said.

But he didn't stop there. The Glen Rovers were remembered with a set of crossed hurleys and a sliotar. Then right above *St Patrick's Breastplate* he carved the top section of Shandon steeple with a big goldie fish inlaid in beech. He said that the fish on Shandon was the only thing that looked down on him in life, so it may as well look down on him in death. He knew Shandon was a Protestant church, that's why he put St Mary's, pillars and all, on the left panel.

When Eddie de Nut saw St Mary's he said it was a nice touch,

– . . .you know, remembering 1916, an' all that.

– 1916? my dad was lost.

– Ya know like, the GPO, Eddie pointed at the coffin.

– The GPO?

– Dat's it there, isn't it?

– GPO? D-d-dat's S-S-St Mary's, Eddie boi.

– Really? Jesus, it looks very like de GPO to me! But now dat you mention it, St Mary's looks very like de GPO, don't it?

Enough said. My dad chiselled the words St Mary's, Pope's

Quay under the carving and so as not to offend the lads of '16 he put the names of the leaders down the right-hand panel. And that wasn't the end of it.

Ronnie Delaney was commemorated by a pair of running-shoes and the words *Ronnie Delaney Olympic Gold, For Ireland and for Glory*. On went Daniel O'Connell, Michael Collins, St Finbarre, Terrence McSweeney, Tomás MacCurtain, Christy Ring, Blackrock Castle, Patrick's Bridge, he even had a *Síle na Gig* at his feet. The work went on until every inch of the coffin was covered, inlay on inlay like a beautiful body mutilated by tattoo.

– N-n-not a dowel i-i-in it! he'd say.

. . .and that's the way it went, tapping away at the coffin whenever he took the notion, right up to the day he died.

\* \* \*

2:15.

– Jeezus Christ! What de . . .

More noise in the hall, I sit up in the bed. The Monk! He's probably locked out of his skull again and fallen over some of his shite in the hallway.

He usually gets after-hours in his local down the Lower Road towards the end of the week. I went there with him once, but it really wasn't my scene. A load of fellas, ex-labourers, road-diggers, contract-workers just flooring the pints and talking about old times.

Jimmy de Monk lives up in No. 5. He spent half his life on the roads and building sites of England and spends the other half talking about it. He had seen such exotic places as Scunthorpe, Northampton and Birmingham. He was one of the men who built the motorways, flyovers and subways, a rough life for tough men. Always on the move, never settling down and somewhere along the line he lost all links with his roots. A contractor's eunuch, that's what Jimmy the Monk was.

At the age of forty-five he came home, couldn't keep up with the the rat-race of the building line. That was when he first came to live on Waterloo Terrace. Ever since, he's been talking about restoring his imaginary cottage out in Carrig na Bhfear, Carrigaline, Carrigadrohid – well it's Carriga' something. He collects bits of broken furniture, cracked toilet-bowls and non-reflective mirrors from skips around the town.

– For the cottage, mate! he says.

Everybody knows there's no cottage and that he's flogging his bits and pieces in the junk shop down on George's Quay. The pile in the hallway gets higher and higher. Anything the Monk does never bothers me. I have enough insanity behind my door than to be worrying about the madness in the hallway.


– Did ya ever tink of gettin' married an' havin' kids? I once asked him.

– Me married? Not likely, mate!

His creamy Tipperary accent punctuated with words like mate or bloke, from his days in England, and of course England was never England, always just plain and simple Over, followed by a toss of his head. Sometimes it was like talking on a CB radio.

– Now don't get me wrong, he continued. – There was never any shortage of wimen Over! he tossed his head.

– Ah, yeah! But do ya ever regret not havin' children?

– Childer', mate? I probably has childer' in towns that I don't even know the names of Over! and a big raw laugh out of him, that was as deep as he got. Over and out.

112

I suppose I feel sorry for him; like a caveman well into his fifties all alone in the world. It just seems like such a waste of a life, all that hard work and for what? Only to live out his days in this kip, drinking himself to death on the Lower Road.

Another loud bang in the hall, and the sound of breaking glass, I think he's heading upstairs.

\* \* \*

2:19.

– Hmm, sounds like ze Monk.

Herman knows the sounds of the night. – Maybe I go talk to him of Pluto.

He listens to the slow deliberate footsteps climbing the stairs. Herman pours what's left of his coffee down the sink, rinses the cup, dries it and places it back on the shelf. He wipes his hands on the tea towel, walks across the room and opens the door. The Monk is staggering on the landing.

– Ah Jimmy, how are you zis evenink?

Jimmy de Monk is puffy-eyed with drink and panting from the stairs.

– Herman, yer not gone te bed yet, mate? I didn't wake ya up, did I?

– No, no not at all, I am ein night person.

– G'night then! and the Monk makes to pass by.

– Tell me? Herman obstructs the landing. – Did everythink seem OK down in No. 1?

– Where? Pluto's, mate?

– Yes! Yes! Pluto's. Did everythink seem alright down zere?

– Well, I didn't notice anything out of the ordinary.

The Monk battles for breath.

113

– But, eh? Has he been out today, mate?

– Not ein sign of him!

The Monk sobers up.

– Jesus, that's almost four days now!

– Zis is vot I say to Brenda, but she say go back to bed, and not to think of such things.

– Four days is serious, mate!

– Zis is vot I think also!

– So, what should we do about it?

– I do not know. I just do not vant a repeat of vat happened ze last time, Herman says, referring to Pluto's last suicide attempt.

– Well, my mind on the subject is, that if a bloke wants to top himself, neither man nor God can stop him, an' if he wants it bad enough . . . let 'im have it. That's what I says, mate!

– But not Pluto! Herman pleads.

– Well, I suppose it's different when ya knows a bloke!

– Phew! I tell you zis, zere is somethink in ze air tonight.

Herman often expresses himself best with a line from a song. The Monk steps back, raises his head and sniffs, knowingly.

– Vould you like to come in and join me for ein cup of coffee?

– Don't mind if I do, mate.

– I also have ein bottle of Hund Harr!

– Hund Harr?

– Schnapps!

– Ah ha! The Monk shows recognition.

The door of No. 4 closes.

# 16

Fatfuka died last Monday. I didn't go to the funeral, don't know why, wasn't feeling the best. The burial thing didn't bother me, we had already said our goodbyes. I think it was more a case of not being able to face the Street. You know like, Mrs Buckley, Mrs Hickey, Pinko, his Mam and Eddie de Nut. I just couldn't face the pain of it.

The Wednesday before he died me and Fatfuka had a bit of a laugh. I was saying to him that I had heard somewhere that the Arabs have fourteen different words in their language for sand,

– . . . fourteen words? Can ya believe it?

– That's nothing, said Fatfuka, – What about the Eskimos?

– Wat about 'em?

– They have over twenty words for snow.

– I suppose dey need all dem words in the desert and de North Pole, cause dere isn't much else to talk about, I said.

Fatfuka laughed.

– It must be fairly boring talking about snow or sand all day.

– Then again the Irish have a lot of words for grass, he said.

– Not really, I mean like grass, is grass, is grass.

– Yeah, but if an Arab saw a field of turnip-tops or potato-stalks, it would all be grass to him, Fatfuka explained.

– Sure turnip tops aren't grass, I said.

– My very point, he laughed. – An Arab wouldn't know that.

– But d'ya know what? De potato! Now dere's one for ya.

– Potato? Fatfuka's eyebrow curled upwards.

– Well! I said. – Like we has potatoes, poppies, taytes, tayters, spuds, mash, smash, boiled, roast, chips, crisps, pandy, colcannon. Not to mention de Golden Wonders, Roosters, Dells, Pinks, Banners, Edwards. There are more names for the potato than there are grains of sand, and that's not counting de sweet potato. Dey say dere are over twenty-five different types a' sweet potato in South America.

– But sure a sweet potato isn't a potato?

– My very point, I said. – An Eskimo wouldn't know that, in fact I'd say an Eskimo wouldn't know a spud if it jumped up and bit him on the hole!

Fatfuka laughed. And that's the way it went for the rest of the afternoon, me and Fatfuka shouting out words for potatoes as they came to us and laughing.

The last time I talked to Fatfuka was Thursday. It was special, nothing too heavy, but deeper than surface. It was like we had talked out all the old days, all the shared memories, all the safe guff. So, the spotlight strayed from other people and shone down on us.

I always wondered whatever possessed Fatfuka to go and join the Christian Brothers, I mean Fatfuka of all people? I could have imagined Pinko or maybe Tragic Ted, but Fatfuka? So I asked him. I don't know why, but straight up I asked him,

– What ever possessed ya to go an' join de shaggin' Brothers?

– That's a fairly loaded question, he said.

– Ah well, ya don't have to answer it, if ya like.

– No! No! No! It's no problem, I've thought that one well out myself, Fatfuka paused for a second. – Really, I suppose there was nothing else for me only the poverty of MacSweeney Street, he said.

– De wha'?

– You know what I'm talking about, Pluto! You remember my dad and his antics. It was like the life of the Brothers had a lot to offer. Anyway my Mother was a bit of a Holy Mary. So, when I mentioned that I was thinking about joining, that was it and no more about it. Sure I didn't quit until after she had passed away. It would have broken her heart. Don't get me wrong now, the Brothers were grand, but it really wasn't for me.

– And what about God? I asked.

– What about him?

– Well, do ya believe?

– Jeezus, you're gettin' very heavy, Pluto.

– S-Sorry, sorry, it's just that, well, I don't know whether I believes or not, I mean like all dat stuff about De Immaculate Conception, de bread and de wine, de creation. . . you know de Angels an' de Devils an' all dat . . .

– You're asking me if I believe in God?

– Well er, yes! I said.

– Ya won't find many atheists in a fox-hole.

Fatfuka pointed to all the hospital hardware, bleeps and graphs surrounding his bed. I wasn't too sure what he was on about.

– You see, if I believe and I die and there is no God, no after-life, it doesn't matter, there'll be no one to laugh at me. Whereas, if I die and I don't believe and there is a God, I'm gonna feel like one Class A eejit, it's not as if we haven't been warned or anything.

117

– But sure dat's a stupid reason to believe, I said.

– Look, that's my excuse for believing, when I need an excuse.

And then all of a sudden he got serious and began to tell me exactly what he believed in. I just sat back and listened.

– You see in the beginning was the Word, he said. – And the Word was God. This leads me to conclude that God is only a word used to explain a concept. Long before humans could communicate with words, God existed. It's a concept older than time itself, and words and books and rituals and funny hats will never fully explain the totality of God.

Fatfuka was beginning to lose me at this stage.

– I see God as a Life-Force, he said. – A Life-Force that keeps blood pumping, lungs breathing, grass growing and the earth turning, not some larger-than-life bearded man in a toga, sitting in judgment up in the sky, that's an ancient concept. To be honest I think it's a bit simplistic to put it in terms of Father, Son and The Holy Ghost. By the same token I think it's pompous for certain individuals, humans, men even, to claim that they alone have a direct line to this Life-Force we call God. That's where organised religion comes in. It's pompous of them and naive of us to believe them. It strikes me that if God is the Life-Force that keeps this big ball of dirt breathing, well then, Man must be the Anti-Christ, hell-bent on destroying that Life-Force. This Life-Force is in all of us Pluto, for all of us; every man, woman, child, animal, plant and this Life-Force, or Spirit, or Soul, or whatever word you want to call it, is God. It is a totally nondiscriminating God that neither requires nor acknowledges sacrifice or ritual, totally self-sufficient in all its needs and doesn't have the ego that's imposed on the God created by established religion. All that is required is to treat the Life-Force with due respect. Simple! Really! Nothing mystical about it! It'd break yer heart to think of all the people who kill in the name of the Life-Force, fighting for the man-made God. You see, the Life-Force lives on through us. We are just conduits of life. We're just the wax in a candle, Pluto. Burning out so that the flame lives on. I mean we are born to die, but life? Life lives. – Do ya know when the Bible refers to God as the Son of Man? Well, I think that's exactly what it means, God is the continuity of life, God is the future, God is eternity, God is the candlewick-maker. There is nothing magical or mystical about God, God is the most natural thing in the world, God is not from some far off place like heaven, God is from earth. God is nature for Christ sake! And Jesus, when it comes to organised religion, you know like Catholic, Jew, and Presbyterian . . . they're just men playing God. You see the whole experience is a very personal thing. It's not as if you can just stroll into a supermarket and pluck God off a shelf. And that's what I believe. . . he said.

I sat there for a second or two, totally blown away. It struck me that Fatfuka would have made a great priest, everything he said about God seemed to make so much sense. Then again he should know, after all he was a Christian Brother.

– And what about death? I asked. – Are ya afraid of it like?

– If you asked me that a few years ago, I'd have said yes. But now that I'm looking death in the eyes, well . . .

. . . and then he went into this big home-spun theory, based on the fact that when two planets are close together and very far away they look like one, when observed from the Earth, I was a bit lost,

– . . . if you walked out that door and met yourself from twenty years ago, you wouldn't recognise yourself, he said. – But because we're in constant communication with ourselves, we don't notice the changes as they occur, and

119

believe me everything changes, it's a gradual change over millions of moments. Everything, looks, size, intentions, principles, tastes, thoughts, feelings; the son begets the father. It's like that person from twenty years ago is dead and gone, all that remains is the name. It's like we die a million times each moment. Life's a series of deaths and rebirths. . . and I'm sure death's no different . . .

– So yer not a Catholic den? I stated the obvious.

– Catholic? 'Course I'm a Catholic! The worst kind! I'm an Irish Catholic! The Irish Catholics are the SS of the Roman Catholics. Stormtroopers that's what we are.

– But I thought . . .

– See organised religion is a cultural thing, you know? Like your history, or your local football team and no fairweather supporter am I! I'm Irish Catholic born, I'm Irish Catholic bred and when I dies I'll be Irish Catholic dead. But I find my God someplace else, do ya know what I mean Pluto?

It was all a little over my head, so I changed the subject rapid like,

– So eh? What about yer wife?

– Who? Valerie is it?

– Yeah, did ya meet her while you were in the Brothers?

– Not at all! he looked surprised. – When I came out of the Brothers I was terrified of women, no real experience, you know, not if you don't count Imelda Kearney. But the day that I literally bumped into Valerie was special. I knew she was the one for me.

I could see he wanted to talk about her.

– You won't believe this, he said. – But I met Valerie in the supermarket . . .

It was as interesting as watching the second-hand on a clock. He was obviously passionately in love with her. There was no doubt but she was beautiful, a little too perfect for my liking, then again maybe I was a little too imperfect for her. I only met her a couple of times at the hospital, she was always mannerly and all that, but a bit plastic. It was like she looked down her nose at me.

– Ah! It was a real whirlwind romance, Ah yes! Love at the deli counter, he sort of sighed.

– I wouldn't mind puttin' my salami into dem buns! I left a big dirty laugh out of me.

Fatfuka didn't get the joke.

– It was a clichéd romance, he explained.

I didn't have a clue what he was on about.

– And when I think back to all the cloak-and-dagger carry-on, you know, about me being in the Brothers before and how we'd break it to Valerie's Mother.

Fatfuka was rambling. I don't think I could have listened to his love story, only for the fact that I knew he was dying. My mind wandered to the beautiful Yvette.

\* \* \*

Yvette . . . ah yes . . . Yvette. She was French from Marseille . . .

There I was trying to find meself. So I headed off to Europe. The plan was: north to Germany and then south to Italy, but the money ran out in Amsterdam.

In a coffee house off Damrak, she was standing there behind the counter, her lips wrapped around a cigarette.

Hair, fair, tossed and shone sorta goldie in the autumn Amsterdam sun, her skin sallow and the most stunning watery blue eyes, looking like they had just rolled from the bed.

She exhaled a lungful of grey and talked puffs of smoke to

121

her work-mate. Her work-mate? A taller black girl probably from Africa or someplace. Yvette chewed, blew bubble, bubble broke, poked gum with thumb, wound around her tongue, chewed, sucked fag, blew blue/grey from lips and nostrels and talked some more.

Strange, it was her friend, the African or whatever she was, that first caught my notice. Hard not to notice a six-foot-two black woman, with a flame-red head shaved to velvet. She was in a green halter-neck, sort of a boob-tube thing, electric green, holding it all together. Cut-off denims, so short that they just about covered the V of her legs, and legs of an athlete, running all the way from counter to floor.

Jesus! I'd never seen anything like her, well not in Cork anyway. I was in love, real love. This wasn't about sex. Not at all! It was love and no more about it. I'm standing there, five foot nine and a half, a twenty-two-year-old virgin and this big black sex-vulture leans over, crotch caressing the counter-mounted bottle-opener. Breasts bursting out like rockets.

I want to save this girl, I want to marry her, take her away from all this. I want to save her from the smut, the filth, save her from herself, save her from all the leering eyes. I want to, I want to . . .

> *I want to hold your*
> *ha-ha-ha-haaaaa-aa-nd,*
> *I want to hold your hand,*

The Beatles zapped crystal-clear from the jukebox.

– Yesss? her blackberry lips puckered not three inches from my forehead.

– Juice? Pawpaw! I ordered.

I had no idea what a pawpaw was but it sounded hip, I

122

mean, a fruit is a fruit . . . couldn't be much different from an apple or an orange. She eye-searched the shelf.

– No pawpaw! she shrugged her shoulders and raised her hands in the air, up went her arms, they in turn lifted her boob-tube, down dropped her melon breasts. My eyes are dragged screaming to those three pre-nipple inches and on to her sleek chocolatey-brown, board-like stomach, untarnished except for the wrinkle of a navel.

Jesus! I really, really, really, really love this girl.

– Passion-fruit? I sucked my stomach in.

– No passion-fruit!

Her screening arms folded.

– Kiwi?

– Kiwi? No Kiwi!

This time she didn't even look at the shelf.

– Melons!

The next exotic fruit that came to mind.

– Listen, sunshine, don't fuck me around, what do you want?

She sounded more north of England than south of the equator, Newcastle or someplace like that.

– Wat've ya? says I.

She points to a menu and walked off, shorts riding right up into the crease of her buttocks.

There were two menus, one with every type of non-alcholic drink, fruit juices, fruit teas, teas from China, India, outer Mongolia, coffee with hazelnuts, almonds, peanuts every type of nut you could think of, coffee with milk, cream, expresso, double milk, double cream, organic coffee, Niceraguan coffee, highland coffee, lowland coffee, coffee with chocolate, even chocolate on its own.

Then the second menu: everything, red Lebanese, Moroccan black, blonde, green, every colour hash under the

123

sun, they had weed, grass, tops, skunky, Thai sticks, heads, big flowery heads the list went on.

I look down the counter, the black girl is back talking to the as-yet-unknown-to-me Yvette. She points in my direction.

Yvette sways up the counter, I grin at her black friend.

– *Bonjour!* she doesn't smile.

– How's she cuttin'?

– So, you see anysink you like?

– Yer friend!

I leave a *yeah hoo* out of me.

– *Pardonnez?*

She stands there looking confused.

– Eh, I'll have a cup a coffee, I say.

– Coffee? she points to the menu.

– Just a normal cup a' coffee, you know like, Maxwell house or something . . .

– One regular coffee, she says.

– Come'ere, wat's de story wit de blow . . .

– *Pardonnez!*

I point to the list on the wall.

– Wat do ya suggest, like?

And she's off, like a schoolteacher explaining the different colours, scents, textures of the ranges of hashes and grasses.

– Zis one will bring you up, zis one down, zis one smooth easy, zis one very happy.

– Have ya got one dat will blow de head offa' me?

She stops, smiles and hands me a ready-rolled joint,

– You smoke zis, a leetle only, yes?

I give her a handful of gilders and wink and smile at her tall black friend.

– An' a cup of coffee, a good strong one, – Yee outcha boi ya!

124

So I'm sitting there looking out on the trams and the Amsterdamonians, waiting for my coffee, they're all moving about heading off to work or whereever they'd be going that time of the day. I run this innocent-looking one-skinner along my lips and light her up. I sit there for seconds or hours. Everything is so clear, clear, clear, clear . . . but nothing makes sense. It's hell, it's heaven. It's *Boney M.*

> *Brown girl in the ring,*
> *tra-la-la-la . . .*

and it gets louder,

> *Brown girl in the ring,*
> *tra-la-la-la-la . . .*

*– Whammo, manohmanohman.*

It's all here in front of me, the why, what, when, where, how. The answer to the unaskable question. My past. My present. My future. My spirit. My soul. Everyone I've ever known and those I've yet to meet here on the back of my hands, pink and white dots beavering away, beavering away. I turn my palms just in time to see my soul filter back between my fingers, back behind the hairline of my wrist, my skin turns from pink, to red, to purple, to blue as the veins buried deep inside surface, from blue to black. Skin bursts to a trembling pulse of raw fleshy, sinewed, foul meat festering in my cupped palm. Jesus! I hold my molten hand over the ashtray and sit there, watching the fluid flesh. My head locked on, can't look away. Left hand painlessly drips in drops to the dirty ashtray.

> *She looks like a sugar in a plum,*
> *Pum! Plum!*

Everything moves inside, must go for a dump, must go now. I get to my feet. Down the café, Yvette is examining the ends of her hair, before I can ask she points to a door. I'm in the toilet. I sit there forever. Oh, this is beautiful! Beautiful, mmmmhhh! Portafleck paint on the back of the door playing cowboys and Indians as the world falls out of my bottom.

*Knock-knock!*

– Everythink is alright in zere, yes? it's Yvette.

Everything is wonderful.

For a change the Indians are winning, probably because they've taken up position safely behind the circled wagons. The cowboys outside riding around in circles, like lunatics, a rantin' and a hootin', shooting into the air and generally doing the bollox. The Indians just crouched there, taking pot shots, picking them off one by one. And just when it seems like the cowboys are well and truly licked, up stands this big, hook-nosed red Indian chief, buffalo-hide head-dress, horns, the lot. He stands there in full view, raises his Winchester up above his head.

– *Remember 1916!* he roars.

Then the sound of a bugle coming from the door latch. I'm concentrating on the dots, expecting to see a Company of the 7th Cavalry charging to the rescue, blue coats and silver steel flashing. But no, not at all, not as much as a brass button in sight. This band of light cavalry charging to destroy, or to their own destruction, are a flying column of the heroes of all the displaced nations of the earth, riding to the sound of the guns. Their hooves hammering out a rhythm picked up by their triumphant war harps playing something from the Ó Ríada Mass. I sit here watching, as the losers of the world charge to the rescue of the Indians who are actually well on top of the situation anyway. Everybody's here, all those who have fought the Good Fight and lost. Asians,

South Americans, Aboriginals, Africans even the Dalai Lama is in there with his regiment. And out in front two squadrons, one of men and the other women, all under a green flag emblazoned with a golden harp, the Irish, led by James Connolly on the left flank, Countess Markievicz on the right, screaming for blood, blue blood at that.

*Knock-knock!*

– 'Ello? 'Ello?

It's Yvette in the distance. Everything is blurry.

It's a mystery to me how I left that cubicle, on my feet or on the flat of my back. All I know is that I woke up next morning in her arms, feeling airy and free and no longer a virgin. That was how I met my wife, the beautiful Yvette.

I remember asking her what was in that stuff I had smoked the day before. She said it was sprayed weed.

– Sprayed?

– *Oui*, sprayed.

– Jeezus girl! Dat stuff's dangerous! Should be made illegal, I said.

– It ez! she said. And the two of us laughed our heads off and rolled another spliff.

Those were days of dreams and ideals, a future of happy ever-afters, poetry. The sun shone down whereon we walked. That was when all in the world was beautiful, young and good, before the darkness set in for the first time.

\* \* \*

Fatfuka was still chuntering on about Valerie, his one and only love.

– Anyway I went along with Valerie to pick out her wedding dress, there was murder! The sales assistant wouldn't let me into the shop. Seemingly the husband isn't supposed to see the dress before the wedding, could you imagine that? he said. – I was never so embarrassed in my life.

– Did ye go de full hog? Ya know like, de dress, de cake, de lot? I asked.

– The works! How about yourself and Yvette?

– Registry office! To tell ya de truth I don't tink I could go trough wit all de fuss of a white wedding, you know de speeches and all dat. I remember at my sister Kathleen's wedding.

She had been planning it for the best part of three years, only the North Cathedral would do. Blackrock Castle was booked for the meal, the Imperial for the wedding night, Lanzarote for the honeymoon, and three cars from O'Connors Undertakers for the day, everything down to a T. But some things you just can't plan for.

On the morning of the wedding my dad was up with the sun and on with the suit, then down the stairs and fell into a bottle of Powers'; got totally plastered. Some said it was because he was losing a daughter. They were wrong. Others thought the wedding brought back memories of my mother, and they were wrong too. I knew his problem, but I was telling nobody.

You see, it's easier to live with a stutter than to have a stutter. I felt it building up inside him for weeks . . . I had heard him in the toilet practising,

– R-r-r-reverend Fathers, L-l-ladies an' G-g-gentlemen . . . shit!

. . . the crowd on the street and the lads up in Mulla's didn't help either, you know asking things like,

– How's de speech commin' along? or, – I suppose yer few words are ready fer de big day?

It all just became too much for him. First he wasn't

coming. Next he was, then he wasn't . . . then he was again and then he did. Locked out of his skull he was.

It's every father's dream to walk up the aisle arm in arm with his daughter , but it didn't work out that way. His arm thrown over Kathleen's shoulder, she sort of half-carried him to the top of the Church.

After the church, he missed the photographs, crashed out in the back of the hired car. When we got to Blackrock Castle he laced into the gargle again. Kathleen broke down, locked herself into one of the rooms upstairs, bawling her eyes out. Aunty Dee the dipso, me dad's sister, outside in the hall hammerin' down the door and shouting things like,

– Come out a' dere dis instant, an' cop onto yerself, yer mother's spinnin' in her grave! Kathleen! Kathleen! Do ya hear me!

Eddie de Nut went looking for my dad, found him outside sitting on a flower-pot smoking a fag,

– Ah Jesus man, straighten up will'a, I mean feck it!

– Y-Y-Ye don't unders-s-stand, Eddie boi,

– I don't understand? La, dere's a hundre' an' fifty guests, sittin' down at th' table inside dat hotel waitin' for a meal, de bride's gone an' locked herself int've one a' de rooms upstairs, she won't come down. . . Wat's dere to understand, boi?

– I-I-I-I-It's m-m-me-me . . .

– I know it's you, you an' a shaggin' bottle.

– N-N-N-no,Eddie. I-It's m-m-me . . .

– Sure isn't dat wat I said? I know 'tis you!

– No, It's m-m-me s-s-stutter, Eddie boi.

– Stutter?

– I c-c-can't face int'v de-de-de speech w-w-wit me st-st-stutter . . .

– Wat stutter?

129

– Wa-wa-wa-wa-a stu-stutter? Wa-wat d'ya t-t-ink dat is, Eddie boi?

– Well granted, ya has a bit of a stammer like, bu-but not dat you'd notice like . . .

– Ah, g-g-get out'v it, Eddie boi.

– Swear to God. Allme life an' I hardly noticed ye had a stutter. Well . . . not until now, when ya just told me like.

– 'T-t-t's easier t-t-ta live w-wi-wi-with a st-st-stutter dan t-t-ta ha-ha-have a wan. D-d-d-ya-ll no?

– 'Tis wat you say wat counts, an' not de way ya say it, Eddie said.

. . . and that's all that was needed, It was like a weight off my dad's shoulders.

– Come on, on yer feet. Dis is Kathleen's day. . .

Eddie the Nut calmly sent everyone back to the function room. He then went up to the room to Kathleen and leaning close to the door he whispered. He explained that my dad was a man of few words and told her some home truths. By the time Kathleen arrived everybody knew the score, you know about my dad and his stutter and all that. One hundred and fifty people sitting in the banquet hall, not a sound, my dad glazed from drink at the top of the table; never touched a bite through the whole meal.

Then the speeches. The best man gets to his feet, a clink of glass,

– . . . and now eh, Reverend Fathers, Ladies and Gentlemen . . . maybe we'll have a few words from the father of the bride, eh, hem, the father of the bride . . .

All the guests sitting there not moving, sayin' nothing. You could cut the tension with a lego brick.

He struggled to his feet and stood there swaying for the best part of a minute and a half trying to get his balance. Not a sound, my dad going from left to right. Kathleen on verge of tears . . .

He staggered a bit, straightened up and pointed to the three bridesmaids. His gaping mouth silent. He stood there like marble. My dad's eyes staring into space, like he was enchanted or possessed or something, face waxen like a dead man. Then from nowhere a sound, as words eased out, hauntingly. It built up force like thunder. But it was a most melodious sound with words so pure . . .

> Dere were tree lovely lassies from Bannion, Bannion, Bannion,
> Dere were tree lovely lassies from Bannion.
> But she was de best of 'em all.
> Yes, she was de best of 'em all . . .

His clutterless voice just filled the banquet hall, like it wasn't of this world at all, magical and eerie, echoing from walls to ceilings. Almost impossible to pinpoint the source of such a beautiful sound as it twirled and looped in the space, like the garlands of flowers, no beginning, no end. Everybody sitting there soundstruck, the verses flowed.

As he came to the final line he walked towards my sister Kathleen, took her hand in his. He leaned forward and kissed her on the cheek. He then stood up straight and took a bow.

The room erupted in applause, a standing ovation. He just returned to his seat and sat down. That was it, that was his speech. Not bad for a man of few words.

* * *

– Phew! says Fatfuka and he paused for a few seconds. – D'ya know, I was very nervous before my speech as well.

Fatfuka was off on another boring story about his lovely Valerie; my mind drifted to Yvette.

131

* * *

Yvette didn't say she was leaving, she only said she was going home, but I knew I had seen the back of her. It had been coming for weeks. The honeymoon was over. I suppose she was too good for me. You see, the Irishman abroad is a strange and exotic animal. He'll throw back his head and sing out a song, he'll raise his fists in defence of the underdog, he'll sleep under a bush, he'll never complain of the harshness of his surroundings, he'll talk about his home, his family, his mother, he'll laugh and cry, and any shortcomings he may have will be just about hidden in the translation from his soft Irish brogue.

At home in Ireland among my own, I'd lose my exoticness and become the beast that I am. I knew it would only be a matter of time before I'd be visible. She'd see me for what I am, amongst my own.

All the same, it cut me right down to the bone, just to watch her sway away from me, across the airport towards the departure lounge. I stood there, helpless and heartbroken. The minutes flashed by on the screen. My eyes begged her not to go, but 14:32 became 14:33 and Flight 204 was gone.

* * *

Fatfuka was still nattering about his wedding day and how lucky he was to have found Valerie.

– I don't know what I'd do without Valerie. I mean like the way she stood by me through all of this. – Ya really need a soulmate to help you through the tough times. You know what I mean, Pluto, sure you were married yerself.

– Don't remind me.

132

I cut him short.

– Was it that bad?

– 'Twasn't dat good! I said.

– Really?

– I was destroyed wen Yvette walked out.

– Really?

– It was like I realised dat de prince didn't necessarily marry de princess and I suppose sometimes de princess might have to kiss a few frogs. And, as for dis dey-all-lived-happily-ever-after bit? Shag dat for a game of soldiers!

– Jeezus! he said.

– When Yvette walked out, I was in bits. I had no future, dat was wen I first found meself deep down under de blankets, deep down in de darkness.

I could see that Fatfuka wasn't expecting such straight talk, but there was no stopping me now.

– Two years dere, two years a' drink, disillusion and delusion, I fell down a lot an' woke up in de most unusual places. Two years a' head space, two years of insanity, out a' body, out a' mind, out a' head. It was my Limbo, and Limbo does exist. It's wen ya lose a love because of ignorance rather dan any wrongdoings. Dat's Limbo for ya!

Fatfuka sat up in the bed.

– Not such a bad place. It's a place where you're free. Free to float around in your ignorance. It's a place of self-assessment. But it don't last forever, it only seems dat way. Sort a' like drowning, when ya stop struggling ya just float gently back to de surface an' everything's hunky-dory.

– Jeezus, it sounds pretty horrific, Fatfuka said.

– Yerrah, I was empty wen Yvette walked, empty an' crushed.

I don't know why I started talking, maybe it was because for the first time in a long time I felt I had a friend, or maybe because I knew he'd soon be gone. Whatever the reason it just flowed.

– I'm not sure whether I had de break-down before or after she left, but Jeezus it took me de best part of three years to come out of it.

By the look on Fatfuka's face, I could see that he wasn't expecting such direct line, but the beast was out.

– Break-down? Fatfuka raised his eyebrows.

– Ya must ha' heard about me stint up in St Anne's?

– Oh that!

I knew he knew. Everybody knew, that was probably why I ended up there in the first place.

# 17

Did you ever have one of those dreams, where you dream you're in a public place, like a bus stop or somewhere. . .

. . . there I was, outside Roches Stores in a queue for the Number 3. I think I was going to school. Anyway, wherever I was going, I was late. Surrounded by people that I knew, but I couldn't put names on any of the faces. That was when I noticed Georgie crossing Patrick's Bridge, and coming in my direction. I hadn't seen Georgie for years, not since he'd died. So I got a bit excited and began to jump up and down, waving my arms in the air and calling out his name. The people in the queue stepped back and just looked at me. So I screamed a little louder. Georgie couldn't hear me. By this time, a crowd had gathered, some of them jeering, others making distorted, contorted faces. I screamed louder, and jumped higher trying to catch a glimpse of Georgie over their heads. That was when the chanting began,

*Eggella! Eggella! Eggella!*
*Eggella! Eggella! Eggella!*

Everything and nothing made sense.

– *Georgie! Georgie! Georrrrgieeeee!* I roared.

Through a gap in the crowd I caught a glimpse of myself in a shop window. I stopped, stood there, didn't recognise myself, naked. I looked at my hands, along my arms, down across my bare chest, my stomach, my pubic hair, beyond my knees all the way to my dirty bloody feet. I crumpled to the footpath into a ball.

Three whole days before I came around. Three whole days of visions, sweats and chills. Three whole days of torment and restraint. Three whole days before I found myself in St Anne's for the second time. It's very frightening when your dreams are real.

\* \* \*

– Sure break-downs are two-a-penny these days, Pluto.

– Don't be talkin' to me, some of de most intelligent people I've met were up in St Anne's.

– And the most sensitive, he said.

– You said it, boi! But I tell ya it's no joke up dere, sorta like a prison.

– And did you just sign yourself in or what?

– Well, the first time, yeah, more or less, you know like. Fatfuka looked at me, he was none the wiser.

– Like, things were getting crazier and crazier, I explained.

– Crazier?

– You know like, dreams an' tings.

– Dreams and things, Pluto?

– I sorta didn't know wat was real, or wat was a dream. It was Yvette convinced me to see a head-doctor. In all fairness, she had a point. I mean like, we were only married about six months, an' I'd dragged her all de way to Belfast.

– Belfast? Fatfuka sat back in the bed. – What were ye doing in Belfast? For Christ's sake!

– Well, actually we were in de lobby of de Europa Hotel, me an' Yvette, an' I was kickin' up blue murder.

– The Europa? In Belfast?

* * *

– Europa Hotel!

The taxi driver squeezed the words out the side of his mouth. His northern accent sounded so exotic. I paid the fare. Even the money looked funny.

– So, zis is it, l'otel Europe?

Yvette was impressed.

– De Europa hotel! I corrected her.

– Oh, whatever.

– Do ya know, dis is one of de most frequently bombed hotels in de world.

– Do not say such things!

– 'Tis only de truth.

– Well, I do not wish to hear ze truth! she headed for the entrance.

By the time I gathered our bags together and caught up with Yvette, she was at the desk.

– I am so excited to meet your mother, after all zis time, Pluto, she whispered.

– You'll love me mudder.

– Where are we to meet 'er?

– Eh! In de, eh! Lobby, I answered.

But I wasn't sure, I knew we were supposed to meet her in The Europa, in Belfast on that day, but the details were all a bit unclear in my head.

– Do you see 'er anywhere?

– Eh, no! I said.

– Ve ask at ze desk, yes?

– Eh, good idea, good idea!

My mother's name echoed around the foyer, no sign of her. We sat there for almost an hour.

– Maybe you phone your mother yes?

– Phone?

– Yes! Phone 'er and see if zere is a problem.

– Eh, phone me mudder?

This was all getting a bit confusing for me.

– Do you have 'er phone number?

Yvette was asking me for my mother's phone number and address. She sounded faint, like she was away in the distance. I could tell by the look on her face that she was beginning to lose the head. It was all getting to be too much for me. I didn't have a number or an address for my mother and for the life of me, I didn't know what she was doing in Belfast. All I knew was, that I was supposed to meet her there in the Europa Hotel to introduce her to my new wife, Yvette. The fact that my mother had been dead for almost twenty years had nothing to do with it. So I stormed up to the desk.

– You! I shouted.

– Who me?

– Yeah! You!

– Pardon me, sir, can I help you?

– I'm lookin' for me mudder.

– Ah! Yes! I'll page her again, sir.

– Don't mind paging her again, I want me mudder now, ya stupid bastard. Where is she?

– I'm sorry, sir, but she hasn't checked in yet.

– Checked in! Checked in, is it? and I threw a fist at him.

– Don't talk to me about checkin' in. I want me mudder! I screamed.

– I'm sorry, eh sorry, he cowered back from the desk.

Something inside me flipped, I reached over the counter and grabbed him by the lapels of his coat.

– Where's me mudder, I want me mudder now!

I dragged him over the counter. All hell broke loose.

By the time the police arrived I was being held to the floor by four of them. Yvette said later that I was like somebody possessed, spitting, biting, kicking and bellowing like a wild animal. When the truth came out, about my mother being dead, all charges were dropped and on Yvette's advice, I went to see a head doctor. He said that I was probably suffering from some sort of Delayed Post-Traumatic Stress, and suggested that I go to hospital for observation, so I signed myself in. It was scary, but fair dues to Yvette, she stood by me.

\* \* \*

– Gowaan!

Fatfuka couldn't believe it.

– Serious! I remember, I asked de head doctor. I says to him, – Tell me straight, Doctor, tell me in layman's language, what's exactly wrong wit me?

– And what did he say? Fatfuka asked.

– He looked at me with his knowing eyes and sort a' cleared his throat. I prepared meself for de worst. – *Ehem, Well, Mr O'Toole*, he said. – *In layman's language. You're totally off your fuckin' chuck!*

Meself and Fatfuka just fell about the place laughing.

– Off yer fuckin' chuck he said! and we laughed all over again.

– But you're fine now?

– Yerrah, I'm alright, but I has me moments.

– Like the rest of us, Fatfuka said.

I didn't tell him about the day I found myself naked, waiting for the Number 3, and I didn't bother telling him about the other trips to St Anne's and I definitely didn't tell him about the day I stuck me head in the oven, he probably knew anyway.

139

– Like de rest of ye, I agreed.

– And your wife?

– Who, Yvette? Yerrah she took off soon after I got over de whole Europa Hotel ting. Who could blame her? She just wanted to go home. A beautiful woman. I don't tink I'll ever get over her. D'ya know, wen tings are good I tink of her, and wish she were dere beside me to share in all me pleasures and triumphs. But Jeezus, when tings are bad, I curse her and anyone who looks like her.

– And have you heard from her since?

– I sent her a few letters, phoned her once, she hung up on me. I had a few letters from her solicitors while de divorce was going through, but that's about it.

– Ah Jeezus! There's plenty fish in the sea.

Fatfuka tried to lighten the conversation. And of course he was right, plenty women too, women like Mags and Veronica.

– I suppose you're right, Fatfuka boi! But there's only one Yvette and I still tinks about her an' if she ever came back all would be forgiven. D'ya know wat I'd love, I paused. – I'd love to have one more crack at it.

– And what would be so different about it this time, Pluto?

– She wouldn't leave me, and no more about it!

\* \* \*

2:21.

– Ha! She wouldn't leave and no more about it?

I look around my hole of a flat, – She wouldn't leave me! I shout, I laugh, – She wouldn't fuckin' want ta!

I cry.

140

# 18

Brenda turns in her bed, for some reason the night-cap isn't kicking in, probably the noise up in No. 4. She switches the light on, it's twenty-two minutes past two, she fumbles for the radio.

– *Click!*

*Candle In The Wind*, Elton John.

Brenda reaches for another cigarette.

* * *

2:23.

Jimmy the Monk is well on, he knocks over Herman's coffee table.

– God I'm terrible sorry, mate.

– Is OK! Is OK! Herman is flustered, he picks up the ashtray and the bits of broken mug.

– See, I was just reaching over for a look of that yoke, mate.

– Yoke? Herman asks.

– Yeah, that yoke there, mate.

– Oh! Ze coffee-plunger?

– Is dat what it is? Never seen one a' them things, an' I've seen many's the queer thing in me time Over.

– Yes, ze coffee-plunger is an adaptation of dere old filter und funnel method.

– De wha'?

– You see, you place ze coffee grind in here, zen you pour in der hot water, put ze plunger in like so. Allow stand for a minute or so until the coffee diffuses.

– Well, I never saw the likes a' that, mate!

– And zen you push down der plunger, not only do make der coffee, but it also separates dere grind and acts as ein filter.

Herman hands the Monk the coffee-plunger.

– Did ya ever try the Maxwell House instant. No messin' about with that stuff.

– Hmmm! Herman is not impressed. He turns up the radio. – Must say I always like zis song, he says. – It's about Marilyn Monroe, you know zis?

Jimmy the Monk is well aware of the fact that *Norma Jean Baker* was *Marilyn Monroe*, but he also knows that Herman is Master of the Obvious, so he leaves him off.

– Gowaan? the Monk looks surprised

– Ah yes, Elton John wrote, *Goodbye Norma Jean*, about Marilyn Monroe, and did you know . . .

Herman is on a roll.

The Monk knows the correct name of the song is *Candle In The Wind*. He also knows that Herman is about to reel out a whole ream of utter scutter, so he changes the subject.

– Gettin' back to Pluto, do ya really think he's a danger to himself, mate?

– Well, I do not know. I just feel it in mein vaters.

– Yeah but you don't think 'e's gonna top himself, do ya?

– I do not know, But I do think there ist ein darkness about tonight.

– Darkness?

– Yes, just like der last time Pluto is low. He leaves his flat tomorrow, he has not organised somewhere to stay. He has not been out of his flat in three, maybe four days, zis is worrying, yes? I worry for Pluto.

– Hmmm!

– I feel I should go down and see if he is well!

– At half-two in the mornin'?

– Zis is vot Brenda says.

– Maybe you should leave it off until the tomorro', mate?

– Maybe so, maybe so, but I just hope ve are not too late. Would you eh like another cup of coffee? Herman's voice fades off into his kitchenette, he's talking about the time he found Pluto with his head in the oven.

– I could smell der gas all over der house, I kicked in de door to Pluto's. He was kneeling down in front of der cooker, half his body in der oven.

The Monk has heard this story thousands of times before. The way Herman disconnected the gas and broke out the windows with a chair, to let some air in, and how Pluto would have died only for the fact that the house had been converted to natural gas and the meter ran out of money.

– Imagine that! Der natural gas vill not gas you, amazing! And did you know, he continues. – Der natural gas has no odour, zey actually mix ein smell in at der Gas Verks so that it can be detected.

Herman has a morbid fascination with gas.

– Do ya mind if I use yer bog? the Monk asks.

– Oh, by all means, be mein guest.

The Monk pulls himself up out of the armchair.

– Oh! Jeeezzus! off balance, he stumbles forward, crashing full force, face first, down on top of the coffee table again, sending mugs, sugar, milk, coffee pot, plate of biscuits and ashtray flying. The table splinters.

143

*Bang – bang! Bang – bang!* Thumping on the floor. It's Brenda the Brasser down in No. 3.

– Herrrmaan! Would ya ever keep de noise down for Christ's sakes! Dere's people trying to sleep down here!

– Is OK Brenda! Is OK! Ze Monk has fallen over! Herman shouts down through the worn carpet.

– What did you just call me? the Monk looks at Herman.

– Sorry, Jimmy, sorry! Herman leans closer to the floor and roars down to Brenda again. – Eh, Jimmy has eh, fallen over! he turns his head and looks at the Monk.

\* \* \*

2:26

Brenda is wide awake, There's no sense fighting it, she decides to have a cup of tea.

\* \* \*

2:26.01

Alison's exhausted. Too tired to sleep. She resents the fact that they all assume being a landlady is a licence to print money. It's hard work and emotionally draining. She's like a mother figure to her tenants. All they do is pay the rent, but she has the responsibility of keeping a roof over their heads and they're a fairly ungrateful bunch.

The kitchen door opens, it's her husband.

– Can you not sleep, Alison? Don't tell me you're losing sleep over that lunatic up on Waterloo Terrace, nobody else would take him, so why should you?

– I know, she says and switches off Elton John – but really I don't think he's got another place to move into.

– Yeah well! That's his problem, he's big enough and ugly enough to look after himself.

– But still though . . .

– Look, this is crazy! he says. – It's going on for three in the morning and you're sitting here worried, while he's up there sound asleep and not a bother on him.

* * *

2:28

I hear Brenda walk across the ceiling,

– Does anybody sleep in this house? I empty the last mouthful of whiskey from mug to mouth and roll another cigarette.

It's amazing how a short, bald guy with glasses and a piano can sing a song and it means so much to so many people. Elton John has always been in there, ever since I remember, turning them out, hit after hit. It's like even his new stuff brings back memories. I don't know if I like *Candle in The Wind* though. A bit over-played, you know like, some brain-dead DJ tells you for the three-hundred-trillionth-time, that the song is about Marilyn Monroe,

– Yeah right! Big swinging mickey!

It's not as if it's the third secret of Fatima. I suppose it's a bit like *Enola Gay*, you know, by Orchestral Manoeuvres in The Dark, good song, but a bit of a gimmick.

*Ah! Yes indeed! All you night people . . .*

He croons in his mid-Atlantic dross . . .

*Tragic story of Marilyn Monroe.*
*From the ever-evocative Elton John,*
*and Candle In The Wind.*
*Bringing the time up to two thirty,*
*in the AM.*

145

*If you're out there partying, working night shift,*
*driving a cab, whatever you're doing.*
*Why don't you give me a call,*
*here on Night Moves.*
*Tell me what you'd like to hear.*
*The lines are open,*
*call me now on 18-50 13-33-33.*
*Ah! Yes indeed! Night Moves comin' at ya.*
*And later on, in the show at three o'clock,*
*we have news headlines.*
*But right now . . .*

. . . and then he has the gall to talk over Queen and the intro to *This Could Be Heaven*. Why do they do that? Why do they insist on talking over a perfectly good record. Records that cost a small fortune to produce. Records that have the best musicians, technology and technicians in the world, and here's this tone-deaf DJ coming out with rubbish like,

– *Take it away, Freddie.*

– Jeezus!

Although in fairness to him, he does play decent music most of the time. Played one last night by Elvis. It was a live version of *The Wonder of You*, recorded in Las Vegas. There's like this black gospel choir backing him and halfways through the song, one of the backing singers gets really carried away. She goes ga-ga, howling and yelling her own particular swirls and yodels. She gets louder and louder and eventually she begins to drown out the King. Elvis just cracks up laughing, stands back and lets her at it. It was a real case of God being made man.

I suppose DJs are a necessary evil really, like imitation superstars. Stardom? Stardumb! Ha! With all the gear from the latest world tour, the sweat shirts, baseball caps and anoraks. Raybans dangling from their necks, spending their days playing other people's music and battling the aging process.

# 19

Fatfuka was telling me that the day he left the Christian Brothers it was like twenty years had been lifted off his shoulders.

– Amazing! There I was, and I felt like a teenager again, he said.

– Dat's love for ya.

– Ah no! That was ages before I met Valerie.

– But it's de same ting, I said. – A new life, a new love, everything changes, everything's new, it takes years off ya. – I remember after Yvette walked out, I threw me hat at love, dat was until I met Veronica.

– Veronica? says Fatfuka. – I never heard about her, I mean, you mentioned Mags and baby Paulo and all that, but Veronica? Never heard about her.

\* \* \*

I wasn't looking for a woman that night but I couldn't help noticing her. She wasn't stunning or attractive. She stood out from the rest though. She had a look of fear and excitement about her as she moved through the Gallery, checking each painting against the catalogue. I was working there on a *Fás*

Scheme, you know two and a half·days a week cleaning, hanging paintings and all that kind a stuff; kept all my welfare and Health Board benefits, a doddle.

I moved in on her at the wine table.

– Great show?

– Huh? she stood back.

– Do you like de work?

– I really don't know much about art, she said.

– Neither do I, but I knows what I likes!

Veronica had never heard that one before, she was impressed. She was looking for culture. I was there for the free drink.

– I'll give ya a tip to get ya out of a sticky situation in a gallery.

– Tip? she repeated.

– See, all ya has to do is, pick out one feature in a painting. For example; see dat big daub a' red paint on dat one over dere?

– Eh, yes? she looked up.

– Well, ya move to de far end a' de room, like where we are now. Den, when you're asked wat ya tink a' de show, just say, – *I think the artists use of the colour red, as in that piece up there, is wonderful, simply wonderful* . . . and walk away. It helps if you know de artist's name. As Louis le Brocquay was only sayin' to me last week, art's all about names.

Veronica thought this was the funniest thing she had ever heard.

The opening closed, we ended up in the Long Valley chatting. After the pub, I asked her if she'd like to come to the Cafe Lorca where we could talk away into the night, unhindered by licensing laws. She said she'd love to, but she had to go home to the baby-sitter.

Now this is a strange one. See the very mention of baby-

148

sitters or kids would usually have sent me diving for cover, but not with Veronica, I just wasn't interested. Don't get me wrong, I had a great night and all that and she wasn't bad-looking, but there was no spark. I walked her to the Taxi stand outside the Savoy. But, just as she was going to sit into the car she kissed me on the cheek. It was like my world stopped spinning. Suddenly it struck me that I would never meet this woman again and a panic set in.

– We might meet for coffee sometime? I grasped at straws.

– That'd be lovely, she said.

– Do ya have a telephone?

She pulled a notebook from her bag, scribbled a number down, tore out the page and handing it to me, she slipped into the back seat. I just watched as the cab drove away. She turned, smiled, waved and faded into the night.

The following Saturday. Lunch-time. The Long Valley: our first date. Not so much a date as a meeting. It was like we'd known each other forever. I was at ease. We talked.

A teacher, that's what she was. She seemed fairly well set up too, her own house and car and all that, but for some reason there was a look of loneliness about her. She told me all about her little girl Julie and how the marriage failed. Her husband was a right waster by all accounts. I told her about Yvette, and how my marriage broke up after my break-down. Veronica thought it very heartless of Yvette to walk out on me at such a stressful time. I agreed with her. We just sat there in the snug in The Valley chatting, no pressure. At seven o'clock she dashed off, late for the childminder.

We arranged to meet again the following Saturday. I couldn't believe it when she turned up. It went on like that for a few weeks, meeting in the snug and nattering away until she was late.

I remember the first time I met her little girl, Julie. The

three of us went for a walk out along the Lee fields. A lovely kid, just like her mother. Soon after that I was having dinner down at Veronica's at least once a week and just hanging around watching the telly and things. I don't remember when we started going out with each other, it just happened. No romance, no fire-lit passion, no real love between us, but we cared for each other, enjoyed each other and wanted to be together, and that for me, in my delicate head-space, was more important than all the candle-lit dinners in Paris.

Love. What is love? Man has been trying to put the finger on that one for ever and a day. It's been compared to mountains, rivers, landscapes; celebrated in song and poem and story; weighed in chocolates and flowers; paid for with diamonds and gold and the highest price of all . . . people have died for love, and still I ask myself, what is love?

I suppose it's all about two people and how they click, and that's it, me and Veronica clicked. A million miles away from the roaring-fire, oxygen-sucking, blazing-white, out of control, insane, unstoppable passion that I knew with Yvette. Well, unstoppable passion until she came up for air, next thing you know she's gone and it's over. A bit like what Neil Young said about *Johnny Rotten*,

*better to burn out than to fade away.*

Me and Yvette got married in a fever, on a fiver. There was no future in that.

But Veronica, now that was different. Like the Church of Rome, the foundations were rock. Commitment developed slowly, it was the intention of a future. The moment of my intention is a hard thing to gauge though, but looking back, I can pin-point it to art.

I had been watching this one ceramic piece, a wall-plaque sort of thing, part of a group show, local artists. Titled, *Blue Moon Full Moon Lunatic*, it was sort of like a burnt biscuit, with a blast of blue and splatters of white across it. I'd be in the gallery two mornings a week, giving the place a brush out, and each day I'd see it hanging there. What first attracted me to it was the price, eighty-five quid. I thought,

– Hey, I can afford dat!

For months, I had watched the cheque-book boys, studying catalogues and buying. Then, there I was standing in front of something I could actually almost afford myself. Red dots were flying up left and right of it. It was like, can I can't I, can I can't I and then I said,

– Yerah, feck it!

It was the day they were taking down the exhibition, the place was crawling with artists packing up. He was on his knees, bubble-wrap all over the gaff.

– Wat's de story wit dat blue plaque ting? I asked.

– Huh?

– Dat dere, I pointed.

– Oh, *Blue Moon Full Moon Lunatic*, is it?

– Yeah!

– Well, what about it? he said.

– Is it still for sale, like?

– Everything's for sale 'cept my soul, he smiled.

– I'd rather me hole dan a soul, I said and laughed. He laughed too.

. . . anyway the deal was done, twenty-five quid there and then, twenty every Thursday for the next three weeks. I walked away with his art, bubble-wrap, the lot; like a young fella who for weeks had my nose pressed against a toy-shop window drooling, wanting, wanting, wanting; and now here it was, under my arm, mine.

After work that evening I met Veronica. She was sitting in the window seat of the Corner House sipping white wine,

151

– What's that? she was talking about the plaque.

A strange feeling came over me, it was like all my wanting and desire for that bit of coloured clay was pointless; art was useless overshadowed by the real thing that was Veronica. So just like that, I gave it to her.

– . . . might be nice on your wall, I said.

And that was it. That was the moment of intention of my love; it was mine for her. I gave her my art.

About six months later I moved in with Veronica and Julie. It was what I had been searching for, no complications, no games, even sex wasn't high up on the list. Two complete strangers just living and caring about each other, absolute contentment, passionless, painless; comfortably safe and controlled. Veronica wanted nothing from me, except for me to be me. I'd collect Julie from school and do other fatherly things – Julie even called me dad – but never any pressure, probably because I didn't have the ambition that a parent has for their child, it was like whatever Julie wanted was fine by me. I suppose if there was ever such a thing as a perfect relationship you need look no further than that first year living with Veronica and small Julie, but then again does perfection ever really exist? – Ask God, he wrote de book on it.

We lived our two lives as one, although we were light-years apart. Veronica liked to read, I'd rather watch the telly. She was vegetarian, no rabbit-food for me thank you very much. Veronica was a political animal. I on the other hand, thought a polling station was where Telecom kept their telegraph-poles; and I must admit I enjoyed my few pints. But all that aside, everything was wonderful. The only time we'd get close to having an argument was when she wanted to talk about feminism. *Women's Issues*, she called it. I mean I'm as much a feminist as the next man, right behind her all the way. It was like she used to get so bloody frustrated or something, but I suppose that's women for ya . . .

– . . . that was when she reached the glass ceiling! Veronica was talking about her friend Geraldine who worked in the bank.

– Glass ceiling? I wasn't exactly sure what she was talking about. – In de bank?

– Yes, that was as high as she could go!

– Unless she went out onto de roof, I said.

– Roof? Yeah, right! Marginalised! That's exactly what they want.

– Who want?

– The fat cats who put the glass ceiling there in the first place!

– In de bank?

– What do you think we're talking about, Pluto?

– I never noticed it myself?

– How could you notice it, she screamed, – You're a man! As if being a man was a crime.

– I know I'm a man, but dat don't mean I wouldn't notice a glass ceiling if I saw one!

– Look, the very principle of the glass ceiling is that you can't see it!

– But you can see through it, can't ya? I still wasn't sure what she was talking about.

– Jesus! What I'm trying to say is that from now on, all Geraldine's promotions will be lateral promotion.

– Ya mean she won't get a wages increase, is it?

– This is not about wages! she snarled.

– Ya mean, she will get paid extra? I was well and truly lost at this stage.

– Look! This is all about the empowerment of women and

the destruction of the oppressive nature of the Old-Boy's Network! Veronica was red in the face.

– De wha'?

– The reinstatement of women to their rightful place in the society!

At last I got a glimmer of what she was on about.

– Ya mean to say dat women should be at home with de kids? Well, I'm all behind dat!

Veronica's face went from red to white.

– Look!

– Hang on! Hang on! I tried to calm her. – Dis is gettin' way out of hand, I thought we were talking about de bank and glass roofs, or something like dat . . .

– Glass ceiling! she screamed and walked out, slamming the door behind her.

But that was as bad as it got. Life was good and as far as I was concerned I would have happily lived out the rest of my days with Veronica and Julie.

* * *

– Hmm! said Fatfuka, – Sounds like heaven.

– 'Cept for the old feminist thing, I said.

– Ah! Sure, you'd get over that though!

– I suppose ya would! But do ya know what?

– What?

– Peter Ustinov ruined my life!

– Peter Ustinov?

– Yeah! Peter Ustinov!

* * *

I would have gladly stayed at home that night. I mean, I love

154

the *Late Late Show*, in fact I was looking forward to it. Veronica was in West Cork, Coolea for the weekend, she took Julie with her. I picked up a few cans in the offy and a takeaway in the Yangtsy River, went home and settled in for a night with the telly. Next thing, who's Gay Byrne's first guest, only Peter Ustinov.

– Peter shaggin' Ustinov?

I couldn't face into a night of that. So, I threw back the last of my Murphy's, smoked a three-skinner, and rolled a nice neat spliff to take with me into town.

Town was buzzing. I hadn't seen night-life in a long time. My plan was to hit all the old haunts, you know like Charlies, The Phoenix, The Donkey's Ears, Loafers, Mojo's and then, maybe on to The Valley or the Hi-B or Counihan's or someplace. I would probably end up in The Cafe Lorca drinking wine until dawn.

Coming out of the Donkey's Ears on my way to either Loafers or Mojo's, who did I meet only small Mags, Mags Horgan. I couldn't believe it. She had grown into a woman. The last time I saw Mags Horgan I was sixteen and she was a child, about eleven. Here she was, twenty-one, looking like a model, sparkling eyes, flashing teeth and a most amazing pair of tits.

– Hi, her lips widened. – Pluto, don't ya recognise me?

I hadn't a clue who she was.

– Ah, how're ya! I bluffed, but she was on to me.

– Pluto, it's me small Mags, Mags Horgan.

No snots, no freckles, no pimples, her jet-black hair framing a tanned face, lit up by rose-red lips and a body to die for. She giggled. And there for the first time since Yvette walked out on me, something moved inside. It was like I had been emotionally castrated, then suddenly I was alive and tingling, like a blood-rush to the head. I reached out, held

Mags in my arms and hugging her tightly I kissed her on the lips.

– Good to see ya, Mags, good to see ya, Jeezus Mags, you've grown into a woman.

– I know, she hissed and placing her hands on her hips she raised her breasts and pouted tartishly.

– Jeezus Christ, Mags, it's good to see ya!

– You said that already, she teased.

– Well eh, would ya like a pint? and I made some joke about buying her her first legal drink.

It was wild, like a teenager again, hormones pumping, my body took over. No clever chat-up lines, just pure raw sex squeezing out the sparks from my pores and she was open to it. I held her hand and headed for the bar.

– So, what will it be?

– Bulmer's cider, she purred.

– Hoi Mark! Two pints a' Bulmers by the neck . . .

It was *Battle of The DJ*'s that night, so we took our drinks out to the quay-side. I followed her, led on by my penis, across the road to the railings, my eyes locked onto every sway of her leggings-cast buttocks.

The river was black as death and full to the brim. We leaned there, looking across to the cherry-blossom-lined South Mall. She told me she was just back from London, working for some Save The Something Fund. She had just got a job here in Cork in a second-hand clothes shop, but was thinking of opening up an Indian Restaurant or a craft shop or something, if she ever managed to get the money together. She said Cork could really do with a good Indian Restaurant. I asked her if she had tried The Delhi Palace, she said she'd never heard of it. She said London was really a wild and crazy place. I said Cork could be fairly crazy too. She said she had heard some years back that I married a French one. I told her that was well and truly over.

– Very sad, she said.

– Hmm, I agreed.

I noticed her fingers inside my T-shirt, gently tip-tapping my skin. I slipped my hand down the back of her leggings, down inside her panties and squeezed, it seemed like the most natural thing to do. Mags moaned a little. I reached further down over her peach-bum, down inside her thigh. And holding her to me, I raised her slightly to her tippy-toes, she turned mouth wide open, and we kissed.

We stood there locked in love forever. From hellish hot to the pleasures of heaven. A splash, my bottle fell to the river and a crash as Mags' shattered on the footpath, but what's cider when you mouth craves the juice of love. It must have been ten minutes before we separated. She smiled and lifted her eyelids.

I took my spliff from my pocket, asked her if she smoked. She just made a short *Mhhhh* sound. I gave her the joint, she lit it, inhaled and putting her lips against mine, the smoke drifted to my mouth. We kissed, smoke wafting. We smiled and laughed a bit. I asked her if she wanted another cider. She asked me if I'd ever tried Ecstasy.

– It's the latest in the clubs in London, she said.

– Yeah, I've heard about it.

– Well, have ya tried it?

– I'm sorta out a de scene at de moment.

I avoided the question.

– Would ya like some?

– Do ya have some? I asked.

She pointed to her bum-bag.

– I don't know if I want to get trippy, I said.

– Not with Ecstasy ya won't, it's a body buzz, she said. – A wonder drug. It's speedy but mellow, trippy without colours. You'll love it, it's a love drug.

We popped the tabs and headed down to Mojo's for another drink. By the time we got there we just kept on walking. Along Union quay, to the footbridge by the old dole office. I told Mags about the time they were putting a new roof on the place and how half the lads working on it climbed down the scaffolding twice a week and into the dole to sign on.

– Aren't Cork people funny all the same, I said. – I mean like see that footbridge there, there are two footbridges along this stretch of the river. This one here was opened by Gerald Goldberg, Cork's Jewish Lord Mayor, it leads from Goldberg's office in the heart of the city to the Synagogue on South Terrace and on into the Jew Town of Albert Road; but the funny thing is that the bridge is known locally as the Pass-Over. Then we have the other footbridge up by the Quay Co-op. It's called de By-Pass, ya see Joe HcHugh was the City Manager at de time dey were building it, and sur poor aul Joe had to go under the knife with his heart . . . de By-Pass, gas or wat?

Mags sort of laughs at the whole By-Pass, Pass-Over thing. I pointed out the oval window of Calanan's, the most beautiful pub in Cork, and the way it jutted out onto the footpath. We stood at the horse trough on Parliament bridge, tracing the shapes of Calanan's woodwork in the air. I told her about the night the whole bar stood to attention as a fella played the National Anthem on a mouth organ . . .

We walked past the South Gate bridge. I pointed up Barrack Street, where Bradley's sold the cheapest pints in Ireland; Tom Barry's where I cheated Pádraic Breathnach, a giant from Connemara, in pool and Ford's who refused to serve the best-loved poet of them all, a neighbour's child . . .

– Come out now, Paddy Galvin!

I roared at a rising heron, and a cormorant vanished under the black-as-stout water near Beamish's.

On we tripped, along Proby's Quay up to St Finbarre's Cathedral; the story goes that if the Golden Angel falls from the gable three times the Cathedral will be given to the Catholics. Mags laughed at the part about the commando raids myself, Fatfuka, Georgie, Ted, Pinko and the lads carried out on the place trying to lasso the angel for the Catholics and for Cork, and how it always baffled us, that the Protestants could believe in angels and not the Virgin Mary, and the way Georgie used say that it wasn't hard for us,

– Sure half the Marys in Cork are virgins anyway . . .

On we went, around by Crosses Green, back to the South Gate Bridge, into South Main Street, down the North Main Street to the Coal Quay. We slipped under Dalton's Avenue archway by Ma Dennehy's to catch a gander of the grotto and the red rows of Corporation Buildings; each terrace with more front doors than houses.

. . . and that's the way we went, talking buildings and stories of people and places. I mentioned that the north channel could do with a footbridge joining the Coal Quay to the northside, I mean like the southside has two,

– . . . maybe they could call it the Danny La Rue, Mags said.

– The Danny La Rue Bridge? I didn't get it.

– He's from Cork, isn't he?

– I still didn't get it.

– You know like, it'd be a Cross-over, like Danny La Rue. Then we'd have the By-Pass, the Pass-Over and the Cross-Over, Mags laughed.

. . . along Lavitt's Quay, across the North Gate Bridge, up Shandon Street, all the way up to Shandon Steeple. At the corner of Bob and Joan's Walk we passed a few whackers, I recognised some of their faces through their older brothers, you know, fellas like Danker and Nickey Flynn. This was my

159

old stomping ground. It was like I was carried here on auto-pilot, all decision-making put aside as my senses worked on the power of Ecstasy. Maybe that's why I ended up in Shandon, under the watchful, unjudging eye of the Goldie Fish weather vane. It turned with every call of wind.

We climbed over the well-worn railings and into the old graveyard. I guided Mags to a bench with a history of teenage lust and lay down, she mounted me like a jockey breaking in the new saddle. She settled, then grappled with the buttons on my 501's, I peeled her leggings down below her knees. She repositioned herself. I lowered my head to the bench, slowly opened my eyes. I could see and smell the Fish, he looked down on me. My dad and his coffin crossed my mind. I smiled. She pushed on me.

– Yesss! I whispered.

Mags moaned. Serenaded by the steeple's bells and the cat-howls from a cider party at the far end of the graveyard, we made mad love.

Later we picked up two tins of Coke in the chipper across from the North Cathedral.

– Diet, if ya have it.

We hopped a hackney on Shandon Street, it carried us all the way across town back to my place, or should I say Veronica's. Still wired, like wild animals, snarling and mauling and tearing at each other's clothing, in the back seat of the cab, like a dream.

What began in the front porch, as I struggled to get the keys from my pocket erupted in a frenzy of passion. We fell half-naked to the hall floor. Power-driven love that carried us through every room, hallway and landing in the house. From floor to table to chair, in the bathroom, on the stairs, we moved through every nook, crevice and cranny of the human body, making love everywhere, everywhere but the bed . . .

– Gi's a fag? she whispered. It must have been two hours later. We lay there naked, sweating, drained and fulfilled on the floor of the hall, the front door open, my keys still in the lock.

– I'm gaspin', she said. – I'd murder another diet Coke.

I struggled to the hallstand and phoned Zico's Pizza.

– Eight cans a' Coke, four regular, four diet, I ordered.

The next morning things weren't the same. It was like there was a stranger in the house. The magic of the night before had disappeared. Mags passed on breakfast, she just gathered up her bits and pieces that were scattered around the house and went.

* * *

– You were haunted she left so easily, Fatfuka said.

– I suppose I was.

– And what about Veronica?

– She never copped on. You've no idea of de guilt I went through. I stood in de shower for over an hour and I could still smell Mags off a' me and around de house for weeks, I could smell her from myself.

– So Veronica never knew at all?

– I'd say she knew dere was something up because I was so freaked out, but she never knew about Mags.

– You're lucky, he said.

– I know, I nearly lost someting dat was very important to me, but d'ya know what de strange ting is?

– What? he asked.

– Tings were never de same between me an' Veronica after dat.

– Not the same?

– Well, I suppose up 'til den, sex was never dat important.

161

But, I was given a taste of it, and how good it could be. It was like de whole Yvette ting just all came rushing back.

– So, eh, did yourself and Veronica break up soon after that or what, Pluto?

– We would have, I mean like de relationship limped on for a while, I really tried to make it work. But I'd seen wat was on de far side of de fence, an' I wanted more.

– So what happened?

– De most amazing ting happened, I said.

* * *

Sometime after that, the phone rang. It was Mags. She said she wanted to meet. I wasn't too sure. Myself and Veronica were just about getting things back together again. Anyway, we arranged to meet at The Farm Gate in the English Market, Tuesday.

By the time Tuesday came, I was up to high-doh. I had a bath, picked out my trendiest shirt, pulled on my new jeans, borrowed Veronica's sunglasses, slicked back my hair and headed into town.

I strolled through the main square in The Market, leaned on the fountain and looked up to the gallery. There was Mags, she smiled and waved. She was stunning. I tipped my sunglasses and winked. Heart doing thirty-six to the second, like Michael Flatley's feet, I made my way to the stairs behind the chicken chokers, trying not to run.

– Hey! How's it going, Mags love? I gave her a big hug.

That was when I noticed the bump. I looked down to her belly.

– Yes! she said.

I didn't know whether to say congratulations or who's the father.

162

– Yes! I'm pregnant.

I stood back.

– Look! I had no intention of contacting you, Pluto. I was going to go through this thing on my own. But things have changed.

– Changed?

– See the landlord don't want babies in the flat, so I'm fairly stuck. Our baby's due in a couple a months, she said.

– Our baby!

I couldn't contest it. It was like my whole world was collapsing around my ears. We talked for a while, I didn't hear one word that was said. All I could think about was how I'd explain this to Veronica. It would destroy her, not to mention small Julie. In the end I just walked away, blown away.

– I'll sort something out, I said. – Leave it to me, I'll sort something out.

\* \* \*

– So, eh, what happened? Fatfuka asked.

– I just walked out ta Fitzgerald Park, sat down on de grass and thought about it.

– . . . and what did you do?

– I pulled de stroke of me life, dat's wat I did.

\* \* \*

I made pasta for dinner that evening. Tomato, garlic and basil sauce, very simple, served with sliced courgette turned in hot olive oil and garlic bread, Veronica's favourite. I even picked up a bottle of wine on the way home. Anyway, over dinner I casually mentioned to Veronica how I had met a neighbour's child, one of the young girls from MacSweeney Street, and how she was pregnant.

– God, that's a tough situation to be in, Veronica said.

– I know, and she was tinking of openin' an Indian Restaurant, an' all.

– And you figure this girl's got nowhere to go?

– Well, de landlord wants her out an' she can't really go home to her mam.

– Does she know who the father is?

– He's with someone else, dat's all I know, I said.

– Bastard! Aren't men right bastards all the same?

– Some men are.

– And what about help during the pregnancy and all that? Veronica asked.

– She really has nobody, sure she's just back from London.

– Ya mean to say she's gotta go through this whole thing on her own?

I knew I was beginning to appeal to the *shag men* side of her brain.

– D'ya know, I was sorta tinking like, maybe she could move into de spare room, you know like, just until de baby's born, like? I cast it out.

Veronica stopped for a few seconds.

– You're dead right! she said, and gave me a big wet kiss on de cheek, – You're just a big softy, and she kissed me again.

– Ah well! Jeezus, you couldn't leave a young pregnant girl out on de side a' de road now, could ya? I said.

I told Veronica the story exactly as Mags had told me, except I didn't mention the fact that I was the father. Within two weeks, Veronica was on side and Mags moved in. She knew the score, Veronica and small Julie were never to know the truth about me being the father of her baby. It was the most perfect solution to a most imperfect situation. I was surprised at how well the whole thing worked, it was like having your cake and eating it. Mags and Veronica really hit it off. Veronica started going to the pre-natal classes with Mags. Julie was thrilled with the thought of having a baby around the house. Before I knew it the box-room was being transformed into a nursery. We were becoming a dawfake family and thriving on the excitement of it all.

Veronica suggested that I put my name on Mags' baby's birth certificate, Mags said she didn't see any reason why I shouldn't. So, it was agreed, that's how I became the official father of my unofficial son Paul. Paul O'Toole, or Paulo as we called him.

But, sometimes the guilt of the lies became too much for my little head, and I just wanted to come clean to Veronica about the whole thing, but most of the time myself and Mags would just laugh at the craziness of the situation.

* * *

I could see that Fatfuka didn't know what to make of all this, there was still a bit of a Christian Brother in him.

– But sure that couldn't go on for ever? he shook his head.

– Well, it lasted long enough! I said.

Fatfuka just looked at me.

– I mean, dere I was sleepin' wit Veronica, Julie's mam, while Mags was wit me own son Paulo in de next room.

– How did Mags feel about you sleeping with Veronica.

– It just never cropped up, I said. – Well, at least it didn't crop up for almost a year.

* * *

Springtime again, it took Mags the best part of the year to get

165

over the whole pregnancy and birth thing. A routine had developed around the house and that in itself was very settling.

Veronica would dash out the door to work at around half eight, meself and Mags would drop Julie down to school. Sometimes we'd bring baby Paulo with us in the stroller, maybe take a bit of a walk down by the Marina, or head into town, and drop into the Harlequin for a coffee or something. Sometimes we'd just go back to the house, roll a joint and play a few games of backgammon. Anyway we were spending a lot of time together. But it was totally straight-up, no hanky-panky or anything like that. I mean myself and Mags were well aware that what happened between us, you know baby Paulo and all that, was only a one-hit wonder . . . well, at least I thought we were.

I remember the morning everything changed. It was pouring, so I brought Julie down to school by myself. When I got back to the house, I was soaked to the skin. Mags had a pot of coffee on the stove.

– There's a video there that Veronica got out yesterday, she said.

– Any good?

– It's a French one and Veronica said it was great!

– Well, she would! I said.

If it was foreign, subtitled, black and white and made on a shoe-string, Veronica would like it.

– What's it called?

– *Toto the Hero!* Mags read it off the cover. – Will we try it?

– Sure we may as well throw it on, I said.

While the trailers were rolling, I lit the fire, Mags organised the coffee and Marietta biscuits and a big fat doobery. We sat on the couch, it was as good a way as any to pass a rainy Monday morning. What a film! is all I can say.

It was just beautiful, made me feel all warm inside. There we were, eleven o'clock in the morning, rain outside pelting the glass, Paulo asleep in his cot, a roaring fire, myself and Mags comfortably numb, curled up on the couch and this wonderful film. Like we were in a bubble, totally unaffected by the outside world, safe with each other.

For over a year we had lived under the same roof but all the time denying each other, but this is how it was meant to be. Mags' body draped across my thighs, her dressing-gown flowing open.

At the part in the film where Toto gets a lift from a truck-driver and he imagines he sees his family in the back of another truck and they're all singing, *Boom! Why Does My Heart Go Boom?* Mags turned her face towards me, looked into my eyes and smiled. I reached down, raised her head to mine and we kissed, a reflex impulse. I kissed her lips, her chin, her neck, her arms, her wrists, her hands, her knees, her nipples . . .

We made love that morning right there, on the rug, in front of the fire – it was beautiful, loving, gentle and overdue.

We lay there on the floor of love, just cradling each other's naked bodies. And then, like Adam and Eve in the garden of Eden the guilt became unbearable.

– Jeezus! What have we done, Pluto?

Mags pushed herself away from me, and rolled off the rug onto the knotty pine floorboards.

– I know! I know!

It dawned on me, that what we had just done could very easily have destroyed the life I had built around me.

– Never again! Mags shrieked, – You must promise me. Never again!

* * *

167

– And was that the end of it? Fatfuka asked.

    – It was, for that day, I said.

    – For that day?

* * *

The house was very strange that evening when Veronica came home. She must have noticed, but nothing was said. Sometimes the house was like that. Mags went to bed early, I went down to The Abbey for a few pints.

    The next morning when I got back from dropping Julie down to school Mags was still in bed. I decided to go up and sort it out with her before things got out of hand and Veronica began to suspect.

*Knock-knock! Knock-knock!*

    – Are ya in dere, Mags? I opened the door.

    – Go away, her voice was low.

    – Alright, I'm sorry, I just wanted to talk about wha happened yesterday . . .

    And I turned to leave.

    – What are ya trying to do to me, Pluto?

    – Huh?

    – What are ya trying to do to me, she sat up in the bed. – You're just playing around with my head, that's what you are! You think you can just roll me around the floor and walk away like nothing happened.

    – Ah, hang on dere now just one minute, Mags . . .

    – You think you can just pick me up and throw me down, like a toy.

    – Dat's not true, Mags.

    I moved close to the bed.

– How do you think it's for me? tears were flowing down her cheeks. – Night after night, to be sittin' downstairs watchin' the telly with yerself and Veronica curled up on the couch? How do ya think it's for me?

– I never really thought about it dat way.

– That's what's wrong with you, Pluto! Ya don't think, do ya? How do ya think it's for me to have the father of me child sleepin' with another woman in the room next to mine . . . How do ya think that feels?

– Jeezus Mags, I dried her eyes with the edge of the sheet. – I never knew you felt dis way.

She wrapped her arms around my neck.

– I love you, Pluto, she whispered. – I always have.

I folded down onto her body. I kissed her neck, her chin, her lips. We didn't make love, we just caressed each other. We lay there, hugging and kissing. It was beautiful. We could hear baby Paulo gurgling in his cot. Mags lifted him into our bed, the most special moment of my life. Me, Mags and our baby, three of us all together. It was the first time in my life that I felt really part of something. We were one, and the feeling was wonderful, and just like that the bridge was mended.

I explained to Mags that the relationship between myself and Veronica was totally non-physical, we hadn't had sex in months, but in our own way we cared for each other. I told her that Veronica was important to me, not only because of the emotional stuff, but also I was living in her house and she had been very good to me. Mags knew that Veronica had been good to the both of us and little Paulo, and without her we wouldn't have a roof over our heads at all.

\* \* \*

169

– Not dat we were using Veronica or anyting, you understand!

I could see by the look on Fatfuka's face that he didn't know if this was a ball-hop or what.

– But I mean, how did Mags feel about that? he asked.

– Well, I suppose she saw de sense in it, I said.

– So that was the end of it?

– Dat was de beginning of it!

\* \* \*

From that morning on, it was rations of passion for breakfast and lashings of it. Veronica would no sooner be out the door to work, I'd drop Julie down to school, straight back home and into bed with Mags. She had a wild streak in her when it came to sex though. A bit of a fantasy queen.

It's a sign of a mature relationship when two lovers begin to talk of the pictures that run through their minds in those fractions of seconds before orgasm. But it didn't happen that way with me and Mags. It was like our third time making love and she tells me straight-up she wants to be called Veronica.

This personality-change bit became part and parcel of our love-making, where each session would begin with Mags being Veronica and me being me. I'd notice that look in her eyes, she'd be standing by the sink or having a cup of tea or something, and all I'd have to do is ask a simple question, put the name Veronica in there somewhere and bingo, we were off. We'd sit there chatting, Mags getting more and more into Veronica's ways; how she held her cigarette, brushing back her hair with her left hand just like Veronica . . . and of course the conversation always came around to herself,

– Isn't it wonderful having Mags living with us? Mags would ask.

170

– Eh yeah, I'd say as convincing as I could, but it's hard to be yourself when the person you're talking to is being somebody else talking about herself.

– So how do you find Mags? Do you fancy her? she'd ask.

. . . and that's the way it was, mad, totally mad.

As the weeks went on she began dressing in Veronica's clothes, even though Veronica was bigger than her. Transexuality I can live with. Tranvestites I can deal with, but transpersonality . . . Mags standing there with Veronica's clothes hanging off her, right down to her underwear; stuffing bra with tissue paper. She insisted I call her Veronica in moments of heightened passion, but most of all she loved sex in Veronica's bed. I'm sure my head doctor would have had a field day with her. Anyway who was I to complain, it was wild and crazy stuff and I was loving every minute of it.

The mood had changed around the house though. It's hard for things to stay the same when you're living a lie, you know those glances across the dinner-table, touches when we'd pass. It was awkward sitting with Veronica on the couch, while the woman I made love to was on her own at the far side of the room throwing eyes at me. Everything changed. Life was exciting but uncomfortable. On top of all that, Mags played it dangerously. You know like – snatching kisses in the hall while Veronica would be in the kitchen, or flashing her breasts at me whenever Veronica's back was turned, totally crazy things like that.

I was spending more and more time down the pub. The front room was getting to be too stressful altogether, and then sometimes I'd get all guilty, thinking I should be at home. I knew I couldn't spend the rest of my life running away from my own front room.

* * *

– Jeezus, that sounds bizarre, Fatfuka said.
  – Bizarre is de only word for it! It was totally bizarre!
  – So what did you do? he asked.
  – Wat could I do!
  – Did you just turn your back on the whole thing, or what?
  – I was inclined to let nature take its course.

\* \* \*

So there I was down the pub one night; just called my second pint. I looked around. It was like *Ground Hog Day*; same faces same places, all these men recycling conversations, camouflaged by cigarette-smoke, hiding from home. I was part of the picture.

  – Shag this! You can cancel that last one, Mick! I shouted, slithered off the stool and left. By time I got home the two women had gone out. They often popped in next door to Norma for a natter and a fag after the kids were put down. I threw on the kettle and went up to the loo.

At the top of the stairs, I stopped. It sounded like one of the kids was still awake, probably Julie. Sometimes Veronica put her into our bed, and moved her later. I could see the glow of the night-light.

  – Are you alright, Julie?
I eased the door open.
  – Julie? I raised my voice and switched on the light.

It was like being hit over the head with a plank. The bed was a mass of movement. I just stood there dazed, my mind unable to make sense of what my eyes were seeing. The two bodies in the bed stopped squirming and sat up in shock.

  – Huh?
It was Veronica and Mags, knotted into each other naked and sweating.

172

– Jeezus! Mags screamed.

– Jeezus yourself! Wat's going on here?

– What are you doing here, Pluto? Mags shrieked and sat up in the bed, she was wearing my shirt.

– I live here! Wat de . . .

I was close to tears. She had my jeans on as well, they were down around her ankles, I could see my boxer shorts tangled at her knees.

– Ah Jesus Christ? she pleaded. – Don't be like that, Pluto!

– Don't be like wat? I needed an explanation. – Don't be like wat? I repeated. – Wat are ya doing wit her? An', an' all my clothes?

– Ah, for shits sake! Veronica snarled.

I had never heard Veronica swear before.

– What's yer problem? You're screwing her, you're screwing me, you're like a fuckin' buck ram in rutting season! Do ya think we're part of your harem or something? Is that it? Women are put on this earth to satisfy men's need to come, is that it?

– Ye're not normal! Lesbians dat's wat ye are!

– For your information I'm not a fuckin' lesbian. It's just so hard to meet men that are any good in bed these days!

I never saw this side of Veronica.

– Please! Please! Mags pleaded. – Please don't be like this.

– How long has dis been going on? An' I don't want no lies!

– I don't see that it's any of your business!

– Please! Please! Mags was in floods.

– Mags! Tell me how long dis has been going on!

– S-s-since the prenatal classes, she whimpered.

– No! No! No! No! No!

– It's none of his business! Veronica shouted.

173

– I've had enough of dis shit!

. . . and I roared and stormed out.

I sat there in the front room, my mind doing somersaults. All this time they've been flahing each other, or riding, or what ever lesbians do to each other. All this time laughing at me behind my back. I had visions of Veronica and Mags flashing their tits at each other every time my head was turned, or snatching romantic embraces whenever I was out of the room,

– Jeezus! Not to mention what went on all the times that I was in the pub.

I was just so hurt.

* * *

– Unbelievable! Fatfuka said.

– You're tellin' me!

– And was that the end of it? he asked.

– More or less, I mean like Mags came down an' begged me to stay for Paulo's sake, she said we could work it out. I tried it for a while, but really, it was a bit too strange for me. – I mean like wen yer going out wit two bisexuals, dere's not much room for fidelity. It's like anything dat moves is fair game, I explained.

– So you just moved out?

– Yep! Dat was just before I moved into de kip I'm in at de moment. It was only a temporary arrangement, I said – Well it was, back den.

– And that's the last you've seen of either of them? he asked.

– More or less, Mags moved back to London soon after dat, sure I told ya about de time I went lookin' for her, and I met Tragic Ted dealing smack?

– Oh yeah!

– I tell ya, Peter Ustinov has a lot to answer for, I said.

Fatfuka laughed. That was the last time I saw Fatfuka laugh. It was the last time I saw Fatfuka.

The nurse came in and said something about something, so I said goodbye. When I called the next day, the nurse said he was with his family, so I didn't stick around. The day after that, she said he was very weak. I caught a glimpse of him through the little glass porthole in the door. He didn't look like himself. I just raised my hand and sort of waved and kept going. I didn't call back any more after that.

# 20

My dad's funeral was a grand affair; lying in state, wrapped in silk, in a casket that would do any mastercraftsman proud. A smug smile on his face, they all came to pay homage, even the Graduate and the crowd from Mulla's were there, most too young to remember my dad, all carpenters; not a cabinetmaker between them. Everybody standing around the coffin admiring it. People pointing out the inlay saying things like – *La', dere's Sonia O'Sullivan* . . . or – *Look a' dat la', de GPO* . . .

. . . amazing people still confused St Mary's, Popes Quay, with the GPO in Dublin.

I was standing there telling them that no nails, screws, or dowels were used, only handcrafted joints handed down from generation to generation. The women of the street *oouing* and *aahing* over Kathleen's silk lining; never the best at talking compliments, she just vanished into the kitchen and rattled a few cups and saucers.

But it was a happy occasion, you know, people telling stories that sort of thing. The priest said that in all his day's burying people he'd never seen coffin like my dad's, this lifted a bit of a laugh . . . and after the prayers, myself, Eddie de Nut and a few others started to shoulder the coffin from the kitchen. It's a strange feeling, carrying your father in a box . . .

– Hoi! Hold it lads! Hold it! Eddie brought the procession

to a halt. – Back 'er up! Here la, try it dis way. No! No! Turn 'er 'round . . .

We tried it sideways. We tried it lengthwise, we even tried it upright, but it wouldn't turn into the hall. One into one just wouldn't go. The crowd that had piled out onto the street waiting, were back in the kitchen again standing around the coffin, advice flying, but nothing moving.

The sound of bottles being cracked open again, big roars of laughter from the back. The Graduate was telling me that the furniture trade had changed since de recession ended.

– It's all quality furniture they want these days, he said – They'll pay a fortune for it. Leave the old dab 'n dowel for the Eastern Europeans that's what I say. But do you know what? he stopped. – You can't get a craftsman these days for love nor money . . .

. . . and he was off talking about something else.

\* \* \*

Eddie the Nut cleared the house and closed the front door behind them. We lifted my dad's board-like body from the coffin and lay him on the floor. And then with the big rusty saw from under the stairs, Eddie cut the coffin in two, right down between *Christ be behind me* and *Christ be before me* . . .

Twenty-eight dowels to put it together again, six top and bottom, eight on each side and he tacked a sheet of plywood to the base. Just in case. We placed my dad back into his masterpiece.

– Com'on! Hurrup! said Eddie. – Wha' he don't know, he won't know.

The front door opened out, and my dad, the master-craftsman, was carried shoulder high, by the tradesmen through the streets of Cork.

The tragedy of death is that it's final. Life and death are similar in that way, you just don't get a second crack at it. I suppose great people live on forever, you know, people like Mohammed, Moses, Jesus and Elvis, but only in the minds of little people. The only way to eternal life is to die, Jesus said that or something like that. Anyway, it took me a long time to understand what he was talking about. There's no future in life, only the present and that's an awful way to live.

I was listening to that science programme on the radio earlier. It'd make you wonder. They were saying that they have telescopes that can see so far out into the Universe, they can see the light from stars that may actually be gone by now. It's like the light from these faraway places takes so long to get here, travelling at some crazy number of light-years, that by the time we get to see it, the star doesn't exist any more. You don't have to be Einstein to figure that one out. We're not dealing with distance any more, were dealing with time. I mean like you can actually stand at one end of a telescope and see something that's happening in the past. I mean, if I know that I am looking at the past, then I must be in the future. And if I can experience the past and the future at the same moment in time? Sure Jesus, that means the present is somewhere way out there between my end of the telescope and that star and not in the here and now, like we're led to believe. Lies, lies and more lies. Amazing! Then again, maybe not so amazing, I suppose really all it means is that the present is the moment when the past meets the future, and sure we all know that.

* * *

*This Could Be Heaven* fades away, he says hello to the night shift up in Apple Computers, he calls the girls down in packaging the Apple Tarts and laughs. They've just been on to Vicky who's manning the phones, he says he doesn't have *Ziggy Stardust* but he'll give it a spin for them tomorrow night. He then makes some joke about getting back to work, because Big Brother is watching you. It's 2:45 AM. He says since the studio clock's gone digital his days are numbered and plays the *Night Moves* jingle, you know the one,

*Night Moves, Light In The Grooves*.

Spare me Please! He plays the Beatles' *Nowhere Man*.

I check the whiskey for a last drop, nothing. I don't feel the half bottle inside me, but like James Brown, I feel good. For the first time in days I want to leave the flat, but where would I be going at three in the morning? I suppose I could always go up and visit Herman. On second thoughts, scrap that.

I miss Fatfuka. Jesus, I really miss him. I think we understood each other. We were from MacSweeneya and that stood for something, not so much the whole MacSweeney Street thing, it could be any street, avenue, dead-end lane or crossroads in the world. You see, life's a journey, we're all just pilgrims, someone said that once. Like snowflakes, no two journeys are the same. But all journeys have a beginning, a starting-point, the place you're coming from. It doesn't matter where you're going, it's where you get on the bus that counts and that's it. Me and Fatfuka were coming from the same place. We knew each other, and that was the painful part. We knew each other too well. I mean like, we all knew that Tragic Ted's real mother deserted him and his father fecked off. That's why he was brought up by the Hickeys. Everybody knew that Pinko's mam lost her mind after Georgie was killed. We'd see her walking the streets bare-foot and deranged, asking people to send Georgie in for

179

his tea; and how often would we see Fatfuka's dad so drunk that he'd piss in a neighbour's doorway, or the nights we'd hear him howling out on the street because Fatfuka's ma would have locked him out. Even my own mother, dragged from the river, misadventure they said, but everybody knew. That was it, everybody knew. That's why it hurt when I met Pinko in the hospital, or when I met Tragic Ted in Piccadilly, or even when I first met Fatfuka in the cancer ward. Nothing had really changed. We were still the same as we were when we played stagecoach on the street, the same downtown dirty faces, it just took a bit of time to drop the mask. It didn't matter what disguise we used, an expensive suit, a crusty, a cancer patient or even a lunatic like myself. It didn't matter. We could see each other for what we were and it hurt, because most of our life's journey was spent getting away from where we were coming from, but you can't hide from yourself. Georgie was the only one who never sold out, then again, he died before he was old enough to know the difference. Death is the one way to stop you growing old . . . just the beginning of a new adventure . . . can't be much worse than the way things are here. Is this what it's all about?

They're all gone, everybody I've ever cared for, gone. I am in this kip of a flat surrounded by hopeless people, thrashing around in the quicksand of dirty bedclothes.

I suppose I still have Pinko, but really I couldn't be arsed, I think it's time to call it a day. I look around me, is this it? Is this what it's all about? I don't think so. Like stop the bus, man! I wanna get off.

I stagger to the dresser, my fingers fumble for the tinfoil with the acid. It falls to the floor.

– Shit!

On my hands and knees, touch-searching the well-worn rug. It smells stale and feels damp. I lie down flat on the floor, my eyes peeled, looking for any blemish on the rough matted surface of the rug. I can hear myself breathing, it's regular and deep. There! There, something shining, the foil. I open it carefully; two micro-dots. I examine their perfection and place the tiny tablets in my mouth. My last night on earth and what a way to go. First class all the way.

I've a few things to do before I leave. I dig deep into my jacket pocket, take out a handful of change and make my way to the door that leads to the bare-bulbed hall. I feel the whiskey as I walk towards the phone, under the stairs.

* * *

– Good morning! *Night Moves*, Vicky speaking!

The coin drops.

– Eh! Is eh dat *Night Moves*? I stumble over the words.

– Good Morning! *Night Moves*, Vicky speaking! she repeats.

– I wants to play a request!

I'm slurring.

– Request?

– Would ya play a requessssst for me friends!

– And your friends names, sir?

– Eh Georgie, Ted and Fatfuka!

– Could you repeat that, sir?

– Georgie and eh, Ted and eh, Fatfuka!

– Pardon me sir, you'll have to speak a little clearer?

– Georgie! Ted! Fatfuka! And you may as well throw in Pinko as well.

– Sorry?

– Just say, for all de lads from MacSweeney Street, alright?

– MacSweeney Street, right! And who will I say it's from?

– Wha?

181

– Your own name, sir?

– Oh me? Eh! Just say Pluto! Alright!

– And where are you phoning from, Pluto?

– I'm under de stairs in de hall, alright!

– Part of town, er, Pluto? she laughs.

– Oh! Eh! Sorry! Eh! Waterloo Terrace.

– Do you have any particular request?

– Play somethin' decent anyway, alright!

– If you tell me what you'd like to hear, sir, I'll see if I can dig it out for you.

– Have ya got *Where Have all de Boot Boys Gone?*

I hear her laughing on the far end of the line. – Pardon?

– *Where Have All de Boot Boys Gone*, you know? By Slaughter and de Dogs, from de North.

– I, eh don't think we have that one, sir.

– Well eh, d'ya have eh, *Waterloo Sunset* by de Kinks?

– I'll see what I can do for you!

– Listen, tell de DJ not to talk over de song, alright, dat drives me mad!

– Eh ha! You sound like you're having a bit of a party up there on Waterloo Terrace tonight, any particular occasion?

– Party? Eh! I suppose it's sorta like a going away.

– OK, very good! Thank you for calling *Night Moves*.

– Thanks very much, alright!

– Stay close to your radio. Good night!

*Click!* The line is dead.

Three whole days since I set foot onto this hall. The place is in shit. I don't know how I spent the last eight years here. It's like a deri, I've lived in better squats.

* * *

A few nights ago I saw Brenda there at the turn of the stairs, that time the landlady gave me all the grief, I was standing here in the hall and I heard a voice,

– Are you alright, Pluto luuv?

I didn't know where it was coming from.

– It's me, Pluto, the voice said.

I turned, there she was on the stairs, her face lit up by the lone bulb; hair wild and yellow-white in the light. And for that glimpse of a second I thought she was the *Bean Sí*, or the spirit of my mother, or death, or something like that. It didn't frighten me though, it was just a fact and I was ready for it.

Me and Brenda talked for a while. I told her about the scene I had with the landlady earlier on, and how, after all of Ireland's long history fighting landlordism, you'd think it'd be a man's right not to be evicted. I told her that we tenants had more dignity under British rule. At least, then we knew who the enemy were. I told her all about Fatfuka's dad and how he'd strut out onto the street when he was drunk and show us the way his father killed the Black and Tans after spending three whole days on the roof of the bank. I end it all by shouting,

– *Remember 1916!*

Brenda stood there listening, then she said that *Remember 1916* was more a plea for help than a war cry.

– Easter 1916 was like a planned mass suicide. You know, a blood sacrifice, a passion play, the resurrection revisited and *Remember 1916* was no more than a pathetic cry for help, from a lost cause, she said.

– Lost cause?

– Ye don't think it was a serious attempt at revolution, do ya?

– Huh?

I didn't know what she was getting at.

– 1916 was like a beaten dog snappin' at the heels of its

183

master, waiting for the flake on the head that'd put manners on it. And as for your friend's dad; there's a lot of Cork people feel hard done by, because 1916 happened in Dublin. D'ya know like, they never had the chance to die with Pearse, Connolly and the lads. But in all fairness, Pluto luuv, I mean like what kind of revolutionaries begin their revolution in a Post Office, a Biscuit Factory, and a public park, and all on a bank holiday Monday?

– Huh?

– All we had was a rising, she said. – See the Irish are dab hands at the aul risings all the same. Been havin' 'em for hundreds of years. But a revolution? Now that's a different kettle a' fish. The French are the boys for the revolutions. See with a revolution ye need only do it the once. Once is enough and all is changed and changed utterly at that . . . but a rebellion, that's only a complaint, and sure the Irish love to be complaining. Did you know that half of Dublin turned up to spit and jeer at the rebels of '16 as they were being carted off to jail. Can you imagine how that must have felt, Pluto luuv? There they were after putting their lives on the line for their country, and their countrymen couldn't give a drunken fart, pardon my French. With nothing but a firing squad, imprisonment, or deportation to look forward to. Jeezus ye'd have to ask yerself? For what? Anyway getting back to the whole *Remember 1916* thing. Seemingly, when it was all over, a prison guard up in Kilmainham found a square of lead flashing under a bunk in one of the cells. It had been ripped from over the window by one of these so-called revolutionaries, and there on that piece of lead punched out with a belt buckle or something was,

*REMEMBER 1916.*

. . . can you imagine? That was no act of defiance. That was no rabble-rousing war cry! Some sixteen or seventeen-year-old country lad, feverishly grinding into that bit a' lead the night before he faced the firing squad. My guess is that he cried that night, cried for help, cried for fear, probably cried for his mother.

REMEMBER ME! That's what he was sayin' . . .

Later that night Brenda came to my room, in a dream. She told me everything would be alright, she rubbed my forehead and lay there next to me, hugging me. My mother was in the bed too, but she just slept through the whole thing.

* * *

2:54

I laugh and make my way back to the door, back to the safety of my flat. The acid is slowly working its way up inside me. I can feel it in my teeth, but it hasn't hit my brain yet. There's a biro over by the sink somewhere and I know I've paper someplace else.

I have the biro but for the life of me I can't think of where the paper is. I search like a mad man. I find the refill pad under the clock radio, 2:55. He's saying something about five minutes till the News at three. I scribble a quick note. I'm beginning to feel the acid, things are getting furry. It sorta looks like the writing is coming from the page. It flows up into the pen and the pen is moving my hand. I've no control over the words as they appear on the paper. Maybe that's what writing is all about, the page communicating with me, rather than the me communicating with the page. I shake my head and try to concentrate on the words. I hear him in the background, saying that Vicky has found *Ziggy Stardust*, and he's gonna give it a spin. It's for the Apple Tarts up in Apple, he says.

I'm writing about life everlasting and life. I can see them all now, the gang on MacSweeneya, my only true friends. It'll probably be Herman who's going to find my body, I scrawl his name on the cover. I'm writing wild. I'm writing about me. It's like my last contact with the living; REMEMBER ME. My mind drifts to the window. I look out onto Waterloo Terrace, lit up by a streetlamp. Everything is blue and white, and one handsome moon smiling down on City Hall. Out over the rooftops, across the schizophrenic river, orangeade Tanora torrents flowing through the city of pain, down into the docks, down among the hoppers and silos. A vanishing beam from the land-locked light-house out beyond Togher on Airport Hill. Each flash like lightning shooting across the silhouetted skyline and stopping at the spire of Holy Trinity. It splinters into colours. Thread-like greens and reds and yellows run along the outlines of darkened buildings. An orange glow; looks like it's coming from somewhere down on the Lower Road. It's red, it's green. A caterpillar glides into Kent station; two more move in the shunting-yard. I pull myself away from the window. The flat is in darkness but it has never looked so interesting. There's a softness about the place. It's like the intro to *Ziggy Stardust* is going on and on forever. I'm a sponge. I move to the sink. As I step into the bathroom it occurs to me that this is the last doorway I'll ever walk through. I smile. There's something comforting in that. Doorways are a bollox. People think they're for getting into a place, but in fact doors are actually put there to keep people out. If they wanted people to come in, why put a door there in the first place, when a gap would do just fine? The design on the crumpled quilt cover is moving, blue streaming through the window onto the rug, its colours are purring, everything bluish.

A pinpoint of red on the dresser takes my notice. Its

intensity grows. The Stratford End on my United mug. I can hear them singing, faintly and it glows, scarves swaying. I leave the bathroom and flow towards the dresser. I sit on the end of the bed. I look at the intense red of the mug. This mug came from the Man United Supporters Club shop at Old Trafford one of the times I was over with the lads, must be almost twenty years ago. In all that time I've never really looked at it. It's the most amazing mug in the world. I always thought it was just a red mug with a picture of the Stratford End, but it's more, much more than that. For the first time I realise that these are real people, holding their scarves above their heads, singing *Storm In A Teacup*, on the side of my mug. They're so happy, it's beautiful, a sea of red and white scarves. A pitter-patter of rain outside on Waterloo . . .

> *Pitter-patter, Pitter-patter, Pitter-patter, Pitter-patter,*
> *One drop of rain on your window pane*
> *Doesn't mean to say there's a Hurricane comin'*
> *Rain may pour for an hour or more,*
> *But it doesn't matter . . .*

I sing along but I can't remember all the words. I never knew I could actually pick out faces in the crowd. Big smiling faces, I think we're losing 2-1 to City, but we're top of the league with four points clear and a game in hand, so it doesn't matter . . .

> *You know it doesn't matter,*
> *It's a stoooorrrm in a teacup.*
> *Brewing up trouble.*
> *But it doesn't really matter any more*
> *Pitter-patter, pitter-patter, pitter-patter . . .*

I can see them now, rosy-faced in defeat.

– Huh! There! What's that?

I think I catch a glimpse of something as a scarf moves to the right.

– There! There again! Behind that scarf!

The scarf sways back.

– There! There! It's Pinko! What no? Can't be, Pinko on my mug? Never! There again! No! Yes! . . . and Tragic Ted, Georgie! There's Fatfuka behind him on the terraces and me, I'm there meself. We're all there singing *Storm In A Teacup*, all together, in the Stratford End, on the side of my mug. I just sit staring,

 . . . meself, Fatfuka, Tragic Ted, Georgie and Pinko on the side of the mug, scarves above our heads, singing in the red sea, we're losing but we don't care.

It's like ink on a blotting-paper, from the edges of my mug slowly the red turns to blue, all around us, blue scarves. We're there slap-bang, me and the lads from MacSweeneya having too much fun to notice, in the middle of about thirteen thousand of them, City fans.

> *Hello! Hello!*
> *City Aggro! City Aggro!*
> *Hello!*

Over and over, a ripple of fear connects with the base of my skull.

The mug falls from my hands, tumbling in slow motion, rotating, flashing red and blue and falling for ages. It looks like it will never reach the floor and it's still falling.

I find myself in the bathroom. I look in the mirror. No recognition. Only my eyes are familiar, my face like rubber, moving, changing, distorting. I see Grandda Buckley looking out at me from my reflection.

– Are ye still playin' Stagecoach down MacSweeney Street? he smiles.

– Stagecoach? I whisper.

– I heard about Fatfuka.

– Fatfuka?

– And Ted, and Georgie, shu' that's life! he says. – Their sufferin's over now!

I look down to the sink, the blade between my fingers. I turn on the hot tap, it's cold. My right hand, under running water; pressing the blade against my wrist. My hands are at arm's length from me. I'm only observing the operation. I slice one deep cut straight across; feel nothing, red gushes out in a cloud into the clear water. I take the blade in my right hand and look into the mirror. My smile becomes the most beautiful face I've ever seen. It's my mother.

– Mam, is dat you?

– Of course it is, Paul. I'm always here, right beside ya, she smiles.

I could never remember hearing my mother's voice, it sounds so sweet.

– Maaam? is all I can manage, but she know's what I want to ask.

– No, of course I didn't drown myself. I just went down the steps by the river to save a poor helpless swan that was in difficulty in the water and I slipped. I wouldn't have gone away from my lovely little man. Never! she smiles. – Come on, Paul love, come on! I'm waiting for you. I'm going to give you the biggest hug you've ever had, just to make up for all the hugs you've missed, my little man.

I look down . . .

The sink overflowing, two wrists pumping.

I glide backwards from the bathroom, fall to the bed.

The life drains from my body. I turn my head.

3:05 in red.

It's blue out there on Waterloo.

– Thirty-three today, Happy Birthday to me, I say.

189

# 21

At four minutes past three he's saying thanks to the newscaster,

*And thank you too, Vicky,*
*For digging this one out*
*Ah, yes indeed,*
*This one goes out to all the lads from MacSweeney Street.*
*That's eh, Pinko, I think it is, Ted, Georgie and the Lads*
*And ye're havin' one hell of a going-away party.*
*Up there on Waterloo Terrace.*
*And this one comes from Pluto.*
*Doesn't say who's going away.*
*Hmmm! Must sack that girl! Hmmm!*
*Anyway, for all of you up there on Waterloo Terrace. This*
one's foooor youuuuah . . . . . .

*. . . Dwang diddy dwang diddy dwang . . .*

\* \* \*

3:05.

*– And it's no, nay, never! the Monk thumps the table.*
*No, nay, never no more,*
*Will I play the wild Rover,*

> *No, never no more.*
> *I went into an alehouse,*
> *I used to fre . . .*

– Shh! Shh! Herman rises to his feet.

– Uh? Wha' is it, mate?

– Did you hear zis? Herman points to the radio.

– Wha'?

– They just announce ein request for Pluto.

– Pluto, mate?

– Ja! He say there is ein party down in Pluto's flat.

– Never! Well wha' are we waiting for?

The Monk grabs the bottle of schnapps from the table and heads for the door.

– Der ist no party!

– But I thought you said . . .

– Der ist no party, but it means that Pluto has come out onto der hall to make ein phone call.

– Big deal, mate.

– It ist ein big deal. Pluto came out for some reason greater than ein request on ein stupid radio programme.

– How do ya mean?

– It ist either good or bad, but certainly not indifferent.

– I don't think it's none of our business, mate.

– I say ve make it our business.

Herman lowers his schnapps.

\* \* \*

3:05.

My body is getting cold, my eyes close.

– Go to sleep, my little man, I hear my mother whisper, – Let me take all your pain away.

I feel her fingers caress my hair.

191

– When you wake, my love, all your pain will be gone, I hear her say.

In the distance, the radio,
*Yes, indeed . . .*
*So, for all the gang up on Waterloo Terrace,*
*Here's The Kinks . . .*
I smile, I drift, I slip from my bed and am drawn to the bathroom one more time.

* * *

3:05.
Herman is pacing the floor.
– Jaysus Christ, mate! Will ya sit down! – Look, just 'cause a bloke puts a request on the radio, it's not the end of the world! That's what I says! the Monk reaches for the Schnapps.
Herman stops, looks the Monk into the eyes, then continues walking.
– If you feel that way about it mate, why the heck don't ya go down there an' see if he's alright?
– I fear it is too late, Herman whispers.
*Knock-knock! Knock-knock!* A rap at the door.
– See there ya are now, Herman mate, that's probably Pluto at the flamin' door inviting us down to the flamin' party!
Herman opens the door, it's Brenda the Brasser, she's looking a bit wrecked, draped in a nightdress, a fag dangling from the side of her mouth.
– Ah Brenda, is everythink alright? Herman asks.
– I'm worried for Pluto, luuv! There was a request for him on the radio. I think maybe there's a problem.

192

She turns her head sideways, smoke wafts from her mouth.

– This is vot I haff being saying all night!

– What do you say we call down and see how he is? Brenda says.

– I thinks th' two of ye are daft! the Monk screams from behind the door.

– Are you in there too, Jimmy? Brenda asks.

– I think ye're daft!

– Good! said Brenda. – We might need an extra strong pair of hands!

– Come on then! says Herman.

– Will you come too, Jimmy luuv?

– I will! I will! But I still thinks ye're daft.

The trinity troop off down the stairs.

\* \* \*

3:07

*Knock-knock! Knock-knock!*

– I hope we're not too late, Brenda says.

The Monk tries the handle of the door.

– It's looks to me like he's gone out, mate!

– At three o' clock in der morning?

– Maybe he's gone for chips or something! says the Monk.

– All I know is that he's not answering his door!

– Und all I know ist, there ist a darkness in the air tonight!

– Maybe you should go out to the front door and try the bell, Herman luuv!

– Is good idea, Brenda.

Herman heads for the door.

– And if that don't work try tapping on the window, luuv.

– And if that don't work, try sliding down th' fuckin'

chimney, mate, jus' like Santa Claus! Jimmy the Monk lets a big laugh out of him.

– What did ya say, Jimmy?

– Nothin' girl! Nothin'! says the Monk.

* * *

I can hear the misfits out in the hall. They torment my spirit. I have no need for them on my journey.

I see a bright light, it's my mother, two white swans at her feet protecting her. She's more beautiful than the photo we had over the fire at home. She guides me in the direction we must travel, her voice clear and sweet. I see faint familiar outlines. I'm drawn towards them. I see Fatfuka, Tragic Ted, Georgie, Grandda Buckley, they're smiling. I see my beautiful Yvette in the distance. I can hear The Kinks, it's the haunting sound of guitar going down and down, on *Waterloo Sunset*. What a way to go? There can come a time when the need to die is stronger than the will to live; I've made the right decision. *Waterloo Sunset* fades away. I breathe my last and drift to peaceful timelessness.

# 22

Did you ever wake up and think you're still asleep?

Did you ever wake up and realise you're still asleep?

Did you ever wake up with *Waterloo Sunset* running around your head? Well, that's how it is . . .

You know how it goes? Guitar intro, *Dwang diddy dwang!* going down. Well, that's how it is when you're Pig's-Head. Dead!

\* \* \*

3:08

– Look I'm tellin' ya, Pluto's alright, the Monk says.

– Would you ever shut up, Jimmy! Brenda shouts, moving her ear closer to the door.

– Do you hear anythink, Brenda?

– I can hear his radio, she says, and she hums along with *Waterloo Sunset.*

– Honestly, I've come across this sorta stuff before, in me days Over.

– What kind a stuff? Brenda barks.

– All I'm saying, mate, is, that Pluto's either konked out or gone out, but he's not dead. The very worst tha' it could be is an attempted suicide, you know like a cry for help like the last time, Jaysus sake 'tis gone three in the mornin'.

– Well, shag off to bed then, there's nobody tellin' ya, ya has to stay!

– Look all I'm sayin' is . . .

– Herman would you ever go out and try the door bell again? she say's. – There's a good lad, and she glares at the Monk.

– Sorry, says the Monk.

* * *

I've come through the tunnel of darkness and everything's at peace, I can still hear the misfits at my door but my spirit is free and the light is beginning to shine through.

*Ding! Dong!*

There it goes again. People were forever ringing the wrong bell, my bell!

*Ding! Dong!*

Jeezus! Will someone answer the bloody door!

I bury my head down between the gritty sheet and grubby cover, deep into the darkness, a winter darkness. Somebody famous once said that the light at the end of a tunnel was probably the light from an oncoming train, that's how I feel. But, I'm beginning to sense a new beginning or is it the beginning of a new end. It's the story of my life, sunshine followed by darkness. Darkness is strange, it's just the lack of light. Darkness doesn't do, it just is. At least the sun has to shine, but darkness sits there doing nothing, just being dark all the time.

The blankets cushion me from the ringing, the laughing, the footsteps on the ceiling, the insanity outside my door in the half-lit hallway and the madness outside the front door, the door out onto Waterloo Terrace, the terrace that looks out across the divided estuary of the city. It's dark down here, my knees curled up to my chin. It's musty, damp and airless, I can't breathe but it is safe, like a caterpillar tucked up in my

196

cocoon waiting for that time when all the responsibility for my safety becomes mine.

*Ding! Dong!*

– *Answertheshaggindoorwillyaanswertheshaggindoor!* I am safe.

* * *

3:08

The Monk shifts from foot to foot in the hallway outside No. 1.

– Vell? Herman calls from the hall door, – Any sign of him?

– Not a peep! Brenda says.

– In all fairness, mate, I'd say he's gone out.

– Sure Jeezus, if he went out I'd have heard the front door slammin'! she says

– So, eh, what do ve do?

– I'd say try the door bell again, and if that don't work, try tappin' on his window. Maybe I'll go up and knock on the floor of my flat, she says.

Herman heads back out to the hall door and disappears into the darkness.

– You stay here, Jimmy, and see if there's any stir out a' Pluto.

– Right! says the Monk.

* * *

I'm dead but the misfits have my spirit tormented.

*Tap! Tap! Tap! Tap!*

I can't believe this! Now they're at my window. I push my head up from under the smelly covers, fish-heads and socks.

*Ding-dong!*

197

– Wrong bell! I roar. – Ring another bell! and then, silence. – Peace at last!

I pull the blanket around my ears, right hand reaching out for tobacco, a twenty pack of Major sitting there where my pouch used to be. I pull a fag from the box and fumble it from packet to mouth and then,

*Click!* of my Zippo.

– Zippo? Never knew I had a Zippo. Major and a Zippo? Lookin' good.

I draw in deep as the cleansing life-giving smoke stretches my lungs. My right hand replaces the lighter on the upturned orange box. I lay back, sucking Major. I flick the ash into my coffee mug.

*Ding-dong!*

*Thud! Thud!*

– Pluto, the door!

*Tap! Tap! Tap! Tap!*

– Ah, Jeezus, this is ridiculous!

So, I throw on my overcoat and slip into my untied boots. I place my hand on the handle of the door that leads to the bulbless hall, the hall to the front door, the door of the bells.

*Knock-knock! Knock-knock!*

– Is there no peace in this world? I jerk open the door. – What!

All is not as it seems. I know that as sure as I'm standing here, I'm not standing here. I know that my lifeless blood-drained body is thrown in a heap on the floor of my bathroom. I know that I've just heard the three o'clock news on the radio and yet, judging by the brightness coming through the fan-light over the door it's morning-time, you know half-seven or eight o'clock. Everything is not right here, I am dead, I am dead! I know that I'm on a journey, a journey to death or life. I'm at Limbo Junction, next stop Heaven or Hell, who knows.

Herman standing there, no sign of Brenda or the Monk. They must be out here somewhere, with all their banging on the ceiling, hammering at the door and ringing of bells. I can't even die in peace.

– What, Herman? What do you want?

– Your door bell, ja? he points at the door.

– I know it's my bell, but you're de one who's ringin' de shaggin thing.

– Huh? Herman looks confused.

– Sure I've been listening to de tree of ye out here makin' a racket.

– Three of us? Herman looks around him, – I'm on my own.

The bell to my flat rings again. Herman points at the door.

– Look, why don't you open de door, you're nearest it, I look at Herman.

– Is your bell, ja?

– Just 'cos it's my door bell, don't mean 'tis my visitor.

There is something wrong here, this is not right. I am dead, my blood-drained body is wrapped around the toilet bowl, yet I am here in the hall talking to Herman. All is not right here and I know it.

* * *

3:09

– He's not in there! says the Monk.

– Or worse. Herman whispers under his breath.

– At least I don't smell any gas, says Brenda.

– Maybe I should kick down der door, says Herman.

– Well, if ye kick down th' door, mate, yer on yer own! The landlady'll have us all out on th' side of th' street.

– To hell with Der Witch.

– Jimmy have a point, Herman luuv.

I stand here in my boots and overcoat getting the last blast of nicotine into my lungs. I'm still confused as to how I'm here in the hall with Herman, because I know my lifeless body is crumpled in a heap in my flat. I stub out my fag. Herman just stares at me, vibing me to go and open the hall door. I hear a door closing upstairs, it sounds like Brenda's.

*Ding-dong!*

– Pluto! Answer yer bell! Tis only eight o'clock in de mornin'.

It's Brenda the Brasser.

– It's O.K. Brenda, I'm in de shaggin' hall.

– Will ya get it, Pluto?

– I'm gettin' it, I'm gettin' it, don't get yer knickers in a twist!

I look up, she's like something out of a mushroom trip. Standing at the turn of the stairs in her pink fluffy slip and flip-flops, pink satin/viscose-mix dressing-gown, her peroxide beehive down around her ears and like me, she strains to get that nicotine hit from a well-burned butt.

– Ah, how are you this mornink, Brenda? Herman smiles.

– I'd be an awful lot better, Herman luuv, if he'd answer his shaggin' door bell! She points at me.

*Ding-dong! Ding-dong!*

– I comink! I comink!

Herman shuffles towards the front door.

My eyes follow him. Brenda, head bent to her waist and turned sideways trying to catch a glimpse of the caller from her obstructed view at the turn of the stairs. I sway from heel to toe, nothing but an overcoat and old pair of boots to cover my nakedness. The front door opens, a dazzling brightness outlining Herman.

– Eh, is me dad there? a small voice asks.

– Your father? Who ist your father?

It sounds like small Julie, Veronica's Julie, and she's still calling me dad.

– Is dat you, Julie? I move to get past Herman.

– Oh Dad! I'm glad. I wasn't sure if this was the right house?

I looked down. There stands Julie. She's the head off Veronica.

– Jesus, Julie girl! I button my overcoat. – Dere's nothin' wrong, Julie love, is dere?

– No! No! Nothing like that, she says. – It's just that me mam asked me to come up.

– Eh, come in, Julie love.

Brenda the Brasser vanishes back up the stairs in a flash of pink, Herman is floating around my door saddle.

– Do ya mind, Herman, I'd like a word wit me daughter.

– Oh, by all means! By all means!

But there is still no move out of him. So, I close the door in his face.

* * *

3:10.

– Tha's De Kinks, says the burly fella, pointing to the radio on the dashboard. – Do ya know one a' dem is married to a girl from Cork?

The fella with the ears keeps his eyes on the road.

– *Delta, Tango, Bravo, Come in, Over!*

*Delta, Tango, Bravo, Come in, Over!*

– Hoi, turn off tha' transistor there, will ye!

The burly fella reaches for the hand-set. The fella with the ears switches off The Kinks.

– Delta, Tango, Bravo, To base. Over! The burly fella speaks.

– *There have been reports of a vehicle on fire up in the Glen*

*Park, reports of youths and joyriding activity in the area, suspected act of vandalism and not an auto accident, Over!*

– On our way. Over!

– *Base Over and Out!*

The burly fella replaces the hand-set. The fella with the ears revs up the engine,

– Hoi, what's yer hurry!

– A burning vehicle! the fella with the ears points to the radio.

– An' yer gonna charge up dere like de bloomin' Light Brigade and save that blazin' car.

– Well, I thought . . .

– You thought! You thought! Look! Listen! And learn! Dere's very little you or I can do to save dat car. De most dat'll happen if we drive in there now is dat we'll get our own windscreen smashed, by one a dem gurriers.

– But the radio?

– La, de best we can do is to turn on de siren and drive up around de Glen, let 'em know we're comin' like, give dat gang of gutties time to disperse, so dat de fire brigade can get in to do deir job in peace and we can identify de vehicle, says the burly fella. – Sometimes it's all about damage limitation, dis isn't a game a' cops and robbers, ya know! he explains.

He turns on the radio and catches the end of The Kinks.

\* \* \*

So, here I am in my overcoat and boots standing in the middle of my kip of a flat. I know this can't be happening. Julie stands there, she still calls me dad.

– I'm not really yer dad, Julie, I mean like, I'll always be dere for ya an' all dat, but I'm not really yer dad . . .

Julie is jaw-hung and wide-eyed. There's a stench of death and decay about the place. It's like a bomb has hit it.

– Jeezus Julie girl, good to see ya. How's yer mam and

202

everybody, eh? Here la, excuse me manners, eh, take a seat, take a seat.

And, like *Norwegian Wood*, she looks around, no seat to be found. So I lift the coffee mug, ashtray and clock radio from the orange box.

– Dere la, I point.

– Thanks, dad.

She was never one for small chat.

– Eh, Dad, it's Paulo's First Holy Communion today and Mags asked me to come up and remind ya.

I haven't heard from Mags and Paulo since I walked out. I didn't even realise that he was old enough to be taking his Holy Communion. This is all a bit of a blast. Julie stands up to leave.

– I suppose I should be getting back and giving me Mam a hand, she says,

– Well, if ya gotta go, ya gotta go! I make it easy for her.

– So, will we see ya later? she wants confirmation on the Communion.

– Oh, chalk it down, Julie girl, but eh, where exactly is the Communion?

– The North Cathedral! she boomerangs it back. It's as if I'm supposed to know these things.

– And, eh, time?

– Twelve o'clock.

– Eh, Julie girl?

– Yes, Dad?

– Eh, what date is it today?

She looks at me as if I'm some class of a langer.

– It's de 2nd of April, Good Friday mornin!

– Holy Communion of a Good Friday? I says. – Are ya sure yer right dere?

She looks through me and turns to walk away. I follow her to the hall door. I mention the dole and the fact that I'd meet her up at the Communion, after I've signed on.

– Look! she stands there brazen-faced. – Be there early, be there late, or don't be there at all! Do you think I give a shit? I'm only the messenger.

Not a girl to mince words, our Julie.

– Ah, no, no, I'll be there, I guarantee ya!

But I don't think my guarantees or reassurances count for much, not with Julie anyway.

– Eh, see ya later so, Julie!

– Yeah! See ya, Dad!

She raises her hand in a dismissive wave. I watch her saunter out of Waterloo Terrace and down into the filth of the city, a woman before her time.

* * *

3:17

Herman reenters the hall.

– Any sign of Pluto? he asks the Monk.

– Not a peep, mate!

– Vere's Brenda? Herman asks.

– If she'd any sense she'd be gone back to bed! Do ye know what time of the morning it is, mate?

Brenda appears at the turn of the stairs.

– I've tried knocking on the floor, she says.

– Look, I say we should call it a night, says the Monk.

– Well, I think Pluto's in trouble, I can hear his radio on in there.

– Vell, maybe I can climb onto his window-ledge and see if he's in zere?

– Good idea, Herman luuv! says Brenda.

– I thinks de lot a' ye're off ye're flamin' chucks, it's almost half past three in the mornin', the Monk snorts.

– Come on, says Herman, – I might need ein hand.

# 23

I don't bother with a shower, you know the way that sometimes you couldn't be bothered with a shower. I don't have a shave either. I know I'm dead but am I alive? Anyway, I don't have that much time. It's half eight and I have to get over to Crosses Green and sign on and then make my way back up to the North Cathedral by twelve for Paulo's Communion. One quick look around the room, everything's off.

– I'll sort out dis mess wen I get back, I promise myself again and I stop. – No, de new me begins here!

I run around the room, scent-checking socks, underpants and armpits. Into a black plastic rubbish bag with everything for the launderette. This way, I can kill a few birds with the one stone.

I map out the morning. Drop my laundry into the launderette on Devonshire Street for around half nine. Cut across by the Opera House, up French Church Street, through the English Market, maybe even have a cup of coffee in Iago's. Give myself until quarter past ten. Then down Tobin Street past Triskel, over to Hanover Street and sign on. I should be out by quarter to eleven. Then it would be just a simple matter of cutting across Washington Street, up the Marsh, back into the North Main Street, up the North Main Street, across the North Gate bridge, up Shandon Street, all the way to the North Cathedral, in plenty of time for the Communion. And, when all that fuss is over, I'd have the rest of the day to myself. Seems like a fairly full morning for an idle man. I throw my black plastic bag over my shoulder, take one more look around the room.

– I'll sort dis place out wen I get back! I promise myself again.

\* \* \*

3:18:02

– I know, Alison explains, – But being a Landlady doesn't sit too easily on my shoulders, probably got to do with being Irish or something.

– I know what you're saying, love, he says, – But really this Pluto fella should have been shown the door ages ago.

– I suppose you're right, she says.

– Course I'm right, this is the same fella that was using the window as a door until the police put a stop to it, the same guy who was convinced that the green carpet in the bathroom was grass and wasn't satisfied until you gave him the bottle of weed-killer, the same fella who burnt holes along his forehead, thinking that there was bushes growing out of his eyebrows, not to mention the time he nearly blew up the house trying to gas himself to death and would have succeeded only for the fact that the money ran out in his meter and to top it all that German lou-la from upstairs breaks down the door and smashes out the windows, trying to clear the gas, thinkin' he's Superman or something. Jeezus, I don't know how you put up with them at all!

The facts bring a smile to Alison's face.

– Look, why don't you take a sleeping pill and a stiff G'n'T, he advises, – Let tomorrow look after itself.

– You're dead right, will you have something yourself, darling? she walks towards the liquor cabinet.

– No thanks, Alison love, I'd only get indigestion.

# 24

The very thought of setting foot out onto Waterloo Terrace has me petrified. But it's got to be done. This is a new day. Paulo's making his First Holy Communion and I'm going to be there.

Out into the fanlight-lit hallway. In the darkness stands Herman.

– Ah, Pluto! Your daughter, yes? he asks.

– Actually, Herman, she's not really me daughter, she's me ex-girlfriend's daughter. I only reared her for a year or two.

Herman looks confused but I don't have the time or the energy to explain.

– More rubbish, Pluto? Herman points at my bag of laundry.

– Laundry!

– You are going downtown, yes?

I explain my plan of laundry, coffee, dole and Holy Communion.

– Wait just one moment, I go with you, I get mein laundry, yes?

– Jeezus! Dis is all I need.

Slowly I step out onto Waterloo Terrace, drop my laundry bag to my ankles. I slump there on the wall waiting for Herman,

– Come on, Herman boi, will ya, I'm mad late!

Spring has sprung and the warm life-giving sun massages the back of my hands. My eyes drift across the calm of the city beyond the two rivers to the silos on the quays. Right over to the grassy rolling hills on the southside out beyond Togher and Ballyphehane, all the way to the Airport.

– *Hermaaaannnn!* I stamp my feet.

I looked down onto the geometry of Kent Station.

– Kent Station, Kent Station, Kent Station, Kent! Kent! Kent!

I mouth it out, always interested in sounds and rhythm. I remember once, on the Cork to Dublin train, the sound of the *clickety-clack* of the tracks and the ticket collector calling;

– *Port-Laois-eh, Port-Laois-eh, Port-Laois-eh,*

sounded to my mind just like Pete Seeger singing *The Lion Sleeps Tonight*, you know the part that goes,

*A-wim-away, a-wim-away, a-wim-away.*

It was just like that. I remember thinking at the time that it must have been something like the way Strauss composed *Tales From The Vienna Woods*. I heard it on the radio somewhere that it came to him as he rode through the woods on the outskirts of Vienna in an open-top, horse-drawn carriage. It was like the orchestration of nature's sounds. The only difference was that the song in my head had already been composed by somebody else. Still though, it's interesting.

– *Herrrman, will ya come on, boi, will'a! I haven't all day!*

The second-floor window shoots open.

– Pluto, will you ever shut up! Dere's people round here trying to sleep!

Brenda is still awake.

– Eh, sorry Brenda, sorry, just waiting for Herman, eh, go back to sleep, eh, sorry.

Her window slams shut. Again, I stamp my feet.

Ah yes, Kent Station down below me. The curved parallel lines of rails and platform. Strange I always assumed the principle of the railway was straight lines, you know, maximum efficiency, maximum acceleration, shortest distance between two points, you know, it sort of made sense. It would make you wonder why they built the platform at Kent Station like a banana. Must be some good reason.

– Come on, Herman!

– I comink! I comink!

Herman thunders down the stairs.

– Keep it down, Herman boi, will'a, will'a! You'll wake Brenda.

– I sorry, I sorry!

He stands there, two black plastic laundry bags, one for whites, one for colours, like only a German would.

– Come on, will'a! I throw my eyes towards the city and we stroll down out of Waterloo Terrace, the early morning sun cutting our long sharp shadows westward.

* * *

3:19

Herman is balancing on the window sill, the Monk is propping him up by the arse.

– Can ya see anything, luuv? Brenda whispers.

– I am not sure, Herman answers, – I think I can see him on der bed.

– Look, mate, will yez make up yer flamin' mind, is he in there or isn't he?

– I am not sure. It ist very dark in there, only der light from der clock radio.

– Ah fer Christ's sakes! Is he in there or isn't he, mate?

209

– I think I see somethink on der bed!

– Knock on the window, Herman luuv!

– What if I break ein small pane of glass, I could lift the latch and go in and see! Herman suggests.

– Jaysus, this is like the flamin Marx brothers! And it's flamin' cold to top it all!

– Look, I'll go in again and give a rap on the door, says Brenda.

* * *

It's about half nine, we're standing outside the launderette. I'm late and Herman's driving me around the twist. He's standing there fumbling from pocket to pocket, jacket to trousers. I know what's coming next.

– You got ein cigarette, Pluto?

Herman has a ritual before he bums a fag.

– No, eh, I try not to smoke till teatime.

– But you smoked one this mornink.

– And why wouldn't I? I was totally stressed out. Wat wit bells ringin', tappin' on de window, bangin' on de ceiling and knockin' on de door. Wat a way to face de day. Did ya ever wake up wit *Waterloo Sunset* on yer mind?

I stretch out my right arm and strum the fingers of my left hand across the fretboard of my imaginary sunburst red Gibson. I make a few tuning sounds.

> *Dwang diddy dwang!*
> *Diddy dwang!*
> *Diddy dwang!*
> *Diddy dwang!*
> *Diddy dwang!*
> *Bab ba ba ba ba*
> *Ba ba ba ba ba ba*

*Ba ba ba ba ba*
*Ba ba ba ba . . .*

– Ya know how it goes?

Herman drops his laundry bags to the footpath and we stand there. Duelling banjos on imaginary guitars. We bang out an instrumental version of *Waterloo Sunset* at least once. It passes the time, but time is one thing I don't have this morning.

– Eh, wat time do dis launderette open?

I lay down my guitar.

– Very soon, Pluto, Herman shrugs his shoulders.

– Very soon? It's half nine an de shagger's probably still in bed!

– It vill not be long, now.

– Well, I tell ya he won't stay in buisness wit dis sorta carry on . . .

– So you have no rollies, Pluto? Herman changes the subject.

– I thought I told you already!

– Is OK, is OK, I go get some. Do you want to go half on a pack? Herman never gives up.

– No!

And I give him a pound coin. He turns and heads up the street towards the shop.

– You keep an eye on mein laundry, yes?

I just grunt and wave and sit down on the laundry bags, comfortable but stressed. I sit there on the footpath, trying not to think of the Holy Communion, trying not to think of the time as it flies by. So I sit there, thinking.

* * *

3:19

The fire brigade are wrapping up. The burly fella is on the walkie-talkie to the base,

– I suppose dere's nothing for it now, only to inform de owner of de vehicle, and ask dem to remove de debris. Over.

– *Very well, Base Over and Out!*

He struts back towards the squad car, puts his head in the passenger side window and says,

– Aren't dey a right bunch a' bastards all de same? When I think of all de pain and expense to de poor creature who owns dis wreck.

– So, what next? asks the fella with the ears.

– We'll just wait for de fire lads to finish up an' den, how about droppin' down to Macari's for a bag a' chips or somethin'?

– Sounds like an idea.

\* \* \*

– Silk Cut purple? Is OK, yes?

Herman's back from the shop with the fags. He hunches down to the kerbside and draws in deep on his factory fag.

– Here, gis one a' dem!

– But you say you don't smoke zis early in ze day?

– Yeah, but I want one now, alright!

– I never understand you Irish, full of contradictions. Zis will be your second cigarette that I witness. Here you are.

He draws a cigarette from the box, – All contradictions, you Irish. I remember . . . he takes a drag, – ven I first come to zis country . . .

The saga unfolds. It's as interesting as bird-droppings on a wall. I'm listening, but I'm not interested, I just can't be arsed changing the subject. All I want is to ditch my laundry into the launderette, get over to the dole and back up to the

North Cathedral for Paulo's First Holy Communion. So, I sit here listening.

Herman can't tell a story to save his life but it doesn't stop him trying. So, he rambles on, from near tears to loud guffaws of laughter with his own storytelling. He relishes the fact that all the crucial changes in his life were brought about by pure chance. Here he is, sitting on the side of the footpath, bumming fags, waiting for a launderette to open. It isn't as if he had reached the heights of mankind with all these uncanny twists of fate. If anything, Herman is on the scrap-heap, and he doesn't even know it. Sick of the rubbish, I stand up.

– Look Herman, I don't tink dis launderette's gonna open today, I'd say yer man was on the batter last night or somethin'.

– It vill open, it vill open. He may be a bit late, he is often late, but it vill open!

I'm sick of waiting and worried about being late for Paulo's Communion and I must lose Herman. He's driving me around the bend.

– Listen Herman, I'm gonna head over towards the dole. I really don't have the time to be hanging around here, well not today anyway.

– OK, we go! Herman moves to get up.

– Me arse you will! What's this *we* business? Sure, you're not signing on. You're on a *Fás* Scheme, Herman boi!

– I haff things to do in town.

What can I say? So, our little parade of black plastic bags strikes off, down Devonshire Street, up Pine street, towards town.

We're cutting across Christy Ring Bridge, I'm up to my eyeballs with Herman. The Red City of Gurranebraher to my right, turned brown by years of weathering. Gurranebraher;

the Brother's short cut, and they too have been tarnished by time. They all look down on Tanora town from their semi-d, where once stood the monastery. Looking down on second city, mind the dog-shit, turd-town.

– Mein Gott! Herman drops his laundry bags.

– What?

– Zere!

– Where?

– Zere . . . zere in der river! his eyes are popping out of his head.

– Wat de . . .

It's one of the most tragic sights I have ever seen. There, way out in the middle of the river, a pigeon. He's floating backwards downstream, on a turned tide, out to sea. He's bobbing up and down, looking as happy as Larry. God only knows how long his unwebbed claws battled the turning tide or how he ended up in the river in the first place.

Maybe reaching for a piece of bread on the North Gate Bridge he slipped, or could he have fallen off the Bailey Bridge, then again he might have been lured to the waters edge by a tasty burger bun thrown into the river by some drunken student out by the Lee Maltings – shaggin students! Or maybe he wiped out on some bushes up along the Mardyke, or did he bang his beak trying to fly through the lattice-work on the Shaky Bridge, or under the arches of Wellington Bridge, or dive-bombing a floating egg-salad roll near the Angler's Rest, or did his wings clip the top of the Hydro-dam out in Inniscarra . . .?

Or maybe he's just sick of it all, condemned to a life of flight when all around him ducks and seagulls and swans are swanning up and down the river, no pressure, on hassle, getting the lion's share of the grub . . .

Whatever the reason, there he is like the rest of us, on a

mystery tour to an almost certain doom, enjoying the free ride and view.

– Ve must do somethink!

– Do somethin'? Like jump in after him or somethin'? Get real, Herman boi, will'a!

– Nein, nein!

Herman always speaks German when he's upset.

– Vot we need is ein rope or ein piece of wood.

... before I could raise an eyebrow or lift a hand, he's off running, and running must be contagious, because I'm running after him carrying the bags of laundry, Sancho Panzaish.

\* \* \*

3:19:51

Alison has popped the sleeping pill and is sipping her gin and tonic.

– It wasn't always this way, you know. I remember when I first came into the property-rental game, I was still at college, third year BCom. My father had just died and somebody had to keep the whole show on the road. But those were different days. I remember, I used go to the parties in the flats and everything, I was one of the gang.

There was one end-of-term party that went totally wild, we trashed the place, tore out the sinks, burned the curtains, painted shoe polish, tomato sauce, mustard, everything we could lay our hands on, all over the walls and stairs and floors, windows and doors smashed, the lot; in one of my own houses, can you believe that? But you can only do those things for so long, and then you get sense or old, or whatever. You get sick of people dodging off without paying the gas, or being shafted for the last few weeks' rent. I've had tenants who were more insane than that Pluto fella, but I'm just worn out from it . . .

Alison rambles on for a little while longer and melts back into her husband's arms asleep.

* * *

I can see Herman up ahead, he's shouting up at the humpers on the scene dock at the back of the Opera House and pointing to the river. A long, maybe twelve-foot-long 3x2 is handed out. With the shaft of wood under his arm, he runs past me heading the opposite direction towards Patrick's Bridge, like a knight, no shining armour . . .

– *Chaaarge!*

Is all I hear, and *whooschhhh* a gust of wind. I follow on.

He's telling me to hold on to his jacket as he climbs to the water-side of the railings on the bridge.

– Herman boi, are you off yer fuckin' chuck or what?

– Hold mein jacket and do not let me slip . . . do you hear zis, Pluto?

So he's leaning there, outside the railings of Patrick's Bridge at forty-five degrees. a twelve-foot length of timber breaking water. I'm locked on to the tail of his coat . . .

– Steady, Herman boi! Steady!

– Here he komes, here he komes . . .

Herman stretches for the pigeon.

– Here he komes! Here he komes!

He's leaning out horizontal, the sole of his right shoe the only contact with the world. It's like I'm being pulled over the railings.

– Come back, Herman, yer tearin' me arms off a' me.

Hearman is reaching further,

216

– Here he komes, here he komes . . .

– Dis is how me mudder died, Herman boi . . .

I can feel him slipping . . .

– Now! Now! Now! Herman lunges towards the pigeon, I tug on the coat-tails, he whips up, back flat against the railings; missing the pigeon by a mile, the 3x2 falls the river.

– *Shhhit!* shouts Herman, and he frog-leaps the railings to the footpath.

– Ya could ha' killed yerself, I point to the river.

But this is no time for arguing.

– Der Dog's Home! Herman shouts, – Zey may have a net or somethink, yes?

. . . and he's off charging down the quays. I'm wrecked from all this running about. I can't believe this, I'm stuck for time as it is and here I am, down around the docks on a wild-goose chase for a pigeon, three bags of laundry hanging from me. By the time I catch up with Herman, he's beating down the door of the Dog's Home.

– Herman boi, dis place don't open for another half hour, by den dat pigeon will be washed out beyond Roches Point to de high seas.

– Quick! To der docks! Ve vill get something there for sure. Come on, hurry. Ve vill catch der pigeon further down.

. . . and once again, he's off like a lunatic over by City Hall, down past Carey's Tool Hire, down beyond the Idle Hour, down among the hoppers and silos and myself like a bigger lunatic after him.

The docker's about five-foot-nothing, built like a block, looks like he's just fallen out of one of the early-morning houses. He's swaying there in his donkey jacket and hobnails. Herman makes a beeline for him.

– A wha'? A pigeon? The docker scratches his head.

– Ja, ja, he est drowning!

217

– Drowning! Where?

– Ja, zere in der river.

Gasping for breath, holes burnt in my lungs from the fags, I stand there amazed as Herman the German explains the plight of the pigeon in pidgin English to the legless docker. The docker nods and shakes hands with Herman.

– So, we get some rope, ja? Herman is waving his hands all over the gaff.

– Rope! Why? the docker asks.

– For der pigeon! He est drowning in der river.

– Sure, what's another shaggin' pigeon? The docker throws his arms in the air and staggers off in the direction of the Marina bar.

I'm inclined to agree with the docker. What is another pigeon. And that's where I leave Herman and his bags of dirty laundry, pleading with a drunken docker. This is where I walk away, today is a big day for me. It's Paulo's First Holy Communion and I'm running a bit late.

# 25

3:20

   – Ah lads this is flamin' ridiculous! the Monk is losing it.
– Sure Jaysus if he was in there he'd have answered the door
by now.

   – But vot if he is not conscious, vot then?

   – Look, come offa' the window. I'm gonna head down to
Macari's and see if Pluto's been down there, mate.

Herman jumps to the footpath and brushes down his
trousers.

   – I'm gonna pick up a sausage supper for meself while I'm
at it, can I get anything for the two a' ye?

Herman shakes his head.

   – Brenda?

   – No thank ya, Jimmy, she says.

   – Are ye sure?

Brenda nods, Herman grunts. The Monk heads off, down
Waterloo Terrace.

   – I'll be back in a minute.

* * *

I see by the City Hall clock that it is just quarter to ten, I am
still okay for time if I skip the coffee at Iago's. A short cut up

219

Oliver Plunkett Street should get me over to the dole in five minutes.

– Hoi! Hoi! Pluto mate!

It's Jimmy the Monk. He's standing at the corner of Beasley Street, a toilet bowl in his arms.

– Ah! Jimmy, how's it goin'?

– Pluto mate, ye couldn't have come along at a better time.

– How's dat?

– Would ya mind obliging me with just two minutes a' your time, mate?

– No problem! But I'm really under pressure, see I must get over to de . . .

The Monk cuts me off with,

– . . . I've just found a great skip, mate. It's over on Father Matthew Quay.

– Look, I can't really go over with ya, 'tis me son's Holy Communion today and I must get down to de dole first.

– I'm not askin' ya to go nowhere, mate! All I wants is for you to hold on to this for two minutes, he nods at the toilet-bowl. – While I run back. There's a brilliant hallstand in the skip, for the cottage like, an' if I don't get it now it'll be gone.

– Ah Jeezus Jimmy! I'm mad late!

– On the level, I'll only be a minute, mate!

Jimmy hands me the toilet bowl and vanishes off down Beasley Street, towards the South Mall. I plonk it on the footpath and sit on it. He won't be too long, I mean like it only takes a few seconds to get over to Father Matthew Quay and back.

\* \* \*

– Dere, dat's it up ahead, pull in dere, says the burly fella.

– Macari's? the fella with the ears mouths the name on the sign.

– Best chips in town! says the burly fella. – Dere, pull in dere.

The squad car rolls to a halt outside the chipper. The burly fella gets out and putting his hand on the roof, he leans back into the car.

– I'm havin' a chips, batter burger an' peas, he says. – How 'bout yerself?

– Eh, I'll just have a chips an' curry sauce, an' a tin a' Coke!

Macari's is quiet. The only other customer there is Jimmy the Monk, he's just about to leave with his sausage supper as the burly fella enters.

– Goodnight, mate, says the Monk. He passes out of the chipper onto the Lower Road.

– G'night, says the burly fella.

The Monk makes his way along the street eating his supper, peas dripping from his fingers and mouth as he goes.

The burly fella is studying the hand-written price list on the wall behind the counter. He raps on the formica with his knuckles.

– Ah, good evening, Guard, Macari pops his head up from inside the counter. – So what can I get for you?

– One batter burger, chips an' peas, an' a chips an' curry sauce on its own, an' a tin a' Coke. Do ya have any milk?

– No sir, only soft drinks.

– Eh, make dat two tins a' Coke so!

– Veronnicca! Throw on a batter burger supper an' a chips an' curry, he shouts through the hatch, and places two tins of Coke on the counter.

– Are dey chilled?

– No cold Coke, Macari shakes his head.

– Fair enough!

– De eh, batter burger will take a few minutes. They're frozen.

– No problems, says the burly fella.

Outside the fella with the ears is sitting in the squad car, listening to the radio. He's tapping on the steering wheel to the beat of the sounds, thinking Cork isn't such a bad place to be stationed. He wonders what's taking his partner so long in the chipper. He's enjoying the break from the constant banter of the burly fella.

– *Delta, Tango, Bravo, Come in, Over!* his peace is shattered, a call from the base.

*Delta, Tango, Bravo, Come in. Over!*

He switches off the radio and picks up the hand set.

– Delta, Tango, Bravo, To base. Over!

– *There have been reports of disturbances at a house up on Waterloo Terrace, suspected robbery in progress. Over!*

– We'll swing up around that way straight away to investigate. Over!

The base give him other details of the situation.

– We're on our way. Over and Out!

He jumps from the car, and dashes into Macari's to get the burly fella. The two guards run chipless to the patrol car. They speed off in the opposite direction to Waterloo Terrace, trapped in the madness of the one-way system.

\* \* \*

I sit, and I sit, and I sit, no sign of the Monk.

– Excuse me,

I stop this guy in a suit.

– What time is it? I ask.

– Same time as it was yesterday only twenty-four hours later! he says.

I sorta laugh. It's an old joke, in fact that same joke was used twice in *Toto the Hero*, he makes to pass by.

– Have ya seen *Toto de Hero*? I ask.

He bursts out laughing.

– I did! he says, – Only last night myself and the wife. It was brilliant! I've been dying to use that line on someone. An oldie, but a goldie! Ha!

– Jeezus I haven't seen it in years, but remember at de start of de filum? Do ya tink Toto an' Alfred were really mixed up at birth in de hospital?

– To tell you the truth, I don't think there was even a fire, he said. – All in Toto's head!

– Gowaan! I never thought of it dat way.

– Sure the guy spent his whole life living in his head, what makes ya think he'd be any different when he was a baby? he explains.

– Ya mean to say he was in love wit his sister all his life? Jeezus I must see dat filum again.

– Ah! One of the best! he says. – So, eh! If you don't mind me asking, what are you doing sitting on a toilet bowl here on Beasley Street?

– Good question, I say. – See I'm actually mindin' it for a friend a' mine, he's just after dashing over to Father Matthew Quay to pick up a hallstand, and I tell ya de truth, I'm sorta under pressure. Supposed to be up at me son's First Holy Communion dis mornin'. Runnin' mad late, and I must sign on first.

– Do you know what? I'm working over there, he points to an Estate Agent's. – If ya want I'll keep an eye on the toilet bowl for yer friend, and maybe you could do me a

223

favour by dropping my video back to ExtraVision, it's on your way!

– Jeezus, would ya really?

– Sure your buddy can't be much longer!

– Dat'd make me life much easier!

– So eh, tell me, what does your friend look like? he asks.

– Ah ya can't miss him. He's a big culchie head on him, and a sorta English accent. In his late forties. Ya can't miss him, he'll be carrying a hallstand, Jimmy, dat's his name. Are ya sure ya don't mind waitin' for him?

– Not at all! Sure it'll save me having to walk into town!

– Well Jeezus, I really appreciate dis, I say.

– Don't mention it. By the way, he reaches into his pocket. – Here, give this to your young fella for his Communion.

He pushes a fiver into my hand.

– Ah! Jesus I couldn't, I say.

– How do ya mean you can't? It's not for you!

– Alright, but I feel very bad about dis.

– Go on, he says. – You'll be mad late!

So, I pick up my bag of laundry, say goodbye again and head off down Oliver Plunkett Street. It's amazing how sometimes you meet a stranger and you strike it off with them straight away.

Time is tight, but everything's under control. It's just a matter of getting the video back, then a quick dart over to the dole; in and out and up to the North Cathedral. The pressure is on.

So I'm beating down Oliver Plunkett Street, my laundry in one hand and yer man's video in the other.

– Hoi! Pluto, Pluto!

My gut instinct is to keep going, but I stop.

– Hoi, Pluto!

It's Pinko. He's standing at the corner of Pembrook Street by the GPO, arms flying.

– Hoi, Pluto! he shouts again.

Jesus. This is all I need, I wouldn't mind but he was one ignorant fucker that day I met him up at the hospital, the day I went to visit Fatfuka.

– Ah Pluto, I'm glad I met ya. I need to talk.

– I suppose you know Fatfuka's dead, I say.

– I didn't see ya at the funeral, Pluto?

– I said me goodbyes while he was still alive.

– I know. Fatfuka told me. He lived for yer visits to the hospital.

– Did he say dat, Pinko? Did he really say dat?

– Only two of us left from McSweeneya now, eh Pluto?

– Dere was nothin' special about Mc Sweeneya, I say. – Only de people who lived on it. Huh?

– You said it, Pluto boi! You said it!

It was just at that moment when Pinko called me, – *Pluto boi,* I saw the real Pinko. The Pinko I used to know down Mc Sweeney Street. The Pinko who lived his life in the shadow of a ghost. The ghost of Georgie, his big brother. A ghost born when a sixteen-year-old boy is crushed by the wheels of a truck in the line of duty. The ghost that lives on to this day selling newspapers at the Coliseum Corner for God and for family.

This is the Pinko I knew before he had spent the rest his life either trying to measure up to his dead brother, or maybe wishing that he himself had been chewed up by that truck.

Pinko's smile just about hides his suffering.

– I gotta talk to ya, he says.

– Well look, I'm in a mad dash right now, eh how about tomorro', Pinko.

– No, now!

I know he means it.

– Well look, I'm very tight on time, I say.

– I just want to tell ya that . . .

– Gowaan so! Gowaan!

– . . . what I'm trying to say is that I know I was a bit edgy up in the hospital, but it wasn't aimed at you. It's me! I'm a mess, Pluto boi!

Jesus, am I hearing this right. He's a mess? This is the big businessman, writing a novel, dressed like a prince and he says he's a mess? So I stop.

– What's on yer mind, Pinko?

– Do ya remember the novel I was writing, the one I was telling ya about . . .

His eyes are welling up.

– De one about de ex-Christian Brother and him falling in love with his old buddy an' den he ditches de buddy for a woman and goes off and marries her, and all dat.

– Yeah!

Pinko's amazed I still remember.

– Well, wat about it? I ask.

– It's true! he says.

– It's true? Wat's true?

– The story! The story's true. I met him after he left the Brothers.

– Met who?

– Fatfuka, Pluto! I met Fatfuka when he left the Brothers. He had nowhere to go. He couldn't go home. He had no money. He moved in with me.

– Ha?

– Me and Fatfuka were lovers! For Christ's sakes!

– Steamers? Gay like?

This is all too much for me to take in.

– Gay is only a word, Pluto boi. We loved each other. Me

226

and Fatfuka really loved each other, and then he dumps me and married that bitch!

Pinko's in floods of tears, sobbing like a . . . well, like a woman.

– You and Fatfuka?

I still can't make sense out of what I'm hearing. Pinko stands there his hands hanging limp by his side, crying uncontrollably outside the Hi-B. I drop my laundry bag to the ground, reach out and hold him. He smells like perfume.

He tells me that each day he went to the hospital hoping that Fatfuka would say that he loved him but it never happened. On the last visit Fatfuka was barely conscious, but he reached out and held Pinko's hand, a tear came to his eye.

– Why wouldn't he say it? Why couldn't he just say "I Love You, Pinko"! Why?

– Well, maybe that's what he was trying to say, when he held your hand, I say.

– At the funeral, his shaggin' bitch of a wife came up to me and said that Fatfuka always talked of me fondly.

Pinko smiles through the tears.

– Did his wife know? I ask.

– Know what?

– Dat ye were well er, steamer . . . er, lovers, like.

– Don't be so shaggin' stupid, Pluto, Pinko begins to cry again, – He thought of me fondly? Fondly? Bitch! He loved me, and she was too thick to know. I just wanted to tell her! Tell her of the nights of passion I shared with her husband. Fuck her! I wanted to tell her about that holiday in Greece! Bitch! It's just so unfair. I can't grieve for him. Nobody knows. Nobody cares. I'm a mess, Pluto boi! I'm just walkin' around like this for days crying! I'll never get over him.

– Look maybe I could meet ya tomorra', we could have a drink and talk about it or somethin'.

– Maybe, maybe, he whispers.

Then he pushes me to one side and heads off up Winthrop Street in tears. I just stand there watching as he fades in the distance. He turns into Patrick Street and heads towards the river. He doesn't look back.

# 26

3:38:42

It's always this way, anytime Alison's wound up, he talks her down. Next thing you know, she's out for the count and he's the one who can't sleep. It doesn't really bother him though. She has a tough day tomorrow, what with making sure that weirdo quits Waterloo Terrace, and all that. So he sits there reading one of Alison's old *Cosmopolitans* by the dim glow of the bedside lamp.

\* \* \*

I can't think of Pinko's heartbreak right now, I'll talk to him tomorrow. I make a small detour into Patrick Street, to drop off yer man's video, then I wonder . . .

– Did he say ExtraVision or Hollywood Video? I take the tape from its case, no ID tag. They'll know at the counter . . .

– Eh! Hello, I'd like to return dis video, I say to the girl.

  – Thank you! she says and grabs it.

  – Bu – Bu – But I'm not too sure if dis is yours or not!

  – Not too sure? she inspects the case. – What's your number?

– I don't have a number, I don't even have a video recorder, says I. – I'm only doin' a favour for somebody.

– And eh what's their name, sir? she asks.

– Eh I haven't a clue, I just met dis guy down Oliver Plunkett Street!

– . . . let me guess, and he asked you to drop back his video? she takes the words out of my mouth. – A total stranger, and he never told you which video shop to return it to! she looks at me as if I have two heads.

– Well, actually we did a trade. See, I said I'd drop back his video if he minded me friend's toilet bowl, I explain.

– He's minding your friend's toilet bowl?

– See, I'm in a mad rush, It's me son's Communion dis morning and I must go over and sign on first, so yer man said he'd look after de toilet bowl . . .

– Eh what's your name, sir?

– Pluto, eh Paul O'Toole.

She punches a few numbers into the computer, looks at the screen and mutters something under her breath.

– Do you know dere's twenty-four pounds fifty outstanding in fines? her eyes dart.

– I don't know nothin' about fines! I plead, she lifts up the phone and dials.

– Look, dis is crazy. All I'm doin' is droppin' back a video, I don't even know dis fella, I never met him before in me life!

– Eh hello, she's on the phone, – I'd like to speak to a Mr John Richardson please.

She examines her fingernails.

– Ah, yes! You'll do fine Mrs Richardson, there's a eh, gentleman here returning the video you have out at the moment. Eh *Toto the Hero!* Yes! Well, he's a bit vague as to how he came across the tape and I'm just phoning to confirm that everything is in order. Eh, name? He says he never met your husband before. Yes, he's a Mr Paul O'Toole!

– Look, dis is crazy! I shout.

– Excuse me, Mr O'Toole, but eh, Mrs Richardson asks me if you're the Paul O'Toole from MacSweeney Street?

– Well eh, I used to be, I say.

– She wishes to speak to you.

I am handed the phone.

– Eh hello, I say, and launch into the full explanation as to how I ended up returning her video.

– Pluto! she says, – It's me!

– You! You who?

– You never lost it, Pluto, it's me Imelda, Imelda Kearney! she says.

– No! Never!

– Richardson's my married name, that was my husband you met!

– Gowaan! I say, – Jeezus I was only talkin' about you to Fatfuka last week! Your husband's some class of an Estate Agent or something?

– That's right, she says. – I heard the news about Fatfuka, very sad. Do you know the last time I met Fatfuka was about fifteen years ago at Grandda Buckley's Funeral?

– He was tellin' me. Yerrah, I was wit him up to de last, I tink he died happy . . . Do ya know, we were talkin' about you, Imelda, I was tellin' him about de night you came to me Grads.

– I was never so nervous as that night! she giggles – I remember you looked like a prince.

– Really?

I'm fishing for compliments.

– Sure all the girls were mad after you, Pluto.

– Well, it's a pity nobody told me, says I. She laughs.

231

She tells me about her two daughters, Ashling and Aoife, I tell her about Paulo and his Communion. She says she had heard I was married. I give her the low-down on Yvette. She tells me she's living on the Rochestown Road, and that I should call out sometime. I tell her how I met her husband and he was really sound. She says John is a good guy. I tell her about Tragic Ted dying of AIDS. She says that was a real tragedy. She says she still meets Pinko every now and then, he's in the same health club as herself and John. I say that MacSweeney Street was never the same after Georgie was killed. She pauses for a few seconds, and then we just carry on talking on old times. Anyway we talk, and talk, and talk, we have a lot of catching up to do.

– Well, I tell ya, Imelda, 'twas great to be talkin' to ya, girl!

– You too.

– I really got to go though, I must get up to Paulo's Communion.

– You'll have to promise me you'll call to see us sometime, especially now that the weather's getting fine.

– I will, Imelda girl, God bless!

– We'll see you then so, Pluto.

– Goodbye, Imelda.

– Goodbye, she says.

She hangs up. I hand the receiver to the girl behind the video-shop counter.

– And you say you never met these people before in your life? she asks.

I don't have the time to even begin to explain to her, so I just say . . .

– Cork's like dat, isn't it? and I walk out the door.

* * *

232

Herman recognises the faint outline of the Monk coming back up Waterloo Terrace.

– Ah! Jimmy!

– Well, any sign of Pluto down in Macari's? Brenda asks.

– Naw, nobody down there 'cept a couple a coppers, says the Monk.

– Well, come on then and give me a leg up onto der vindowsill.

– Ya any chips left, luuv?

– Dere all gone.

– Ya ate them all! Ya greedy gut! What are ye?

– Jaysus, ye said ye didn't want any.

– Come on over here und give me some help.

\* \* \*

I'm late, but I hesitate for a second at Princes Street corner, a busker treats *I Know My Love* with care.

I cut through Mutton Lane into the Market, the scenic route to the Grand Parade. The Market is glowing. It's like when *The Wizard Of Oz* turns to colour. Vegetables freshly dug from unpolluted country gardens tumbling from stalls. Chickens, rabbits, wood pigeons, pheasants, ducks, strung up in clusters. Trays of eggs from every caste of farmyard and water fowl stacked to the canopy. An art student sitting on the fountain sketches moving-life. The knobbly knees of café society poke through the railings of the ceiling-slung Farm Gate Restaurant. The air is thick with sound and scent. The most beautiful aroma of exotic herbs and spices from Mr Bells' spice Emporium, hot breads from the Yukon bakery, cheeses, pestos, chorizo, bitter balsamic vinegar, sweet olive oil, freshly sizzling crepes, fish and all creatures of the

Atlantic Ocean and meats – more meat than you could shake a stick at. All this blending beautifully with the sing-song sounds of people talking.

A fuss at the olive stall, another TV company trying to capture the soul of The English Market. Blackmarket shop assistants, dash and hide, dole-dodgers caught on camera. I move in for a closer look. It's some continental station, sounds like the fella with the mic is speaking French. They're blocking the whole walk-way. So, I decide to head back around by the Fish Market – that's when I see her, clipboard in hand.

– Yvette? Yvette? Is dat you Yvette? my heart drops.

– Pluto? she turns.

– Jeezus, Yvette, I'd recognise yer smile anywhere.

– *Mon petit Pluto!* she reaches out to me, I kiss her on the cheek and hug her, in truth I have never stopped loving her. I step back, holding her hands. I look her up and down.

– I have gained some kilos, oui?

And yes she had gained a couple of stone, her face was softer, skin looser, hair a bit more structured. But those eyes, sparkling, more beautiful than ever.

– You look wonderful, I say and I kiss her again.

– Where have you been, Pluto?

– How do ya mean where've I been? I've been here in Cork! Where d'ya tink I've been?

– But I have searched for you many times since our divorce! she says.

– You've searched for me?

– Oui! After our divorce I realise I have made ze biggest mistake of my life!

– Mistake?

– I wanted you back, mon Pluto, I came here looking for you, but you had left our flat.

234

– Gowaan? Dat must've been de time I was goin' out wit Veronica!

– Veronica? And now? she asks.

– Naw! I'm sorta' between girlfriends at de moment.

– Would you like to take an old friend for a coffee?

I can't believe this, after all these years, Yvette turns up on the very day of Paulo's First Holy Communion. I suppose I could always skip the dole.

– I'd love to have coffee with ya! I say.

Yvette turns to the camera crew and shouts something in French. There's some mumbling and the lamps are switched off.

I explain that all I have is the fiver given to me by Imelda Kearney's husband.

– *Oú est Imelda Kearney?*

– Ah, she was de girl I took to me Grads.

She links my arm.

– *On-y-va!*

– Iago's the best in town. I say.

Two coffees and an amaretto biscuit later, she's talking about her search for me. She says that at one stage she thought that I must have been dead. I tell her that I'm made of tougher stuff than that. She talks about the years of emptiness since our divorce. I just stand there at the counter as her velvety voice wafts around my head-space. I study her eyes and every movement of her lips. A wave of emotion builds up inside me. Now I know why I fell in love with her, that first day I saw her in the cafe/juice bar off Damrak. That love has not died. I still love her and always will.

– What I am trying to say, Pluto, is, I still love you and I want you back, she says.

– Jeezus, I love you too, Yvette.

I reach over and kiss her on the lips. I taste her bittersweet tears as they blend with mine at the corners of our mouths.

She tells me that she has to get back to the TV crew but she will be wrapped up by around one o' clock. I say that's perfect, because I should be finished with Paulo's Communion by then. She asks about Paulo. I tell her the whole story of Veronica and Mags and how two lesbians made a langer out of me. I laugh, she doesn't get the joke. I arrange to meet her in Le Chateau bar at around one o' clock. She moves closer and kisses me one more time and whispers,
 – *Je t'aime*.

* * *

3:46
   The squad car sneaks into Waterloo Terrace.
   – Now keep yer eyes peeled for anything out a' de ordinary! says the burly fella.
   – Look! Look! There! he points – There, two fella trying to climb in the window of that house there.
   – Well, what are ya waiting for! Put de boot down.

# 27

Coming out of the Market, onto the Grand Parade, five to eleven by Hilser's clock. That's when I see them, they're heading straight for me, like something out of Tarantino; Tony Tabs and two of his henchmen, all in black, sunglasses and slicked hair. I suppose the Devil you know is better than the Devil you don't.

– Howzit goin', Tone?

– N'too bad! Yerself, Pluto?

– Pluggin' away.

I make to pass by, but for some reason Tony decides to stop and chat.

– Jojo, Dutchy, Pluto.

We're introduced.

– Howzit it goin'? I say.

Dutchy raises his Raybans. Jojo just says, – Pluto!

– So eh, what are ya up ta, Pluto man? Are ya still up in the other place?

– Eh, ya?

– So how's Blackrock treating ya?

– No! No! Tone, dat was de place I was in before I moved in above to me new gaff.

– But I thought you said you were still in the other place.

– Well I did, but I thought you were talkin' about me new gaff.

– But yer still with the same aul doll?

– Which one are ya talkin' about, Tone?

– Eh, the French one?

– Naw, dat was about twelve years ago!

– How's about the schoolteacher, Pluto? Ya know the one with the kid?

– Naw dat was about eight years ago, sure I told ya all dis when I met ya before Christmas, Tony boi!

– Oh? Is that the one ye were talkin' about?

– I'm not too sure, I say. – I thought you were talkin' about Mags, me other aul' doll. De schoolteacher was de ex-ex one, if ya know what I mean.

– Why? Is there a new one?

– Well, dere was, I say. – We had a kid an' all. A boy. Paulo we called him.

– Congratulations, Pluto boi.

– Tha' was about eight years ago though, we're split up now.

– Jez! Sorry to hear that, Pluto man!

– But you'll never guess who I met today?

– Who?

– Me ex-wife.

– Ex-wife, Pluto?

– Ah, yeah, de French one.

– I don't remember her, Pluto man.

– 'Course ye do . . . Yvette, remember, Tone?

Anyway meself and Tony Tabs are rapping away about nothing. I can see Dutchie and Jojo, they are totally lost.

– Do ya want to try a line a Panama Power Powder? Tony asks.

Cocaine is the last thing I need, I'm running late as it is, so I throw a few excuses at Tony.

– Ah come on, come on, he says.

Before I know it, we're standing at the bar in Canty's. The barman's at the far end, down by the cold-plates. Tony sees his opportunity. Shielded by the pillar, he throws out a mole-hill of coke dust, out onto the brass corner of the bar, a quick chop-chop with the one-sided blade. Dutchy and Jojo, busy rolling their crisp twenty-quid notes. And there lined up, on the brass, four finger-thick lines of powder.

– Gowan Dutchy, he orders.

In one greased movement, Dutchie raises the rolled note to nostril, left index to nose, head dips and in a smooth swoop snorts it into his brain.

– Jojo! Tony snaps his fingers, points to the coke.

Jojo moves in like a hawk.

I'm fumbling through my pockets, all I have is the fiver given to me by John Richardson, Imelda Kearney's husband, and like all fivers it's totally maggoty, ripped, cellotaped and silver thread stripped at both ends. I try to roll it; looks like a limp dick.

Jojo steps back, Tony hovers over the counter, and then hoovers.

– Pluto! Gowaan!

I move in, a bit self-conscious, put my mangled roll on the line. I sniff, get nothing.

– Gowaan, Pluto boi, will'a, will'a!

I snort again, this time with such force the fiver shoots up my nose. I lift my head, Jojo nudges Dutchie. They laugh.

– Stop muckin' 'round, Pluto boi, will'a.

I remove the fiver and clear my sinuses, inwards.

– Great tack! Hey Dutchie? says Tony.

– Feelin' good! says Jojo.

To be honest, I'm getting nothing from the coke, the boys were probably flying before I met them anyway.

– How're ye now, Pluto boi? Tony asks.

I just smile, but in all fairness, I don't feel great. For one thing, the coke is doing nothing for me and for another, I always feel odd about taking lines from people. See I can never really afford to repay it, makes me feel like a bit of a bum.

– Ya feelin good, Pluto?

– Tell ya de truth, Tone, I got nothin' outa tha'.

– Ha?

From nowhere the barman appears.

– Gentlemen?

– Three coffees and a mineral water! Tony snaps his fingers and points to the counter.

One mineral water and three coffees are put in front of us.

– I'll get it, I say.

This is a good pay-back opportunity. I pull out the fiver and hand it over. The bar man, a real sharp dude, places a sugar bowl, jug of milk on the counter. He takes the fiver, with a flick of his wrist it's unrolled. It's like slow motion, as the five-pound note stretches in mid-air up goes a cloud of jungle powder that had been trapped in its manky folds. Jojo drops his sunglasses, our eyeballs follow the coke mist as it rises above the bar. Dutchie laughs.

– Gowl! Tony pushes me.

The barman turns and heads for the till, as the coke cloud settles to a white film over the counter. Jojo and Dutchy run their fingers along the surface and picking up the powder, they rub it into their gums.

– Shag ya! says Tony. – Ya got nothin' out a' that line!

– Lost it in me fiver! I explain, and point to the counter.

– Fuckin' fiver! Come on! he says.

I follow him down to the end of the bar and into the toilet.

Tony checks the cubicles, the place is empty. He steps into

the first one, lines up two ridges along the back of the cistern. He then rolls up two twenties.

– It's very uncool to snort from another person's note these days, he says.

He sucks one line into his face, calls me in, pushes the door out, bolts it and hands me the other twenty. I dip my nose to the porcelain and whip it up.

– Great tack! he says. – Straight off the block!

I stand there for a second or two, waiting for it to hit.

– Great tack! Wha? he repeats.

I'm looking at Tony, I'm standing so close to him that I can see his eyeballs as they dart around behind the red-tinted shades, so close it's hard to recognise him. It's like I don't know this guy at all, I mean, we're only nodding aquaintances and here I am in the cubicle of the toilet in Canty's, not two inches from his face and it's like he's a total stranger . . . But yeah, great tack and I feel good, too good to care.

– Jeezus . . . Tony whispers.

Tony turns to leave. But as he puts his hand on the door latch, the main door into the toilet springs open, it sounds like about four guys.

– Fuck! says Tony.

I think he's more worried about being found in a toilet with another man, than the whole cocaine thing.

– I'll stand up on de toilet bowl, I whisper.

– Shut the . . . !

We hear the intruders shuffle around on the tiles outside. One of them makes a wisecrack, something about two steamers in the loo. They laugh. Tony's face stiffens, and as it tenses up it's like I don't recognise him at all. Strange, I've known Tony Tabs all my life and here I am, not three inches from him and I suddenly realise he's a total stranger.

The lads outside, lined up against the wall emptying

bladders, still laughing and slagging, calling us botty boys and things,

– Bate it up his arse! and they all laugh.

Tony's face contorts, like a wolf's. I decide to chill the situation.

I make the sound of an elevator bell, and push the cubicle door open.

– *Ding!* – Is this the first floor or the basement? I ask and lead the way out towards the bar.

The four lads laugh. But just as we reach the door, one of them says something about arse-bandits, they laugh louder.

Tony turns. He heads straight for the wisecracker.

– Do ya see somethin' funny, he says.

The funny man doesn't answer, his hands occupied down by the urinal.

– I'll show ya somethin' funny, says Tony.

And just like that, he grabs your man by the hair, clings his face to the tiles. A splatter of blood. Then whamo off the sink and straight up, full force against the mirror, shatters it. I've never seen the likes of it. It was like, *Duff! Duff! Duff!* Three seconds. That's all it took. He falls to the floor fumbling with his zip.

– Laugh now! Go on! Laugh now!

Tony kicks him a few times.

– What're ye lookin' at? Tony paces towards the other three. They turn their faces straight to the wall.

– Come on, Tone! Come on!

– Fuck! Tony whispers and barges past me, out of the toilet.

This is when I realise I don't know Tony Tabs at all.

Back at the bar, Tony never mentions to Dutchy or Jojo what happened inside in the loo. I'm a bit shell-shocked. I tell them about Paulo's Holy Communion. I thank Tony for the line of coke and say goodbye. One thing about the Devil you don't know, you won't unless you do and it's an odd feeling when the Devil you don't becomes the Devil you do . . . know like.

– See ya later, Pluto man, says Tony.

– Yeah, later, Tone.

The effects of the coke has been numbed by what happened in the toilet. I make for the street and air.

By now I'm running so late that I don't have the time to sign on and get up to the North Cathedral. I decide to skip the dole.

– Shag 'em if dey can't take a joke! Dat's what I say.

So I head up towards the Coal Quay.


– *Yoo! Whoo! Pluto!*

It's Brenda the Brasser. She's across the road by The Roundy House. I wave and keep going.

– Pluto! she calls again. – Come'er, boi, will'a?

Caught by the curlies, I cross the road.

– Brenda, how's it goin'? I'd love to stop an' chat, but Jeezus I'm under fierce pressure!

– Listen I won't delay ya at all, boi! It's just that on me way down Waterloo Terrace I met de Monk and he was cursin' you.

– Cursin' me? Jeezus what did I ever do to him?

– He said that you were supposed to mind a beautiful toilet bowl for him, but when he got back you and the toilet were gone. Do ya have it, luuv?

– Do I look like I have a toilet bowl?

I open my jacket, and shake it showing that I have nothing to hide.

– Well, he's gonna do his nut! Brenda runs her finger across her throat.

– Jeezus Christ! As if I don't have enough on me mind dan to be lookin' after him and his toilet bowl!

243

– Hey hold it! Hold it! Brenda says. – Don't talk to me in that tone. I'm only the messenger.

– Sorry Brenda! Sorry! See, I'm going off me head today.

And I start to tell Brenda all about Paulo and his Communion, and how Herman had delayed me with the whole pigeon in the river thing, and then Jimmy the Monk and his blasted toilet bowl, not to mind my chance meeting with John Richardson, Imelda Kearney's husband, and the crazy phone call in ExtraVision. For some reason I don't tell her about meeting Pinko, Yvette, or Tony Tabs, Jojo and Dutchy, I just don't have the time. But I explain to her that John Richardson, Imelda Kearney's husband, is minding the Monk's toilet bowl down in his Estate Agent's office.

– Who's Imelda Kearney? she asks.

– Ah! She was de aul' doll I took to me Grads.

– Hmm!

– But if dat don't beat everything, I'm runnin' so late I tink I'm gonna have to skip de dole.

– Skip the dole? Ya can't just skip the dole! They'll cut ya off!

– Well, look I must get up to de North Cathedral for eleven, and if I go over dere I'll be dere for de day.

– You'll have to phone 'em! Brenda says.

– An' wat am I gonna' say?

– Look, I'll phone 'em for ya.

– Would ya! Would ya really!

– Here, gis twenty pence.

– You're like a mudder to me, I say.

– By the way Pluto, wha's that in the black plastic bag?

– Oh dis? I raise the bag to knee height. – Dis is me laundry.

– Here show me that too! she says. – Now go on ! Get going or you'll be late for the young fella.

I cut across Castle Street onto the North Main Street, and turn my feet to Shandon.

# 28

3:46.

*Tap! Tap!*

– *Pluto!* Herman shouts.

– Ah! Come down offa dat windowsill, mate. Yer wastin' yer time.

– I am sure I can see der shape on der bed!

– Look, mate, it's almost four in the mornin', it's freezin' cold, and here I am on the side of the street with me hand up a German's hole.

– Oh, stop complaining and hold me steady, Pluto could be dying in zere.

– Me arm is fallin' offa me, mate.

A cop car screeches onto Waterloo Terrace, lights flashing, doors open. Two Guards on the case.

– Hoi! You! Hold it right there! says the fella with the ears. They shine their torches, the Monk turns to face them.

– We're just . . .

– Who told you to say anything! Git up against the wall dere!

The burly fella pushes the Monk.

– Hoi, easy with that thing, mate!

– You heard him, up against the wall. – Are you deaf or something? he shines the torch on Herman. – Get down offa that winda!

– But you say to stay vere ve are! protests Herman.

– Are you trying to be smart?

The fella with the ears pulls Herman by the ankles.

– Sorry, officer! You'll have to excuse Herman, the Monk tries to explain.

– Who asked you anything?

The Monk is shoved back against the wall by the burly fella's baton.

– Wha's yer name?

– Herman, Herman Muller!

– Well, Herman Muller, is that your winda?

– No it's not, but . . .

– Well, what are you doing up on top of the sill at three in the morning? he sneers.

– I think Pluto may be dead in zere!

– Dead?

– Suicide, mate!

– Who asked you anything? again he pushes the Monk.

– Suicide? What makes you think there is a suicide in there? asks the fella with the ears.

– I can feel it in ze air tonight, says Herman.

– Are you on drugs or what? the burly fella shakes Herman.

– That's exactly what I'm saying all night, mate!

– Shut up you! again he pokes the Monk with the baton.

– Hoi! Hoi! Easy with that thing, mate!

Brenda appears out of the hall door, onto the terrace.

– Wha's going on here?

– Who de hell are you? asks the burly fella, shining the torch in her face.

– I'm Brenda Healy, I live here, so do Herman and de Mo . . . eh, Jimmy!

– Well eh, what's going on? Dere have been reports of a bit of a commotion.

– I think we have an emergency! she says.

– Emergency?

– Well, we think Pluto has maybe done away with himself! Brenda explains.

– Why? Because this guy here feels it in the air, is it?

The torch lights up Herman's face.

– There's actually more to it than that, luuv.

– Tell them about der radio request, Brenda.

– Enough out a' you! the fella with the ears points to Herman. – Now carry on, Missus.

– Well, Pluto's been through a pretty hard time lately what with his butty dying and all that. He's also being thrown out of his flat tomorrow, he hasn't set foot outside his door in four days, and what's more he's tried to take his own life a few months ago.

– It was Herman, here, found him that time, mate.

– I thought I told you to stay up against the wall and shut up! he pushes the Monk.

– Tell them about ze radio request.

– Would you ever be quiet, the burly fella roars. – What's dis about a radio request?

– Well, it's nothing really, just that there was a request on the radio about an hour ago and it was sorta' odd like, it was for some of Pluto's old friends and a few of them are actually dead, like, Brenda says.

– Jeezus, dat's fairly odd, fair enough! says the burly fella.

– The DJ said there was a going-away party up here.

– Hmmm!

– And what makes ya tink he's dead in dere?

– Well, to be quite honest with you, Guard, I don't know. It's just that everything points to it, you know like, we've been knocking on his door for the last twenty minutes, and there's no sign of him.

– Sure if he hasn't been out of the flat for days, maybe he's just gone down to the chipper for a bite of food! says the fella with the ears.

– That's what I've been saying all night, mate!

– I thought I told you! shouts the burly fella.

– Sorry, mate! Sorry!

– I'd have heard him going out, says Brenda.

– Maybe if you shine your torch in der window, ve might be able to see if he's in zere, suggests Herman.

– Here you! the burly fella points at the Monk. – Give him a hand there up to the winda'.

– Com'on, says the fella with the ears, – Gis a leg up.

* * *

I'm just on time. Shandon says one minute past eleven. I cut across Chapel Street and up Chapel Lane. The North Cathedral stands there in front of me. My view of the Cathedral in all its splendour is blinkered by the narrowness of the street. I can just about see the mid-section of the gable end of the building. And there in the distance I make out the shape of two women; Veronica and Mags. I wave, they don't recognise me.

– Hey! Veronica! Mags!

Mags does a double take, she nudges Veronica. Veronica looks at me. I wave again.

– Pluto? – Is that you, Pluto?

Veronica looks better than the last time I saw her, but Jesus, Mags has aged something terrible. It's only been a few years and she looks twenty years older, like she's fifty or something, must be the stresses of child-rearing.

– How's it going Mags? Yer lookin' great.

She doesn't answer.

– Look, I know I'm a minute or two late, but Jeezus you've no idea of de kind a' morning I put down.

I give her a quick run through of my morning's escapades. I tell her about Herman and the pigeon in the river, the Monk and the toilet bowl and how I met Imelda Kearney's husband. I tell her about the madness in the video store and the telephone call to Imelda, the mad meeting I had with Pinko, I mention that I bumped into Tony Tabs and finally I tell her how Brenda the Brasser saved the day by phoning the dole and taking my laundry to the launderette. Mags just looks at me.

– Pluto? her voice raises in pitch. – Is that you, Pluto?

– A' course it's me.

– I thought you were dead!

– Dead?

– You died about twenty years ago, Pluto!

– Jeezus, you're de second woman today to tell me dat dey thought I was dead, I laugh. – Did I tell ya dat I met Yvette dis mornin', Yvette me ex-wife . . .

– How did you know about today? Mags asks.

– Sure didn't you send small Julie up to me flat dis mornin' to tell me.

Veronica just looks at me.

– Veronica, your daughter Julie! I explain the obvious.

Veronica looks confused. – I am Julie, she says. – Veronica was my mother.

– Wa'? Is dis some kind of a sick joke, Veronica?

– I'm Julie, she says it again.

– Ah Christ!

– Veronica died of leukemia, three years ago last February, Mags says.

I look at Julie, or Veronica or whoever she is. She's a woman, maybe not Veronica, on closer inspection. She's younger, more beautiful, she's the head off Veronica though, but she's definitely not the kid that called to my flat this morning to tell me about Paulo's First Holy Communion.

– Small Julie? I whisper.

– Who are ya, and what are ya doing here? she raises her voice.

– I'm Pluto, for Christ's sake! Look, de only reason I'm here is because Julie called up to me flat dis mornin' and told me.

– Listen, mister, I'm Julie, and I wasn't near any flat this mornin'. I don't even know you!

– You know who I'm talkin' about? Small Julie, Veronica's little girl.

– I was Veronica's little girl, she insists.

– What age are you, Pluto? Mags says.

– Thirty-three! It's me birthday today, 23rd of April.

– What age do you think I am? she asks.

– Is dis a trick question or something, Mags?

– Trick question?

– Jeezus, I don't know! What is it, about six years between us. I suppose you're about twenty-seven? I guess.

– Do I look twenty-seven to you? I'm fifty-one! she says.

– Ah, come off it! Look I don't know wat's goin' on here! All I know is dat Julie called up to me flat dis mornin', and told me it was Paulo's First Holy Communion, dat's all I know, and dat's why I'm here.

– Holy Communion? Mags steps back. – Paulo's gettin' married today!

– What? I'm totally stunned. – Gettin' married?

– Who are you?

– I'm Pluto! Is it dat ya don't remember me?

– Pluto's dead! says Julie.

– How could I be dead? Amn't I here talkin' to ya?

– I saw them carry Pluto's body out of his flat the morning he died, I was there. I was only a child, isn't that right, Mags? she says. – I was there, I remember!

– That's right! says Mags, – The morning of Paulo's Communion!

– Dis morning! I add.

– Yea! Only twenty-four years ago, she smirks.

– Look honestly, I don't know wat's going on here, all I

250

know is dat I'm Pluto, and dat's me son Paulo inside dat church getting married. Maybe I'm twenty odd years late, I don't know. Now if you don't believe I am who I am, well I'm gonna' turn around and walk away.

I stare at Mags and then Julie. They hesitate.

– Ah, for Christ's sake! Ye must remember me! Jesus, Mags, remember de first night I met ya in de Donkey's Ears. Remember you had Ecstasy and we took it an' we ended up havin' mad sex, on a bench over dere.

I point to Shandon graveyard. – Den we went back to Veronica's house for a night of de wildest passion. Jeezus, ya must remember!

Mags is stony-faced, she says nothing.

– Remember when you were pregnant with Paulo you moved into de house with meself an' Veronica an' small Julie. Remember Veronica didn't know dat I was Paulo's father at all?

I'm beginning to sweat.

A glimmer of recognition comes over Julie's face.

– What about de winter morning dat I dropped small Julie down to school, an' wen I came back, we watched *Toto de Hero* on de video, an' had wild an' crazy sex on de rug in front of de fire! Ya must remember, Mags, dat was de beginnin' of de end of our, one big happy family! Jeezus!

Mags doesn't blink an eyelid.

– Mags?

I am close to tears. – You know exactly who I am, we know each other from MacSweeney Street.

I turn to walk away.

– . . . I remember, Julie whispers.

I stop.

– I used call you dad, when I was a small little girl, she speaks softly.

– You remember?

– You were the only father I ever knew, and I remember

251

you used always tell me that you weren't my real father, that I was Veronica's little girl, but if ever I needed you, you'd be there for me.

There is no more to say. Do I stay or walk away? The three of us stand there in silence for what seems like eternity. Then Mags says,

– I suppose you'd better come in and see Paulo on his wedding day.

– Come on, Dad! says Julie, and she plaits her hand under my arm.

– I'm not yer dad! I protest. She just looks at me. – But if ever ya need me, I'll be dere for ya, I whisper.

* * *

3:47

– Hold me steady! shouts the fella with the ears.

– Well, can ye see anything? asks the burly fella.

– Will ya hold me steady!

– I'm flamin' well holdin' ye, mate!

– None a' your back-chat! the burly fella nudges the Monk.

– Is he in there, luuv?

– I can't see too clearly. But I'll tell ya, his place is in an awful mess, wherever he is, looks like there's a big mound of sheets on the bed, but I can't be too sure.

– Maybe ve should break down der door yes?

– Dere'll be nobody breaking no doors down! D'ye hear me!

– We're gettin' nowhere in a hurry here! says the fella with the ears.

– Do ye mind if I let ya down, mate, me flamin' arm is killin' me, says the Monk.

– What did I just say to you! shouts the burly fella.

The fella with the ears calls the burly fella to one side, – Look, he says. – If we break down the door and there's no stiff in there we're in big shit back in the station . . . I mean like

252

this is my first night on the job and lookin' at this bunch a' Martians I'd say yer man Pluto's just gone out or somethin' . . .

– Ya has a point, says the burly fella. – Is there a spare set of keys? he shouts.

– The landlady has one, says Brenda.

– Do ye have her number?

– It's upstairs, she says.

– Ye can't phone her this time a' the mornin', we'll all be evicted, mate.

– Shag that witch! is all Brenda says. – I'll give her a call.

– Ve can all come up to mein flat for some coffee and Hob-nobs, Yes?

– Sounds like an idea, says the burly fella.

– Alright, come over here an' help me down offa this window! says the fella with the ears, – Hurrup!

– Aaaaah! sighs the Monk shaking life back into his arm.

* * *

I haven't been in a church in a long time, but I feel comfortable. The only thing that gets to me is, that I don't know if I'm supposed to be sitting, standing or on my knees, and because I'm in the front row I can't follow anybody's lead.

I hear a surge of movement from the congregation. I stand up. I'm standing there for a good thirty seconds and I feel Mags tugging my jacket sleeve. I look across to my left. The whole front row is seated. I look behind me and the church is half up and half down like myself, the lapsed Catholics obviously following my example. I snigger.

– Shut up and sit down! Mags squeezes my arm.

– I don't believe in all dis standin' up an' kneelin' down business anyhow! I whisper. – Sure wat kind of a God would have ya walkin' around on your knees, and he after creating ya with feet?

253

Mags begins to laugh, Julie giggles, I shake trying to control myself. We spend the rest of the ceremony avoiding eye-contact, afraid we'd set each other off and crack up laughing, making a mockery of Paulo's day.

When it's time for Communion Mags nudges me,

– Are ya going to receive?

– I'm not practising, I say.

– How much practice does it take, says Julie. – Are ya fasting?

– Well, I've had nothing to eat today only a few cups a coffee an a couple a' amaretto biscuits.

– Go on, you'll be fine, she says. – It's Paulo's day.

– Right!

I've just spent three hours running around town trying to get here to Paulo's First Holy Communion, and somewhere along the way I've lost over twenty years, and I'm the one who's taking Communion for the first time in a long time, then again life's like that, but then again life's not. How can this be, when I know I'm lying dead on the lino in my toilet . . .

The three of us move out of the pew, and head for the altar. I don't know how long it has been since I received Communion, but the ritual has changed drastically.

My memory of the whole thing was: you knelt at the altar rail, closed your eyes, opened yer mouth. Hands under the altar cloth so as that you wouldn't contaminate the host if it fell from the priest's hand; the priest pops the host into yer mouth, Bob's yer uncle, Fanny's yer other uncle. The chances of the host landing on the altar rail was fairly slim anyway, because the altar boy used to have a thing like a big round brass plasterer's trowel, to hold under your jaw.

I'm watching the priest working his way through the crowd, this new ritual is freaking me out totally. People are taking the host in their own hands, and eating it, actually chewing it. They're gulping back the wine straight out of the chalice. Their eyes are wide open, they're not even kneeling for God's sake! The whole thing seems blasphemous. It dawns on me that we're like a bunch of pagan cannibals waiting for our share of the blood sacrifice. A cold sweat is running down my neck. I can't just stand here open-eyed and munch into the body of Christ, not to mind swilling it down with a mouthful of his blood. It just seems so bloody sacrilegious. By the time the priest gets to me I'm totally stressed.

– Body of Christ?

I freak, drop to my knees, shut my eyes and stick out my tongue. Nothing happens. I open one eye, the priest is looking down on me,

– Body of Christ!

I can't remember the response.

– Body of Christ! he says it again.

I can't think of the word. It's just one simple word. My mind is full of religious catch-phrases, like *Lord graciously hear us!* or, *Go forth in peace!* but I just can't seem to think of that one word.

– Body of Christ!

I can feel the tension building in Mags and Julie next to me.

– Body of Christ!

– Thanks! I say and reach out, take the host in my hand and pop it in my mouth.

The priest doesn't bat an eye-lid, he probably thinks I'm part of this liberation church theology movement we hear so much about on those religious programmes.

– Blood of Christ?

– Thanks again! I say, and take a mouthful from the chalice.

As I struggle to get up, the priest has moved down the line.

– Body of Christ! he offers it to Mags. She takes the host in her hand and says,

– Amen!

– Aaamen! I say.

* * *

3:58.

– So tell me, asks the burly fella. – Does dis Pluto guy have any family?

– He have a sister in England somewhere, but his mam and dad are dead, luuv.

– D'ye know what, mate, he was tellin' me about his fadder. Seemingly his fadder was a cabinetmaker, master-craftsman. But when they started using the wooden dowels up in the factory instead of proper wood joints, he turned his back on the craft. Anyway he decided to make his own coffin at home in the kitchen.

– In the kitchen? the fella with the ears doesn't believe the Monk.

– That I may be struck dead, mate! His masterpiece, like a monument to his craft. Anyway he built one hell of a coffin, not a screw, nail or dowel in it. All joints handed down from generation to generation. Then he started carving and inlaying on it, covered the whole coffin so he did. But d'ye know on the day of the funeral, and they carrying the body from the house the bloody coffin wouldn't turn between the kitchen door and the hall.

– Ah, come off it Jimmy luuv, yer havin' us on.

– On me muddur's soul. They had to take Pluto's father's body out of the coffin. They sawed the masterpiece in half, right down the middle, mate!

– Serious?

– On the level, mate! But do'ya know a funny thing about it, the lad's from the furniture yard put the coffin back together with dowels. Twenty-eight dowels, mate. Six top and bottom, eight on each side and they tacked a sheet of plywood onto the base. Just in case.

A roll of a laughter runs around the table, and Herman states the obvious,

– Just goes to show, ve cannot plan for der future.

After the wedding Mags introduces me to Paulo, he looks just like me.

– All these years and I thought you were dead, Dad.

– I know, I say. – One day yer makin' yer Communion, next yer gettin' married.

Paulo is as excited as I am. He introduces me to Claire, his beautiful bride.

He's shaking my hand, and introducing me to his friends.

– What age are ya now son?

– Twenty-eight, he says. – You're lookin well yerself, what age are you, Dad?

I pause. I mean like I know I'm thirty-three today, but it makes no sense, especially, if Paulo was born when I was twenty-five, that makes him only eight years of age, and here he is, standing in front of me a young man in his twenties. Then again if I am his father, it means I was only seven when I made Mags pregnant, possible, but that would more or less wipe out my whole life with the lads on MacSweeney Street, and the chunk of time I spent with Yvette, not to mention my time with Veronica.

– Well, dad, what age are ya? he repeats the question.

– When ya get to my age, son, ya stop keeping count.

Paulo is hanging on every word that comes from my mouth and all the time I just want to hear him speak. He tells me about his life, and what it was like being brought up by two lesbians.

He tells me it didn't feel any different from a hetero family, but then he says he'd no idea what a hetero household would be like anyway.

– I suppose normality is a very personal thing! he says. – I mean like I remember, I kissed Julie once!

– Kissed? Yer sister!

I wasn't sure what he meant by kissed.

257

– Yeah the full thing, when I was about fifteen, he says.

– Ya kissed yer sister?

– Sure technically speaking, Julie isn't my sister at all!

– Hmmm! I suppose you've a point.

– Don't get me wrong, Dad, says Paulo, – She mightn't be my sister but I'm always there for her.

– But ya only kissed her just the once? I ask.

– Ah! We were only kids, he says, – But I remember when Julie was about eighteen, one day the four of us were sitting around the table at supper-time, Veronica, Mags, myself and Julie. Anyway, Julie was just starting to go to dances and things, and Veronica asks her, how did the disco go for her. There was a silence for a second or two . . .

Well? Veronica repeated. – How was the disco?

Julie raised her head sheepishly.

– Mam, she said, – I've something to say. Now don't get mad, mam.

– I won't.

– Promise, Mam.

– Ah, go on Julie, for Christ's sake, spit it out.

– Don't get mad now, but I think I'm a heterosexual . . ., and he laughs. – Do ya get it? Paulo shoves me, – Julie telling Veronica that she thinks she'a a heterosexual.

Paulo laughs louder. I stand there, sort of missing the point.

– Do'ya get it, Paulo says. – She said . . . I think I'm a heterosexual!

– Is dat a true story? I ask.

– Jeezus! 'Course it's not! and he laughs again.

I smile. He tells me that he couldn't have wished for better parents than Mags and Veronica. He says he's a qualified social worker, and working for the Department of Social Welfare. I warn him to treat poor people with respect. He nods his head. I tell him all about Pinko, Georgie, Tragic Ted, Fatfuka and the lads from MacSweeney Street. I tell him about Grandda Buckley, and Eddie de Nut. I tell him how his grandmother died trying to save a beautiful white swan from the river and how every year that swan comes back to nest in the Lough out of respect for the woman who saved it. It's a wonderful thing when a father and son talk. I don't mean trading words, we were standing there listening to each other speak.

We're separated when they drag us into a soul-stealing photograph. Paulo manages to say that he'll see me at the wedding. I ask him if I'm invited. He just shouts, – See ya later, Dad.

Mags asks me if I'd like to come to the reception. Julie butts in and says,

– 'Course he would.

– Where is it? I ask.

– Down in Sherkin.

– Sherkin Island? Sure that's miles away.

– I know, says Mags. – But it's a cousin of Paulo's girlfriend, oops! Wife – I'll never get used to that. A cousin of Paulo's wife owns the hotel down there.

– So are ya coming, Dad? asks Julie.

– I wouldn't miss it for de world, I say. – But eh I'm supposed to meet Yvette in de Le Chateau at around one. Would it be okay if I bring her along too?

– Mags? Julie asks.

– I don't see why not, says Mags.

– You're an angel, Mags, Julie kisses her on the cheek.

– Eh! What time is it anyway? I ask.

– Just twelve o' clock.

– Look I'd better run down and get Yvette, I say. – We'll make our own way to Sherkin. By de way wha's de name a' de Hotel down dere?

– The Garrison, says Mags, – There's only one on the island.

– I'm gonna go, I'll see ye on de Island.

– Make sure you come down, Dad, says Julie.

– I wouldn't miss it for all de tea in Newcastle.

– Or the coal in China, Julie laughs.

I strike off down Roman Street, down into the bowel of the city.

\* \* \*

3:59:57

When the phone rings this time of night, it always means trouble. He lifts the receiver immediately so that it won't wake Alison. The Cosmopolitan falls from bed to carpet.

– Eh, hello? he whispers.

– Hello, I'm sorry for eh phonin' this time a' the morning, but eh, can I speak to Alison please?

– Well, she's actually asleep, is there anything I can do for you? I'm her husband. Eh, who am I speaking to?

– S-S-Sorry, my name is Brenda, Brenda Healy, I'm one of the tenants.

– And eh, which property are you in, Brenda?

– I'm up in Waterloo Terrace.

He should have guessed.

– Look, it's important I get onto herself, because we've a bit of a problem up here.

– Well, can it wait until the morning? he asks.

– I don't think so, I think Pluto down in No. 1 might have, eh, killed himself.

– Huh? Wha'? Killed?

– The Guards are here an' all, and they're lookin' for a key to get into the flat.

– Eh, can you hold the line for one moment.

He shakes Alison. She's in a death-like sleep.

– Alison! Alison! Wake up Alison! Alison, There's a problem up on Waterloo Terrace! Alison wake up! Alison! Alison!

260

# 29

At Dominic Street I catch a glimpse of Shandon. It's quarter past twelve, don't have to meet Yvette until one. For the first time since morning, I've a bit of time to myself, so I decide to take the long way into town. I cut down the Skeety Bars steps to John Street and head for Cypress Street towards MacSweeneya. I often go through my old area, drawn in by the blended scents of the brewery and Linehane's sweet factory, like a wassie to ice cream. A lot has changed, you know like, some of the houses are falling down and most of the small shops are gone. They died soon after the first wave of supermarkets. Punch's Bridge is gone and Karl's Quay, the stretch of water where the swans sheltered, is covered over – it's now a highway link road, the families have vanished too, squeezed out by the motor car, out to the Corporation Reservations on the Northside. Progress they call it, but I don't know . . .

With all the changes, there are traces of what once was. A faint scent, a long-forgotten sound, and in the ghosts of the past, the soul of MacSweeney Street lives on.

At the corner of Cypress Street, I stop. A gang of lads are kicking a ball against a warehouse gate. I didn't think kids still played ball on the city streets. I stroll down for a closer look.

– Pass the ball! Pass the ball! I hear him shout. It rings familiar to my ears.

– On the head! it sounds like Tragic Ted. I walk closer. – On the head!

It is Ted. I can't believe it! It's Tragic Ted, Georgie and Fatfuka, they're just tapping around.

– Ted! Ted! Is that you! Hoi, Ted!

He turns.

– Hey, lads, look who it is!

– Pluto! How's it going, Pluto boi? Georgie reaches out his hand.

– Jeezus Georgie! How're ya doing? I thought you were dead, I say.

– Dead? Me? Do I look dead to you? Georgie hugs me. – Good to see ya, Pluto boi.

– De tree a' ye are dead! Jeezus, Fatfuka, I don't believe this!

– Listen, Pluto boi, life's like death. It's only a state of mind, Fatfuka smiles.

– Dis is really weird. Already twice today, I've been told by people dat dey thought I was dead.

– Come on, Georgie! Tragic Ted roars. – Chip in de ball.

– Georgie's as stingy as ever with de ball, Fatfuka laughs.

– Just 'cause I can hold de ball longer than de two a' ye.

– Ah listen, lads, am I alive or dead? I ask.

– Dat depends on wat state of mind you're in, Georgie laughs.

I make a dash up the inside, steal the ball from Georgie cross it in, on to Ted's head. He clings it into the corner of the gate. The Kop's on fire . . .

> Six foot two,
> Eyes a' blue.
> Tragic Ted is after you!

> *An' we love him, we love him!*
> *We do.*

After the tap around, we sit on the footpath, chewing the fat. Georgie is telling me that I've just missed Grandda Buckley. He says that Grandda Buckley usually heads down to the church this time of day to light a candle for the living.

– Dey need it more dan we do.

– An' who's gone down with him? I ask.

– He's gone on his tod.

– With nobody to push de chair?

– Chair? What chair? Sure dat was years ago, Grandda's legs are perfect now.

None of this makes sense to me, but I know I'll never understand it with a simple explanation, so, I just laugh and the conversation continues.

It's not like old times, it's not like we're trying to catch up on the past. It's not like anything, It's just the way things should be. We're winding each other up and putting each other down, slagging all the time. Ted is saying that if ever he's caught smoking he'd be mombolised at home. Georgie says that his dad lets him smoke as long as he can pay for them himself. Fatfuka says they're bad for yer health.

– Says who? Georgie raises his voice.

– Says all de doctors in de world!

– Sure look at John Wayne! Georgie says.

– What about him?

– Well, he smokes!

– John Wayne's dead!

– Is he really?

– Cigarettes! Fatfuka smiles.

– Listen lads, I've always wondered why am I called Pluto?

– A name's like a hat! says Tragic.

– Yeah but I always thought I was called Pluto because of me name, you know, Pluto, Paul O' Toole, P-L-U-T-O, like.

The three lads fall around laughing.

– But den somebody told me I was called Pluto after Mickey Mouse's dog.

The lads laugh louder. – So eh, what's de story?

– Disneyland! says Fatfuka.

– Disneyland? Why Pluto?

– Figure it out for yourself.

– De only thing special about Pluto is dat he's de only cartoon dat don't speak. I mean like dey're all animals, aren't dey? – Even Donald Duck talks, not de best mind ya, but at least he talks!

– Pluto can't, says Georgie – So dat means dat Pluto is . . . ?

– Dumb? Are ye saying I'm dumb or something? Is dat what it is?

Ted pushes me, Georgie wraps his arm around my shoulder.

– Dumb you? Not at all! Yer called Pluto cause you've a fuckin' tail! he cracks up laughing. Fatfuka locks onto my head and pulls me down the road.

– Would ya rather be called Mickey? he howls.

– Let me up I can't breathe!

I'm gasping for breath, in fits of laughter.

– Breathe dat! shouts Tragic Ted, and he farts into my face.

– Ya disgusting bollox!

Fatfuka releases me. Ted makes a run for it. I'm after him like a greyhound.

– After him!

Georgie and Fatfuka join in the chase. We corner Ted at de end of the street. I tackle him to the footpath.

– Don't ever fart in my face again! Do ye hear me?

– I won't!

– Promise!

– I promise! I promise! Ted is hysterical. – Let me up!

– Double promise!

Fatfuka and Georgie rip Ted's shoes from his feet.

– Ah, lads! Ted is screaming.

– Let him up! Let him up! shouts Georgie.

Georgie runs off with the shoes. Ted after him like a greyhound, meself and Fatfuka join the pack.

– After him! shouts Ted. We catch up with Georgie at the far end of the street and the whole thing begins again, puppy dogs at play, making up the rules as we go along.

* * *

– Don't mind if I do, Mam! The fella with the ears reaches across and takes another Hob-Nob.

– How much longer did the landlady say she'd be? asks the burly fella.

– She won't be long. When I mentioned the Guards were here, it put the skates under her, Brenda says.

– Although it'll take her a good twenty minutes to get in here from the Model Farm Road, mate.

– Anyone for more tea or coffee? Herman shouts from the kitchen.

– I'll come in and give ya a hand, luuv.

– So tell us, what's this Pluto fella like anyway? asks the fella with the ears.

– If ye ask me, mate, 'es a bit of an odd-ball! Y'know what I mean eh?

The Monk spirals his index finger to this head.

– That comin' from you, says something! the burly fella laughs.

– He's not dangerous or nothing, mate, but he's not really the full bob either.

– Hmmm! Interesting, I think we've come across him down at the station before.

– Sure I'm tellin ya, he's no trouble to nobody else, Pluto's only trouble to himself, mate.

– We usually come across most of the head-cases. Jaysus, I've an awful feeling he's de fella we caught comin' out de window of dis house a few years back . . . bringin' his bike out a' de window he was . . .

– More tea anybody?

Brenda's carrying the pot to the table.

– You can throw a drop in there, Missus, says the burly fella.

– Pardon me, Missus, but you wouldn't have an ashtray, would ya? asks the fella with the ears.

– Herman! she shouts. – Where's the ashtray!

– I am just cleaning it now!

* * *

She's sitting at the counter sipping something white. I'm trembling, she looks absolutely amazing.

– Ah Yvette! I slide up on to the bar stool beside her. – You're here?

– So how was your son's Communion?

– Jeezus, I was a bit late, by de time I got dere he was gettin' married, I must have got de dates wrong, or something.

– *Non?* she says.

– Yes! But anyway, we've being invited to de reception. I mean like I'll understand if you don't want to come, Yvette.

– I would love to come, she says.

– Really?

– But, of course! Eh, where ees zis wedding?

– It's on Sherkin Island, de Garrison.

266

– An island? *Trés exotique*.

– It'll be magical!

– My car is outside, she says.

I don't know much about cars, never had one, never had use for one, can't remember the last time I sat into one. All I know is that this is a car and a half, great sound system, sun-roof, the lot. She hands me a pair of sunglasses from the glove-box and slips a CD into the player. M People.

– Do you know, I once met Mike Pickering? I say pointing to the tape. – He was here in Cork years ago, a House DJ in Henry's before he made it big. Although when I say I met him, I suppose really I was only standing next to him at the bar. I was fairly twisted the same night.

I look to Yvette, her fingerless leather driving-gloves clenched tightly to the steering wheel. She nods her head, I don't really know if she's listening to me or just keeping time to the music. Her eyes are fixed on the road ahead. I put on the sunglasses and melt back into the seat. We speed out along the beautiful Bandon Road under the monumental viaduct, hair blowing wildly in the wind, sun on our shoulders . . .

> Search for the hero inside yourself,
> Then you'll find the key to your heart.

– Dis could be heaven! I whisper.

Colourful country towns flash by. I sit there, pointing out standing stones, ring forts, castles and ambush sites, all notches on the belt of Ireland's bloody story. Yvette's eyes don't leave the road, but every now and then her left hand reaches out and touches my thigh.

\* \* \*

– That could be her now, Brenda stands up and looks out the window.

– Well, is it? asks the burly fella.

– Here, gis a look! the Monk barges past Brenda.

– Well? asks Herman.

– It looks like her car, luuv!

– 'Tis the landlady alright, mate.

– Come on then! the fella with the ears reaches for his cap.

To a clatter of cups, they head for the door, Herman leading the way to the landing and down the rickety stairs.

Herman opens the hall door. Alison's standing there, key in hand. Dangling from the key is a chain with about thirty other keys strung on it.

– Ah come in! Come in! Herman says.

– What's going on here? she's fuming.

– Mornin', mam! says the Monk.

– It's four in the morning. What's all this talk of the Guards being up here? she shouts.

Herman opens the door a little wider, the two guards step into the light.

– Oh! she says.

– It's suspected dat one of your tenants may have had a mishap, the burly fella points to Pluto's door.

– Who? Paul O' Toole?

– Yes! Pluto! says Brenda.

– Mishap?

– Dead!

– Dead? she fumbles through the keys. – What makes ya think he's dead in there?

– Well, he's not answering his bell.

– We were wondering if you had a spare key, you know to save us knockin' down the door! says the fella with the ears.

– Hang on! she says. – I think this is it!

She sticks it into the lock, wrong key. – Naw! Here I'll try this one.

# 30

We're sitting outside Bushes, looking down on Baltimore Harbour. I'm supping a pint of Murphy's, Yvette's on brandy and port. I point to the old Abbey on Sherkin and tell Yvette the story of how it was sacked by a bunch of gold-digging, blood-crazed, Algerian pirates back in the sixteen-hundreds. She's amazed when I tell her that they were shown the way to Sherkin by a fella by the name of O'Driscoll from Dungarvan.

– But sure that's Dungarvan for ya . . . I say.

– Dungarvan?

– Yeah, in County Waterford, says I. – I've cousins down dere, an' do'ya know dat Dungarvan was founded by a Monk by de name of Garvan, from Cork, Pope's Quay to be exact . . . just around de corner from where I was born on MacSweeney Street.

– *Non!* she says. – You Irish have such a deep understanding of your history.

– Ah! Well, 'tis hard not to when it's all around ya.

The ferry is ploughing its way towards Baltimore. It'll be a while before it gets back in port to carry us across to the island. We're sitting in the sun, sometimes talking, but mostly saying nothing, at ease, soaking up the comfort and pleasure of being in the company of the one you love. It feels so good it almost hurts. I find myself staring at her. She turns her head, raises her shades and smiles. I smile too but it's more a smile of disbelief. I feel dirty in her presence. I mean she's perfect in pastels, I sit here in my grubby army parka, manky jeans and boots, and from the odd glimpse I'd caught of myself in the shop windows I know that my hair is long and greasy and I haven't shaved in a few days.

– All me good clothes is in de launderette, I point to my jeans. – Dese are only me workin' clobber!

She just smiles.

– Pluto my love, you are perfect.

I sit back.

– I used to be somebody, you know! But somewhere along de line it all went terribly wrong. Do ya know what I mean. I had a future. I had friends an' family, but now it's all in de past.

– Past! Future! Paaa! Yvette throws her hands in the air. – Some people say that there is no past or future, only the present, and we must enjoy the present.

– De only present I ever enjoyed was a Christmas present! and I laugh.

She doesn't really get the joke.

– Sometimes I think, she continues, – we live and die many thousand times each day. And with each moment that passes we die a little, likewise we are reborn with each moment as it arrives. Nothing else matters, but what you are at zis moment in time.

– Do ya know, Fatfuka was sayin' something like dat just before he died. Ya might be on to something dere, dey were sayin' on de radio dat de mayfly lives for only one day as an adult, and in dat day, dey mate, lay eggs and molt twice, and do ya know wat? Dey don't eat at all, in deir whole life dey don't eat one mouthful a' food. And sure how could dey? Dey don't even have a mouth. Den again it'd be hard to live very long if ya didn't have a mouth . . . Anyway, I tink I know what ya mean, I say.

270

But when does anybody truly know what somebody else means. We finish our drinks and stroll down to the pier, towards the ferry.

Sherkin is a magical place. It has a pace and rhythm all of its own, everything fresh and green and untouched. We head up the hill towards the Abbey, just taking it all in. By the time we get to The Garrison the meal is over. We walk into the function room as the speeches are about to begin. I am a prince, the beautiful Yvette on my arm. I point out Mags, Paulo and Julie. I tell Yvette that Julie is the head off her mother Veronica. Paulo is making his speech. He's thanking everybody, I'm so happy for him, proud of him.

– And finally, he says. – What makes today so special, is that my dad is here. A round of applause for my dad, Pluto.

. . . and then he points at me, I'm totally choked up. The cheering begins. They are chanting my name, and clattering glasses and cutlery off the tables. I feel Yvette's hand at my back pushing me out from the wall. I step forward, remove my sunglasses and wave my right hand in the air. I can see the top table, with Julie, Mags and Paulo on their feet, clapping and smiling through the tears. Julie blows me kisses.

– I love you too! I mouth.

I'm crying without shame. I step back to the wall.

– Seize the moment! Yvette whispers in my ear and pushes me back out to the floor. Silence fills the room.

– Ah hemmm! I clear my throat, – Reverend Father, Ladies and Gentlemen, Ahem! I would just like to say a few words.

An uneasy shuffling around the table.

– I left home dis mornin' with de intention of going to Paulo's First Holy Communion. By de time I got to de North Cathedral it was three hours later, an' Paulo was gettin' married!

They all laughed.

– No joke! Somehow I lost twenty years, runnin' around de town tryin' to organise tings for de Communion, and my little boy became a man.

You could hear a pin drop in the room.

– As you all know, Paulo was brought up by Mags – I point to Mags – and Veronica, God rest her soul, and I tink dey done a mighty fine job of it. Wat I'm trying to say is dat I wasn't dere for Paulo over de last twenty years, but dat's my loss, not Paulo's. Listen Paulo. I've never given you advice in your life, so I'm not gonna start now, but here's an observation.

Son, life's but a series of memories and den yer pig's head. It's up to you to decide whether you want yer memories to be happy or sad. It might seem fairly obvious to most people, but it took me a lifetime to learn dis. If ya want a happy life ya need happy memories, and if ya want happy memories, ya gotta be happy right now. Wat I'm tryin' ta say is dat life is only not worth living wen de present is unbearable.

The room is totally silent, a hush of anticipation, but I've no more to say. I've run out of words. Slowly I walk towards the top table, and taking Paulo's bride's hand in mine, I kiss it. She rises to her feet. I can see my own father, he is nowhere definite in the room, but he is smiling down on us,

– Gowaan! he whispers. I point to the two bridesmaids.

– G-G-Gowaan! Will ye! I can hear him. I open my mouth and begin to sing. It's like the words are coming from nowhere,

> Dere were tree lovely lassies from Bannion,
> Bannion, Bannion.
> Dere were tree lovely lassies from Bannion
> An she was de best of 'em all!
> An' she was de best of 'em all!

I lean across and kiss Paulo on the cheek. Julie's in floods,

– I love you, Dad, she whimpers.

– I'm not yer dad.

– I know. But you'll always be there for me, won't you?

– Chalk it down, Julie girl! Chalk it down!

– A toast to the Bride and Groom!

The best man rises to his feet.

– To the Bride and Groom!

He raises his glass above his head.

– To the Bride and Groom!

\* \* \*

*Click!* The key turns.

– Ah! At last, says the burly Fella.

The landlady pushes open the door into Pluto's flat. They stand back.

– Would ya look at the cut a' this place, mate?

Brenda, Herman, the Monk, the landlady and the two Guards slowly ease their way into Pluto's room. An unearthly stench is thick in the air, everything is up in a heap. The fella with the ears switches on the light.

– Oh my God! Brenda points at the bed. It looks like it's drenched in tomato sauce.

– Jeezus, Mary and Joseph, de burly fella whispers.

The place is covered with the stuff, from the bed all the way to the bathroom. The bathroom door is daubed red with drips running down onto the matted carpet.

– Jaysus!

The Monk pushes open the bathroom door.

– Holy fuck, he steps back.

– Jeezus Christ! screams Brenda. She rushes past into the toilet. Pluto's lying there, his bluish-green body splattered red.

– Call an ambulance! Call a shaggin' ambulance! she screams.

The burly fella's on his walkie-talkie to the base, the fella with the ears trying to console Brenda. Alison on her knees, cursing and bandaging Pluto's wrists with towels.

– I think it is too late for an ambulance, whispers Herman.

– Hoi, Mick! the fella with the ears shouts to the burly fella. – Call a priest.

The Monk begins saying the Act of Contrition into Pluto's ear.

> *Oh my God, I'm heartily sorry*
> *For having offended thee . . .*

Then he stops,

> *Oh! my God, I'm heartily sorry*
> *for having offended thee . . .*

He repeats, again he stops,

– I can't remember the words. What comes next, he looks to Brenda.

> *Oh my God I'm heartily sorry . . .* she mumbles. –

Jeezus, I can't remember. I haven't prayed in years.

She's panicking. The burly fella blesses himself and says there's a priest on the way.

– Say something, for Christ's sake! Brenda screams.

The Monk leans over the body, and raises Pluto's head from the ground.

– Look, God, he says. – I don't know what's a sin or what's not a sin, mate, but I do know what's right from wrong. An' Pluto here is just a poor wretched creature, living a tortured life. I know that most of his troubles are of his own makin', but Jaysus Christ in all fairness, he did no harm to no one else. There was nothin' more for poor aul' Pluto in this life only pain. I'm sure you'll understand God. He just wanted off the bus, mate . . .

The Monk eases Pluto's head gently to the floor. Herman covers the body with the least stained sheet. The landlady reaches for the clock radio and escorts Brenda from the room. The burly fella is still on the radio. The fella with the ears removes his cap, rubs the back of his head and sighs.

274

# 31

– One! One-two! The bandleader taps the microphone. – Testing, One! One-two! Can ye hear me down there? One! One-two! Ladies and Gentlemen, I'll ask ye to put yere hands together, for the bride and groom, and maybe they'd lead off with the dancin' now! Thank ye!

The band strikes up with a selection of old-time Irish waltzes and polkas. Paulo escorts Claire, his new bride, out onto the floor. Slowly with uncertainty they move, gathering momentum and confidence. They glide as one across the crystals.

– The best man and the maid of honour, please! the band leader calls from the stage.

Paulo and Claire are flowing and swirling.

– And the parents of the Bride and Groom! he shouts.

Claire's mother and father take to the floor.

For a moment I hesitate, I feel Julie and Yvette's arms around me.

– Gowaan, Dad, Julie whispers, – Mags is waiting.

I look across the floor. I see Mags. She's smiling at Paulo and Claire.

– Go on, Pluto! Yvette pushes me.

I step out onto the dance floor and move towards Mags.

I'm halfways across when she turns her head, our eyes meet. I stretch out my hand, she smiles and reaches towards me.

– Would ya like to dance, Mags?

Her left hand takes my right and we move together. I lead her out, we sway together a few times finding our rhythm, we begin to dance. Paulo catches my eye. He's looking at us over Claire's shoulder. He winks. I just nod my head.

– Now everybody, take yer partners and onto the floor please! the bandleader shouts.

The dance floor fills, as Mags and myself glide across the maple in ever-increasing circles to the sound of the squeeze-box hammering out the tune of *Billy Jenkin's Old Boots*, to the rhythm of life.

# 32

*Click!*

The landlady switches off the polka coming from the radio. The burly fella asks the fella with the ears if this is his first time dealing with a suicide. He shakes his head and explains that he used to help his uncle after school . . .

– Yer uncle? asks the burly fella.

– Hmmm, me uncle the undertaker . . .

Medics lift Pluto's corpse onto a stretcher. The fella with the ears is asking Brenda if she knows of any next of kin. Herman picks the blood-spattered refill pad from the floor.

– Wha's tha'? asks the burly fella.

– I don't know, says Herman. He flicks through the pages. – It ist full of writing, a lot of it ist scribbles.

– Here show us tha'! the burly fella reaches out. – Probably some class of a suicide note.

– He has my name written on der cover, I vill read it, Herman takes a deep breath and begins to read.

*Sometimes the need to die is greater than the will to live . . .*

*When I was three years of age my mother went down to Pope's Quay. She sat on the bench across from the Dominican Priory, took off her rings and shoes, walked down the steps into the river Lee and drowned herself. She could have crossed the road to the church, but I suppose she must have tried that once too often. Nobody ever told me. I just always knew, but sometimes I wished they had lied, for Christ's sake they lied about everything else. Why the hell couldn't they have lied about my mother? Tell me she died saving a beautiful white swan and that the swan lives on to this very day and winters each year in the Lough out by Ballyphehane, where she rears one small downy cygnet. Tell me the swan comes back to Cork each autumn as a sign of respect to a courageous and beautiful woman who sacrificed her life that the most graceful of all God's creatures should live. Tell me a lie . . .*

– Gowaan, Herman luuv, what else do it say?

– Der handwriting gets hard to read from here on, It est like der scratches, der rantings of a mad man.

– A tortured soul, says the Monk.

– It makes no sense, Herman flicks through the refill pad. – Looks like der story of a life.

– Pluto's life, mate?

*Ding-dong!* the door bell.

– I vill get it, says Herman.

Herman walks to the hall, opens the door and looks down at a young girl standing there on Waterloo Terrace. The ambulance men shuffle by, with a stretcher carrying Pluto's covered body, out over the Monk's rubbish in the hall. The girl steps back to make way.

– Ah sorry! Can I help you, Herman asks.

– I'm Julie, she says. – I'm lookin' for me dad.

– Your dad?

– I thinks he lives here.

– Vot is your father's name?

– Paul O'Toole, most people call him Pluto, she says.

– You are Pluto's daughter?

– Not really, well sorta'.

278

Herman just stands there. She says something about her mother sending her up to remind Pluto of her brother Paulo's First Holy Communion.

– Eh! Sorry, says Herman. – Could you just wait here for one moment?

He turns and vanishes into the darkness that's the hallway.

– Brenda! Brenda! she hears him call.

# 33

The sound of the *céile* from the wedding is faint in the stillness that's Sherkin. Yvette and myself take a walk across the island, arm-in-arm down past Horseshoe Harbour, past The Island House, out beyond Silver Strand all the way to Cow Strand, not saying a word, holding hands. And we walk and walk, barefoot over land and sea, all the way back to the beautiful city. I point out Seamus Murphy's water trough for dogs and red Gurranebrahar. We step onto Patrick's Bridge.

– When you're standing in the middle of Patrick's Bridge; then, Patrick's Bridge is the centre of the Universe, I say.

– Tell to me another McSweeney Street story, she says.

– One big family, dat's what it was like. D'ya know, when I was about a year old, me mudder was headin' down to dat church dere one night, I point to St Mary's.

– an' she came across dis couple huddled in a doorway. Dey had a small baby with dem. A small little creature as pale as a swan me mother used say, an' de baby was wrapped up in a blanket asleep, with only an old drawer as a cot. Me mudder didn't go to de Church dat night, she did de Christian ting an' brought 'em home. Dey moved in with us for a while. After a while dey found deir own place 'round de corner down Cypress Street an' do ye know who de little fella in de drawer was?

– Who?

– Georgie . . . Pinko's brudder, Eddie de Nut's son, 'member I was tellin' ya, de fella dat was killed by de truck.

– Ah? Ze young paper-seller, yes?

– Young? Sixteen's as old as ya get, if sixteen's when ya die . . .

I ramble on for a while telling stories about the old days, MacSweeney Street and the lads who lived there . . .

On Patrick's Hill I look down into the goldfish bowl, I don't turn to salt. Yvette tugs my hand and leads on to the brow.

We climb the wall at Bell's Field. I stretch out my arms embracing the beautiful Northside laid out before us as it vanishes over the hill at Knocknaheeney and Blarney Street.

– Breathe it in! I say.

She's just standing there, eyes bulging like they're trying to capture everything at once.

We walk through the knee-high meadow and nestle down into a sheltered hollow. We're sprawled there barefoot on a grassy ridge above the city, saying nothing. My mind travels across brewery valley, passing each laneway, step and steeple; from the Bishop's Palace right over to the dome of City Hall. Bolts of pleasure and pain as memories stop off along the way at the North Mon, the Cathedral, Eason's Hill, Murphy's stack, Poulraddy Harbour and Shandon, then all the way back to Redemption Road and over the city to the spiked spires of Holy Trinity, St Finbarre's and the green tops of St Francis. Off in the distance the County Hall scraping clouds, picking up the gold of a dying sun. I stare out westward, out along the Lee Valley to the Carrigrohane Straight. There, like a last grasp at life, a setting sun sends flames of red, and orange, and yellow licking high up into the sky.

– Looks like Ballincollig's on fire, I say.

Yvette snuggles into me.

My city is a Royal town, dressed up in crimsons and gold in the distance, through the mists of coal smoke; the cry of an *Echo* boy, the movement of a bus, car, cyclist; people walking home from work, the chimes of an ice-cream van across on Spangle Hill, the bells of some cathedral or other, the yelps of children from Roches' Buildings playing ball along the road. There is a harmony of movement and colour and sound. Everything as one; the aromatic blending of Murphy's brewery, Linehan's sweet factory and Donnelly's bakery . . .

– Dis could be heaven, I whisper.

– Could be, she smiles. – Could be . . .